5/12/16

D0130196

60000350714

Also by Jeff Povey

SHIFT

JEFF POVEY

DELETE

SIMON & SCHUSTER

Typeset in the UK by M Rules
Printed and bound by CPI Group (UK) Ltd, Croydon, CR0 4YY

www.simonandschuster.co.uk
www.simonandschuster.com.au

First published in Great Britain in 2015 by Simon & Schuster UK Ltd
A CBS COMPANY

1 3 5 7 9 10 8 6 4 2

Simon & Schuster UK Ltd
1st Floor
222 Gray's Inn Road
London WC1X 8HB

Simon & Schuster Australia, Sydney
Simon & Schuster India, New Delhi

A CIP catalogue record for this book
is available from the British Library

PB ISBN: 978-1-4711-1870-8
EBook ISBN: 978-1-4711-1871-5

Prin   don, CR0 4YY

www.simonandschuster.co.uk
www.simonandschuster.com.au

*This is for my big sister Mandy Evitt,
and my little brother Tim Povey.
Bet you weren't expecting that.*

HOW TO KILL AN ENTIRE TOWN

There's an alien staring at me.

And trust me, that's not as weird as it sounds.

I'm sixteen, I have dyed pink hair and I have seen and done things I still can't really explain. There were nine people in school detention. Eight pupils and a teacher. But typically the teacher got up and left a second before a bright light whisked the rest of us away to an empty world. Empty that is, but for extreme copies of ourselves. Creatures I am now calling aliens. Super-powered and from a world that is exactly the same as ours – only it isn't.

Of the original eight only three of us made it back alive.

Me. Reva Marsalis.

GG. A glorious gay who it turns out is braver and more determined than almost anyone I know.

And the Ape. A lumbering, rude manboy who fought everyone and everything to keep me safe and alive.

Lucas the boy wonder died first. Hanged himself. Thought he was all alone in the world and threw in the towel. God, that still turns me inside out. Lucas had everything to live for and

1

if we'd just got to him a few minutes earlier ... He was still warm when the Ape and I found him.

Mean girl Carrie died in London. Cut down by the utterly evil alien version of GG. Sliced to ribbons by steel talons that will haunt my dreams for the rest of my life. All of the aliens possess them. That and metal teeth. Their dentists must double as metalworkers.

For a while I thought Billie, my best ever friend, the Moth, a brainy paraplegic, and Johnson, the only boy I could ever call world class, had also died. Buried under a thousand tons of rubble when the alien version of our Ape punched a hotel down around them.

That's right.

He punched it.

BOOM! That was the sound his punches made. *BOOM, BOOM, BOOM!*

To my eternal shame we were convinced they were dead and ran for home, back to our world. Only problem with that is we never actually made it home. Instead we were shifted back to the alien world.

And, if that's not bad enough, we then learn that Johnson, Billie and the Moth aren't dead after all. They're still trapped in the empty world. So that's two major wrongs and they certainly don't make a right.

'Talk to me, Reva.' The alien version of my mother is now standing right in front of me, gripping my wrist tight.

I'm tingling all over. My personal alarm is going off like a thousand sirens.

Wait.

Did I mention Other-Johnson? The exact copy of the world-class Johnson who stole my heart?

2

'Reva?'

I'll have get to Other-Johnson later.

If there is a later.

'What?' I ask her. I mean *it*.

The alien looks identical to my real mum. She is a carbon copy from head to toe. Just like I'm an exact copy of her real daughter.

'Where did all those cuts and bruises come from? Have you been in a fight?' she asks.

Have I been in a fight? There's an understatement to end all understatements.

'A fight? Me?' I say and try to look perplexed and condemning in the same breath. 'When did I ever get into fights?'

My non-mum is scanning me now, taking in all of the little cuts and bruises, her maternal worry animating her face. I can feel the low throb of the beginnings of a black eye from where GG punched me in the face – not because he wanted to, but because it was the only way he could get me to leave the others behind. I also have about a hundred other burns, scars and bruises, all of which I didn't have when I left for school this morning.

It seems that no time has passed in this world. I've come home from detention at the exact same time I would have done on any normal day. But I've spent at least two or three days fighting for my life.

So time happens differently in different worlds. That's something to tell the Moth when I see him again. He'll like that. It'll excite his big space brain.

But I won't get to tell him anything if I don't get out of here. I seriously need to find the Ape and GG because I left them to go home, or at least to what I thought were their homes.

'Anyway – uh, Mum – I was reading Dad's papers, you know, that thesis thing he wrote,' I tell her. The same thesis thingy that has turned my world upside down, not to mention, inside out. But it's the only thing that can help.

'You were? When?' My non-mum frowns.

'The other day.' I shrug, trying to sound as calm as I possibly can. 'Found it and started flicking through it.' I'm trying to sound casual and I think it's working.

'But you can't have been.'

I stop dead.

'No?' My voice catches.

'They're not here any more. There was a charity collection so I looked out some old clothes,' she continues, 'and found the papers at the bottom of the wardrobe. I don't know why, but as soon as I saw them I felt like I wanted them out of the house. So I rolled them up and shoved them into the sleeve of one of your dad's old leather jackets. Seeing them almost made me cry, Reva.' My non-mum has the same look in her eyes as my real mum when she talks about my dad – which is actually pretty much never these days. The same sadness and pain from twelve years of not knowing why her husband left without a word and never came back. 'You helped me pack the clothes into a bin liner. Remember?'

This is migraine-inducing. In the empty world Other-Johnson had found the papers in this very flat. Or a copy of them. In what he said was Rev Two's – my hugely inferior double's – bedroom. But that isn't this world. Which means I can't have been reading them.

Which also means I've made Huge Mistake Number Three.

4

'Duh, what am I like.' I force a smile and then remember that's not a good idea. Like I said, in this world people have talons *and* metal teeth, and God knows what would happen if my non-mum saw that I don't have either. They are a violent and aggressive race and tend to slash first and ask questions later.

My phone beeps with a message.

It's lying on the floor on charge but I can still make out the text. It's from the Ape. My big hairy hero who is probably the only reason I'm still alive.

where r u?

I slip free of my non-mum's grip, grab my phone and text as rapidly as I can.

don't talk to any1! don't look at any1! wait 4 me!

'Anyway.' I turn back to her, pretending to be chatty and sweet. 'What charity shop was it?' But there's an unmistakable quiver in my voice. I'm surprised she can't hear my vocal chords twanging.

'Just one of the shops in town. I forget which.'

I do a quick Google Earth search in my head and come up with at least four charity shops in the town centre alone. My insides are churning now. If I don't find my dad's papers – no, not *my* dad's papers, they'll actually be my other-dad's papers ... God this is worse than sudoku – then it is officially game over.

I glance at my phone. It's only charged to three per cent but I yank it and the charger from the wall and pray the small amount of power will hold until I find the Ape and GG. I rush past my non-mum and step out into the hallway. As I dart past her, I catch a faint whiff of her understated perfume. It's the same brand my real mum wears. So weird.

5

I head down the hallway with my non-mum padding behind me. The talons on her bare feet click-clack on the fake parquet floor and it makes the hairs on the back of my neck stand on end. Why have her talons come out?

'Reva,' she says. 'I know when something's wrong.'

But I can't stop now. I'm out of here, I'm going, I'm running, I'm ... I'm not moving. I can't move a single muscle. I can't even blink. What the hell is this?

'Wait.' My non-mum's voice is gentle, caressing. She's doing this. This must be her power. She's frozen me to the spot, wrapped me in invisible bonds. The perfect power for any parent with an errant teenager.

All of the aliens we have encountered so far seem to have a special power. To them it is normal, but to us meek humans it is horribly scary. And it doesn't help when you don't always know what that power might be.

Her hand lands lightly on my shoulder and I feel her talons slide out and curl round me.

Her grip tightens. 'Talk to me, Reva.'

But even if I wanted to, I can't tell her anything because I can't even move my jaw. I am completely immobile.

My non-mum comes round to face me. Even though my eyeballs are as frozen as the rest of me, in the periphery of my vision I can see her talons. Is this it? Is she going to cut me down?

She takes me in, scrutinising me. 'Sorry,' she whispers.

I try my best to move but it's like I'm encased in concrete. 'I shouldn't do this.'

I feel the bonds she has trapped me in slip away and I'm mobile again.

She looks a bit ashamed. 'I know I'm stupidly over-protective, but you're all I care about.'

I was sure she'd realise I wasn't her Reva, but maybe her eyes only take in what they want to see. I'm – well, the other me – is all she's got in the world and that's all that really matters to her. But that doesn't stop me secretly looking around for a weapon. Thanks to the Ape and his remarkable instinct for fighting and violence, we discovered that these versions of ourselves have a major weak spot. Go for the throat hard and fast and you've got a chance of beating them.

I can't believe I'm looking for something sharp to drive into any version of my lovely-loving mum. But I've seen what these creatures can do.

My non-mum blocks the way to the front door. But I have to get out of here. Now.

So I do the only thing I can.

I hug her.

I couldn't hurt this alien, *this woman*, in a million years. So I slip my arms round her and give her the most loving, caring hug I can.

'I love you,' I whisper.

Which distracts, maybe even surprises, her because when I look into her eyes, there are tears in them.

She smiles awkwardly. 'Silly.'

I hold her gaze. 'I do,' I tell her. 'I really do.'

There's something clawing at the back of my mind. If I do get away from this world, then this woman might never see me or her real daughter again. She'll spend the rest of her life wondering where her Reva Marsalis disappeared to. She's already spent twelve years wondering where her husband went and she's about to lose a daughter too.

I look into her warm eyes and I feel my eyes tearing up now.

'Mum?'

'Yes?'

But no words come. I just stare at her and wish this was so different.

I head swiftly down the concrete steps that rise alongside the rows of nineteen-fifties flats, taking them two at a time. As I do I phone the Ape. He takes an age to pick up and I'm worried I'll never get to say what I want before my charge gives out.

'Yowza to the yowza.' His deep man's voice booms across the airwaves.

'Did you phone GG?'

'Nah, couldn't be bothered.'

'Ape?'

'Gotcha!' He laughs.

This is no time to make stupid jokes, but the Ape has a mindset that only he will ever understand. Though even that is doubtful.

'I'm right here, Rev.' The sound of GG's voice lifts me as he takes the phone from the Ape.

'OK, listen, meet me at—'

'Use your own phone!' The Ape snatches the phone from GG. 'I'm on Pay As You Go.'

'And Rev called you, so it doesn't matter,' replies GG,

snatching the phone back. His voice is panicked, an octave higher than usual. 'Rev, I went home and no one was in. But then I saw my next-door neighbour ... She came out of her house, yacking on her mobile, and she had teeth that could chew through an aeroplane!'

'We came to the wrong world, GG.' My voice is flat and lifeless.

I hear him suck in his breath. 'I am never doing a bad thing ever again. No more detentions for GG.'

'Meet me at the charity shop next to the perfume shop on the high street. You know it?'

'Why there?'

'I might have a plan, but listen—' I lower my voice. 'You have to be so careful. They don't know we're not the same as them. But the second they do ...'

'It's Talon Time,' GG finishes for me.

I hang up. There are aliens everywhere and after spending a few days in a completely empty world it feels weird being back amongst people again. Only trouble is there seems to be lots of them. This might be a small town, but from what I can tell it must be a summer market this evening and that seems to have brought a flood of visitors.

I half jog, half walk past a huge second-hand car dealership and cross a busy main road to reach a packed car park that sits directly opposite.

A car horn sounds, making me jump. I glance up at the driver to gesture an apology for walking into his path, but he winds his window down and yells at me furiously.

'IDIOT!'

See. I told you they have the shortest fuses in the universe. I scoot between two more cars before finding the steps that lead down to the market. A small shallow river curls past the busy stalls and flows around a huge fourteenth-century church that dominates the town. Three teenage boys head my way and, recognising one of them from school, I bow my head and pretend to browse a music stall until they pass.

After they're gone, I head as quickly as I dare through the market and walk up a small arcade of shops before emerging into the cobbled town square where a tall blue clock stands proudly. I scan the area, looking for GG and the Ape.

Where the hell are they?

A young mother and her chocolate-devouring four-year-old brush past me and I yelp. Even with the merest of contact, she's electrocuted me in some way. She turns, looking surprised, as if I shouldn't have reacted like that, or she doesn't know why that happened. Her coal-black eyes scrutinise me and I quickly turn away.

I keep walking, feeling her eyes on me as I do. All of the aliens have black eyes, dark pools that are definitely not windows to the soul. Which shows how much my non-mum only saw what she wanted to see. Mine are bright blue.

'Hey!' the electric woman calls out.

'Stop looking at me,' I mumble to myself. 'Please, I'm nobody.'

'Hey, Pink Hair!'

I decide that now is the time to run but I'm saved by the woman's little boy screaming his head off. The noise is so ear-piercing that it makes nearby windows rattle. The mother forgets about me and possibly electrocutes her kid, because he stops screaming quite suddenly. She's probably got some taser power and set herself to 'stun'.

I start dialling the Ape's number, but before I can finish I see him and GG emerge into the square. GG is tense beyond words.

'I swear everyone's staring at us!' I hear him hiss at the Ape.

'Stop wetting yourself,' the Ape responds.

'Who in their right mind wouldn't be?' GG replies.

GG is wearing the same outfit as he was back in the classroom. Bright yellow jeans, a fur-lined combat jacket with the word *WAR(M)* on it and a cheap tiara. Together with the oversized Ape in his vast black overcoat, they make the least inconspicuous pair I have ever laid eyes on.

Before the detention that went so spectacularly wrong I barely knew them. GG was always the life and soul of the school, a relentlessly upbeat and excruciatingly funny boy who everyone adores but who no one really knows that well. The Ape is probably the most hated person at school. Both by the kids and the staff. And probably every parent. I was among them until I got to know him a little better. To my surprise I discovered the Ape – or Dazza as he always tries to get us to call him – has the biggest, bravest heart, and there is something inside him that never gives up. No matter the odds he always expects to win.

I can tell GG is ready to scream at the Ape, so I quickly herd them into the charity shop. 'Move.'

The shop is empty apart from an elderly lady dozing behind the counter with her mouth open. Her false teeth have slipped and it sends a quiet chill through me when I see that even they are metallic and sharp.

I keep my voice low as I whisper to GG and the Ape. 'OK, we're looking for a brown battered leather jacket. It was my dad's and in one of the sleeves, rolled up tight, is our ticket out of here.'

'We need a ticket?' the Ape asks.

GG ignores him. 'So, find the jacket, find the thesis . . . And you'll understand what your dad wrote?'

'I'm his daughter,' I say hopefully. 'Maybe some of his cleverness will have rubbed off. But let's be quick and not draw any attention. OK?'

'Del!' the Ape suddenly shouts. 'Hey!'

GG's eyes almost leap out of his head in horror. 'What are you doing?'

'That's Del,' the Ape says simply and bangs on the glass door to get the attention of a skinny boy who is passing the charity shop. 'Hey, Del!'

'Stop that! It's not Del!' I hiss at him.

The Ape looks at me and the lonely cog in his brain shifts another millimetre as he realises what he has just done.

'Oh, yeah.'

THE MIND HAS A THOUSAND EYES

'Dazza!' Not-Del grins broadly as he heads into the charity shop. He has lank greasy hair and wears a battered biker jacket.

The Ape falls completely silent.

Not-Del's grin reveals what look like rusty teeth. He clearly doesn't floss. 'What you doing in here? Robbing the place?'

The Ape stays silent.

'Say *something*,' GG hisses through his lips to the Ape.

'Dazza?' Not-Del's brow creases. He doesn't understand the Ape's silence.

I nudge the great oaf. Hard.

The Ape finally responds. 'Shopping.'

What a genius.

'Yeah? For what?' asks Not-Del.

'For . . . shopping.'

'Shopping for shopping?'

'Yeah.'

The Ape's alarmingly blunt and unfriendly conversation skills are not helping so I link my arm through his.

'Sorry, Del, we're sort of busy right now.'

'You with her?' Not-Del looks surprised and I realise that by linking arms with the Ape I've made it look like we're a couple.

'Yeah,' the Ape responds. 'Till I find something better,' he crows.

GG is all but dancing on the spot he is so nervous. 'Rev, we need to, uh . . . you know . . .'

Not-Del hasn't really noticed GG until now. 'GG?' he says and swallows hard.

'Hi.' GG nervously waggles his fingers.

But Not-Del is experiencing fear on a massive scale as he looks at GG.

And then it dawns on me. When we met Evil-GG, the super-powered, super-bitchy version of our GG, he bragged that he was the worst of the worst. Judging by Not-Del's reaction he was right on that score.

All I know about Del is that he was held back a year because he barely showed up for class. But this version of him obviously has history with Evil-GG. His talons are shooting in and out of his fingertips, a nervous reaction.

'You're friends with GG?' Not-Del asks the Ape.

'We're bezzies.'

Not-Del looks between the two of them. 'Why are you so small?' he asks the Ape.

The Ape from this world is huge, over seven feet tall and probably just as wide. I see GG's eyes widen with worry.

'I ain't small,' the Ape says.

'Yeah you are.'

'No *you* are,' the Ape says defiantly.

'Eh?'

'*You're* small.'

15

Not-Del seems to have become totally confused. Thank God he missed at least half his schooling.

GG takes a big breath and steps closer to Not-Del, channelling all the Evil-GG he can muster. 'You got a problem, Del?'

'No, GG! No, no, no, I swear.' I have no idea what Evil-GG has done to this poor boy, but it's obviously not pleasant.

'Then why don't you let us finish our shopping?'

'Yeah, absolutely, totally.' Not-Del's face is draped in panic as he takes one last confused look at the Ape. 'Always thought you were bigger than that.'

'You were always smaller,' the Ape tells him.

'On your way, Del.' GG flutters his fingers at Not-Del, who turns and hurries out of the shop. 'Bye-bye now.'

GG takes a moment for the *moment* to settle then giggles. 'Did you see that? Did you? I am officially the scariest boy in town. Oh, we have to stay here now. Let me dream the dream.'

I allow GG three seconds of omnipotence and then yank hard on the Ape's arm and together with GG we move deeper into the shop.

'We've got to be quick, all right? Quick and . . .' I study the old lady who is still dozing '. . . quiet.'

'She's farted.' The Ape fires a disgusted look at the snoozing woman as he waves at the bad air. 'Gas butt!'

'It's the smell of the clothes,' GG tells him.

'I know fart, and that is fart.'

'For God's sakes, can we just look for the jacket?' I hiss.

The Ape breathes in deeply, like he's the equivalent of an expert wine-smeller. 'Definitely fart.'

The old woman stirs, opens her eyes and sees us.

'Hello.' She smiles, then realising her false teeth have

slipped she pushes them back into her mouth. In a world of such gifted people, some of whom can heal, it comes as a strange comfort to think they can still lose their teeth and grow old and decrepit.

'Can I help?' She glows red from embarrassment.

'You can open a window,' the Ape replies.

The old lady stiffens a little so I try to steer her attention my way. 'I'm looking for a jacket. My mum and I accidentally donated it with a lot of old clothes.'

'We have a lot of jackets.' She smiles and waves towards the rear of the shop. 'But, if you find it, it's yours.'

'Thank you,' I say and head for the row of old jackets and musty unfashionable trousers lined along one of the rear walls.

GG comes with me, keeping his voice low. 'What if it's not here?'

'We'll try the next charity shop and the one after that.'

'But, Rev, what do we do if we can't find a way home? It won't take long before someone notices we're different,' he says.

'Let's not give them the chance. We're getting out of here and that's that.'

Something shifts in the room. I don't know what it is but my secret inbuilt spider sense is not happy. Ever since I was in the empty world I've had this warning signal. If I'm near danger my shoulders start tingling. So far it hasn't been wrong. Which is both good – and bad.

'That's odd,' the old woman says.

I stop in my tracks.

'Very odd.'

I turn back to her. 'Odd?'

GG's breath catches in the back of his throat and his eyes

open wide. The Ape is busy sniffing a cheap naked figurine. 'Why's everything stink in here?'

'*Well*.' The old woman takes a moment before her eyes find mine and look directly into me. '*You three are odd*.'

The old woman's lips don't move when she speaks.

'We are?' GG and I speak at the exact same time. She has entered both of our heads simultaneously. That's a feat Other-Johnson hasn't mastered. He's a telepath too. He can grab people's minds and put them in other people's heads. He can also steal girls' hearts, but I can't afford to get sidetracked thinking about him. As far as I know he's dead and that's just too heartbreaking to contemplate.

'What's odd?' asks the Ape five seconds later.

The old woman is reading our minds and to her credit she doesn't panic or scream. 'Well, well,' she says.

'Please,' I urge her. 'We know we shouldn't be here.'

'Just want to be on our way,' says GG.

The old woman takes a moment to think about whatever she's seen in our minds.

In that moment a talon slides from her finger.

'Hold on a sec, we can explain,' GG urges her.

The old woman drags thoughts and images from our heads. I feel them torn from me and even though I try my best to think of something else she tears out snapshots of the last few days. The awful moment when we ran a train over the Moth's double. Yes. A train. Then there was Carrie's double who I crushed and flattened with a wheelchair. It fell from the top of a hotel roof and hit her smack in the face. It was an accident but the old woman is already scrolling to images of Other-Johnson lying dead in the middle of a town square identical to the one outside her shop. That was really down to my evil

18

double, but we're so similar it looks like it was me who did it. So all in all I'm not coming across that well.

The old woman pales at the images.

'Please,' I say again, and this time I have tears in my eyes because the image of the dead Other-Johnson has ripped through me. 'We're lost,' I tell her. 'We're totally lost.' Which is true in so many ways.

But the old woman isn't listening. She is too scared. 'Wha-what do you want?' she stammers.

GG puts up his hand to get her attention. 'To go home, that's all. We want to be back in time for supper.'

There's something in her black eyes, a rising fear of us, and she seems to be particularly frightened of the Ape. Whatever she has found in his head has disgusted her. 'You,' she spits, 'you are a horrible creature.'

'You're the one farting,' says the Ape.

The old woman gets to her unsteady feet. 'Stay away from me.'

'We're not here to hurt you,' I tell her.

'*I need help,*' she mutters.

'We're the ones who need help,' GG pleads with her.

'*Hello, are you there? Anyone? Can you hear me?*' I realise that she's trying to mentally transmit an SOS to as many people as she can. And she's going to bring them all to the charity shop.

'*Hello, hello?*'

'Rev.' GG can sense it too as the old woman gathers her strength.

'Please!' I say for a third time. 'Look closer. We're good people.'

The old woman continues to gather her power. '*Please*

19

come!' She starts to shake and tremble; the transmission is taking all of her strength.

'Don't,' I plead. 'Please, please don't do this.'

She is ready, though, ready to summon a town of vicious creatures.

'Ape!' I yell, truly wishing it didn't have to be this way.

The Ape is huge, overweight and slow. But put a weapon in his thick stubby-fingered hands and he turns into one of the Three Musketeers. He grabs a metre-high porcelain statue and is ready to smash the old woman with it when she lets out a low whimper. Her nose bleeds with drops of black oily blood as she collapses back into her chair.

'I'm not what I was . . .' she mumbles as her eyes roll back in her head and she slips into unconsciousness. The exertion was too much for her and to my absolute relief we are safe. For now.

That doesn't stop the Ape from raising the porcelain statue above his head to bring down on the old woman. 'Eat this.'

'No!' I yell.

GG moves quicker than I have ever seen him and he gets in front of the old woman. 'We're OK, Dazza,' he urges. 'She can't do anything to us.'

The Ape takes an eternity to come to a decision but eventually even he can see that battering a defenceless old woman with a statue isn't exactly polite behaviour.

'She got lucky,' is all he mutters.

I turn to the clothes section in the very vain hope of finding my dad's jacket.

'Quick. Help me,' I tell GG.

GG starts grabbing at jackets. 'This one?' he asks.

I shake my head.

'This?' Another shake of the head.

'This one?' The Ape has picked up a woman's raincoat.

'That is not leather,' GG quietly admonishes him.

We find five more jackets but none of them are my dad's.

'We need to try another charity shop,' GG declares, up to his knees in fallen leather.

'The next one is over there.' I point diagonally across the square. 'But remember some of those aliens can read minds so keep your heads clear of anything that might give us away.'

'Maybe we should just send the Ape,' offers GG weakly. 'They wouldn't find a thing in there.'

I ease the door open. 'Ready?' I ask.

'Wait.' The Ape grabs three sets of sunglasses from a box of second- and third-hand eyewear.

'We're looking for a leather jacket!' GG tells him.

'They've got weird eyes.' The Ape hands me a pair of cheap Ray-Ban rip-offs. 'We haven't.'

I am stunned into silence. The Ape has moments of genius that still astonish me. Of course we should try and hide our eyes. Why didn't I think of that?

GG slips on a pair of aviators and immediately checks his look in the nearest mirror. 'Well hello Top Gun.'

The Ape has a pair of thick-framed glasses on now and looks in the mirror too. 'Yowza,' he says.

THE SQUARE DANCE OF DEATH

The town square isn't large, but moving through so many people who could potentially kill us might be one of the hardest things we'll ever do. We start walking as casually as we can. The Ape even tries whistling but it's tuneless and brings sharp looks so I nudge him and he stops.

I start scanning the square. I have no idea how many different types of powers people have in this world. Knowing our luck there's bound to be someone who has the nose of a shark who can sniff us out from a thousand different odours.

'I think I need a tinkle,' whispers GG.

'Cross your legs. You'll have to wait,' I whisper.

The next charity shop is little more than forty metres away down a side street that leads off from the square.

We can do this, I think. *We can make it. We have to*.

'Yo, Pink!'

A voice calls through the air and I'd recognise it anywhere. It's Ella. One of the banes of my life at school. She's a big lumbering girl who basically hates any girl who is smaller and skinnier than her. Although, of course we're in the other world, so this is Not-Ella.

'Keep walking,' urges GG.

'Hey!' Not-Ella shouts louder this time and because I don't want people looking at us I reluctantly turn round and see a group of girls sitting on a bench by the tall blue clock in the centre of the square. They're all in my school year and Carrie's hatred of me only just trumps what these four feel about me.

Not-Ella likes to squeeze herself into ill-fitting clothes rather than admit she's actually two sizes bigger. She has hated me since primary school. I was chosen to play Archangel Gabriel in the school nativity while she was cast as the cattle shed. In truth it's the teacher she should have a problem with but the Ella in my world doesn't see it that way and it seems that neither does this version of her.

Not-Ella gets to her feet and her aggressive acolytes follow suit.

The Ape stares down Not-Ella. 'What d'you want?' he says in his dull aggressive tone.

Not-Ella walks over and comes face to face with us. Her spiteful little friends hang back a pace or two and I'm scanning them wondering what sort of powers they may possess.

'I was talking to her,' Not-Ella hisses.

'And now you're talking to me,' the Ape responds.

There are many, many things wrong about the Ape but when it comes to confrontation then he's the fiercest, most capable person in the world. And that's any world you care to mention.

Not-Ella hesitates. The Ape from this realm is unbelievably strong – he practically tore a train in half when we first encountered him – and she's obviously well aware of this. Even if he is a lot smaller now.

'I'm just saying.' Not-Ella is less confident.

'And I'm just saying it too.'

As the Ape stands his ground, I feel hugely protected. With him by my side I don't think anything could hurt me. Ella weighs up her options, then gives me the bird and turns away.

'Laters,' she spits.

I allow myself a second of relief and then set off again, quicker now, eager to reach the next charity shop.

GG speaks with his hand cupped over his mouth but even through it I can hear the fear in his voice. 'Rev? I think they're looking at us funny.'

I look up and everywhere I turn I meet someone's eye. It definitely feels like they are all watching us. There are pairs of staring black eyes everywhere I turn. Thank God we're wearing sunglasses.

'C'mon,' I urge and we set off, moving as fast as we dare. But faces are stopping to stare and it really does seem that every time I look up I catch someone else's eye. They don't look at all friendly and my danger-alarm starts to quietly scream inside me. It builds steadily as more people take a moment to double take as we push through them.

The square seems packed now. Every centimetre of it is full like Oxford Street at Christmas.

'Almost there ...' I whisper, more to myself than the others.

But the faces are everywhere we look and the people are crowding around us. There's so many more of them than before and it's getting harder to push through.

'Excuse me, sorry, excuse me please ...' They step out of the way but for every one we squeeze past another two seem to be blocking our route.

I see the taser woman with the chocolate-obsessed four-year-old stare directly at me but I look away. Her son starts to wail again and the shrill sonic scream fills my ears. GG is grimacing from the noise, but the Ape seems indifferent, probably thanks to all the heavy metal he listens to.

I can't actually see the side road where the next charity shop is located. There are just too many people in front of us and I'm becoming disorientated. I can smell the musk and sweat and perfume of the hostile creatures whose numbers are thickening around us by the second. It feels like we've been walking for at least ten minutes and yet we don't seem to be able to find a way off the small cobbled square.

'How come the square is so big all of a sudden?' whispers GG.

'It can't be much further.' Panic is wrapping itself round me and I'm starting to think that someone has got a power that plays with perception and they're holding us in its sway.

I don't know which way to turn because it seems as if there is no end to the square. It just goes on and on and the more we push through the less we seem to get anywhere.

Someone is definitely doing this to us, I am sure of it. I can almost feel them inside me, showing me a gap that we can head for but then it suddenly closes and we have to turn and find another opening somewhere else. But that closes too and I know we are being turned round and round in circles.

The square is packed now, heaving with their version of their humanity. We're getting jostled and pushed around and the faces are uniformly unforgiving and accusing. I don't want to look at them because I'm scared they'll see how horribly anxious I've become.

I look at the Ape and his slow-moving brain is having

25

trouble computing what is going on. 'How far is this stupid shop?'

'Ape,' I say.

The Ape turns. 'It's Dazza.'

'We need to get off this square. And you need to clear a path.'

The Ape couldn't look more delighted. He twists his neck, making it crack, and then gets ready. 'Which way?'

I turn round and try to pick a path. But as I do I give in to the totally worst certainty ever.

'Oh God, they know,' I breathe quietly. 'They absolutely know.'

GG dares to look around and when he does every face is staring straight at us and we are trapped in the middle of them all.

'They know what?' says the Ape, frowning.

'Who we are.'

'*What* you are, you mean.' The voice is high-pitched and shrill. Not-Del pushes through the crowd.

END OF THE ROAD

I spin around looking for an exit or an escape route but all I can see is an army of angry aliens, all of them focused on us.

The Ape bunches his fists. 'I got this.'

The Ape's famous catchphrase is back. Have to admit I've kind of missed it, even if it does usually herald a fight.

'Excuse me?' GG is stunned.

The Ape shrugs. 'I got this.'

'There must be a hundred of them!' I hiss.

'More than that.' GG swallows.

'Maybe we can talk to them,' I say without a single trace of belief or hope.

'Get ready to run,' the Ape says. 'I can hold them.' The Ape is completely serious and I have to admire his utter conviction and fearlessness.

'No, Ape, no way.'

'Get ready.' He flexes his muscles under his coat.

'Let me talk to them,' I suggest.

'And say what?'

Which is as good a question as he has ever asked because

27

there is no talking to these creatures. We've seen it over and over first-hand. They do not stop for a cup of tea and a chat.

'Go.' The Ape is circling GG and me watching the creatures.

The thing that scares me the most, the one thing I have grown to hate more than anything about these 'people' are their talons. Their sharp metal talons. I have seen the mess they made of Billie's face and Carrie's entire body.

'Where exactly are we supposed to go?' asks GG as the creatures continue to stare unforgivingly at us.

'Get out of here, Rev,' urges the Ape.

Deep down in his Neanderthal brain is some never-say-die spirit, and it is a part of him that dwarfs anything I have ever seen in anyone else. Johnson and GG come very close but the Ape's deep well of spirit and fight is God-like.

All I wanted was to get us back to the other world. To save our stranded friends and find my beloved Johnson – both of them. Somehow I've been clinging to a crazed notion that, like in every book I read and every film I ever watched, the boy and the girl will end up together. It's a universal given.

Until now.

Turns out that apocalyptic reality isn't like the movies.

'You can't take on an entire town,' I tell the Ape.

'Yeah I can.'

'No, Ape, you can't. We're in this together.'

GG puts a gentle hand on the Ape's thick wrist. 'We've got nowhere to run.'

The Ape stares at the gathering of aliens. They bare their teeth and a thousand steel-tipped talons slide from their fingers.

They've been unusually patient. They should have attacked us long before now but maybe they're drawing mental straws to see who gets first slash.

'Then you'd better get behind me,' the Ape tells us.

GG's hand remains on the Ape's wrist as their eyes meet. 'God I love you.'

'Stop that!'

I feel a sense of calm spread over the square, as if the creatures have come to a decision.

Some of them part and out of the masses steps Not-Ella who joins Not-Del. She can barely contain her joy. 'Yo, Pink.'

'The old woman in the charity shop,' Not-Del says, his high-pitched voice making my skin crawl. 'Her thoughts got out. They were swirling around until someone picked them up. And that someone can sends texts without a phone. So we *all* know what you did.'

'Wait,' I say. 'Aren't any of you curious about why we're here? Don't you want to know about the other worlds out there? There could be hundreds of them.'

'Yeah, it looked like the world you just came from was great. Visit and die.' Not-Del laughs but it's not a nice laugh.

'That was just a big misunderstanding,' I say. 'Well – maybe more than one.'

'And we're talking humungous confusion,' adds GG, babbling again.

'D-don't any of you get it?' I stammer. 'It's the eighth wonder of the world.'

'And you've got friends stuck there,' GG adds.

'Friends?' Not-Ella laughs. 'That's not the word I'd use.'

'Your people, your, uh, your kind, they can be healed. You all know that.' I try and make eye contact with Ella, hoping she'll see the humanity in me. 'And we can go and get them and send them back. I promise you. I absolutely swear that's

29

what we'll do.' I blink the well of tears from my eyes. 'You could even come with us.'

'Don't you get it? No one likes any of you.' Not-Ella is enjoying this way too much. 'We don't want any of you – and that goes for both versions.'

'My mum'll miss me,' I tell her.

'Your mum's a nobody,' says Not-Del.

The words sting and I can't believe the whole town think of my non-mum and my real mum in such a callous way. God I hate them. I hate them all.

'My dad'll be furious,' offers GG.

'Your "dad" is driving a train to the coast.'

'And your mum and your sisters were seen driving out of town earlier.'

GG immediately pales at this. 'You can't do this to them. They love their little GG.'

'I don't recall anyone loving you,' says Not-Ella to GG without an ounce of compassion.

'Sorry, Dazza.' Not-Del shrugs an apology to the Ape.

'You're the one who's going to be sorry.' I watch the Ape stand tall, taller than he's ever been. He towers over Not-Ella and Not-Del, fixing the entire square with the bravest, most defiant look I have ever seen. 'You think you can take me?'

I feel a huge swelling in my heart, and a surge of strength flows straight from the Ape into my tired, battered body. I take a moment, then pull myself as upright and as proud as I can and stand head to shoulder with him. GG sees and follows suit, puffing out his skinny chest, and together we turn and form a small triangular circle, if there is such a thing, our backs to each other, waiting for a whole town to come at us.

The Ape continues to eye the creatures. 'Rev?'

'Yeah?'

'Fight or die.'

The Ape cracks his neck again. He is ready for war. And GG and I are going to stand right by him.

It's the only way. The Way of the Ape.

'Why don't you let us make this quick?' Del is completely bewildered by the Ape's lack of fear.

'Why don't you stop talking and do something?' The Ape has no step back in him. He is all forward thrust and bring it on. He will never be a model citizen but I think a tiny part of me has fallen for the model he is.

'*We've* got this!!' yells the Ape as he charges forward. Talons glint, teeth are bared and I surprise myself by staying tall. I'm not going to give them anything but all the fight I've got in me.

The Ape ploughs onwards, plunging headlong into a maelstrom of creatures who quickly fall on him.

Despite my best intentions I turn away, unable to watch.

DON'T MESS WITH MUM

'Nobody touches my daughter!'

The voice erupts over the lethal gathering of teeth and talons.

I open my eyes and find that the world has stopped.

Everyone in the square is frozen. Their slashing talons, their snapping teeth, every part of them is frozen in suspended animation.

GG's eyes find mine and he's just as confused as I am. The Ape crawls out from under at least a dozen clawing creatures, miraculously none of which managed to touch him before becoming frozen.

He gets to his feet, triumphant. 'Told you I had this.' He grins at us.

'Reva!' My non-mum's voice breaks through the mass of static bodies.

I turn and see her pushing through the frozen masses. Her walk is a weak stumbling stagger as if she's drunk.

I go to her and catch her just as she falls into my arms.

'Go! I can't hold them for long.' She can barely get her words out, she is breathing so hard.

'You did this? You stopped them?'

She can barely catch her breath. 'Wherever you came from, you need to get back there.'

GG and the Ape join us. GG is so excited, so relieved, he squeals. 'I thought we were so dead, I did. I thought I was going to GG heaven.'

My non-mum clutches my arm. 'Please, you've got to go.'

'I don't understand. I'm not even – I'm not your Rev.'

'But maybe ...' She has to take a moment to catch her breath again. 'Maybe you can send my Reva back to me.' She looks into my eyes and then reaches up and touches my face. 'Send her home. Please.'

GG casts his eyes around the square, taking in the non-moving creatures. 'How long have we got?'

'Ten minutes, maybe less.' The pressure of freezing an entire town is showing on her face.

'I don't know what to do,' I tell her. 'Not in ten hours, let alone ten minutes.'

'You have to get away,' she says

'But—'

'You have to do this for me. I want my daughter back.'

GG starts to pull me away from the frozen crowd. 'Let's find the jacket and the papers.'

'They could be in any charity shop and I don't even know what good it'll do if we find them!' This is hopeless and futile. 'I pinned my hopes on those papers because I was desperate but I have no idea what difference finding them will make. The Moth would understand them but he's not here.'

'Let's go back to the classroom,' suggests the Ape.

Which stuns me into silence.

'It's how we got here,' he says. 'Probably get us back.'

'You think another light will just come along and sweep us up? From out of nowhere?' I ask, disbelieving.

'Why not?' He shrugs.

I look at GG who looks as incredulous as me that the Ape has said two sensible things in the last ten minutes, but then he nods. 'It's better than anything I can think of.'

'But why would the light come back?' I ask.

The Ape shrugs again. 'Why wouldn't it?'

My non-mum grips my arm tighter. 'Hurry. I can't hold them!'

As if to prove her point, one of the aliens staggers closer, fighting hard against the bonds.

My non-mum urges me with determined eyes and I think of my own mum and how she'd be right here fighting for me as well. I haven't had time to miss her but now, more than ever, I'm determined to get back and be the best daughter ever.

I can't help myself and stop to kiss my non-mum's cheek. 'She's coming home. I promise you. I'll send your Reva home.'

Running through a town of frozen yet deadly creatures is a long way short of pleasant. Most of the town's residents have unsheathed their talons and some probably have exceptional powers. Whoever heard the old woman's weak message has transmitted it to everyone in town, and that is one pretty powerful alien.

GG and I try to duck and weave round them while the Ape just ploughs straight through them, shoulder-charging them out of his meaty way. 'Coming through!'

The school sits at the top of a steep hill and time is flying by too quickly. I'm not convinced that ten minutes will be enough.

A skinny middle-aged jogger suddenly moves, lashing out with a clawed hand, and I am forced to duck at the last second.

'She can't hold them!' yells GG.

'Yes she can!' I yell back. 'She's my mum.'

A man in a suit moves stiffly towards us, but my non-mum must get a hold of him and he freezes again. Some see us coming and start to fight the bonds they are held in, but we keep going, pumping our legs, darting round and past the everyday folk of a nightmare world. My legs are aching as we head through the school gates. School has finished and there are fewer creatures in the grounds. We are lucky to meet only a few half-frozen teachers who are now struggling furiously against the bonds my non-mum has wrapped them in.

I fear what they might do to her when they break free of her bonds. And I'm wondering if we should have taken her with us, but I can't go back for her now. To pause, to even think about pausing, will be the death of us. I just pray that Rev Two comes home and finds her mum is still here.

The Ape crashes into the school, shattering the glass in the doors, and almost gets decapitated by Mr Allwell who manages to swing slow-moving talons his way.

GG sees it coming and, using all of his strength, barrels into the Ape and shunts him to one side. 'Ape!!'

The metal talons embed in the wall.

GG dances round Mr Allwell and takes the first stairway we come across. The classroom we had detention in is on the top floor and we have to weave between hateful teachers and a group of violent-looking drama pupils who form pretty much the same doppelganger group that Billie and I were thrown out of. We have to be careful because on the stairs we are forced by the narrowness of the stairwell to pass close to them. A few even manage to take some painfully slow lunges at us as my non-mum's hold over them starts to falter.

The Ape barges a few over the side of the banisters but because of the way they are made the rubbery-skinned creatures shrug off their landing, then snap themselves back into place and, moving as if they are trudging through treacle, start to come back up the stairs.

By the time we have reached the top floor it's painfully obvious that my non-mum's hold over the town has all but bled away.

The noise of increasingly fleet footsteps coming up the stairwell is filling the school as the Ape kicks open the classroom door. GG and I burst in after him and start piling desks and chairs up against it. I know it won't be any use as we hear footsteps in the hallway outside. The Ape smashes a chair against the floor over and over until all he is left with are the metal legs that he now intends to use as a weapon of some sort.

The only weapon GG can find is a mid-sized globe of the world and he gets ready to wield it as the first thud crunches into the barricaded door. I try to put all my weight behind the piled desks but the door shudders again and I'm shunted back, my feet slipping and sliding on the polished floor.

There's another massive shunt and the door flies off its hinges, scattering the desks and throwing me into the middle of the room.

Vicious angry faces appear at the doorway as GG drags me to my feet. The Ape tosses me a chair to use as a weapon.

GG stands with us, globe at the ready, as the creatures weigh up what they're going to do next. I could pretty much spell it out to them but they always seem to hesitate first. As if they know we're doomed and that there's no escaping them.

'Rev?' asks GG.

'Yeah?'

'Say the light did come, how would we know it was taking us to the right place?' I hadn't even thought of that. 'I mean, it could be worse than this.'

'Oh, yeah, GG. Loads worse. This is nothing.'

Our eyes meet and for the briefest of moments we share a smile. *We've come such a long way together*, I think, and it's a total crying shame it has to end now.

The Ape studies the creatures. 'Come on then!'

They couldn't have received a clearer invitation and the creatures begin to pour forth.

They're quick but the white light is quicker.

ARE WE THERE YET?

The classroom is empty.

There is just me, GG and the Ape. We're still clinging on to our makeshift weapons but wherever we have gone there are no longer any creatures crashing in.

The door to the corridor remains open and the only sound I can hear is of my own laboured breathing.

It's empty. The school is empty, I'm sure of it. Which means, hopefully, we're back in the empty world.

'You did it, Ape, you were right.'

'It's Dazza.'

'Is that the first time you've ever known the answer in a classroom?' quips GG. 'Because if it is then I love you more than ever.'

'Stop saying that!'

The Ape cranes his great thick neck as he looks around scanning the room.

'I think we're back,' I tell him.

But the Ape is wary; he has ultra-keen instincts. 'Shh,' he says. 'Can you hear that?'

38

He falls silent, listening hard.

I fall silent with him, listening as hard as I can. 'There's nothing.'

He raises a large slab of hand, silencing me. His near perfectly square block of head scans from left to right.

GG is holding his breath. 'I can't hear anything,' he whispers.

But the Ape is convinced there is something – or someone. I can tell from the way his grip tightens on the legs of the school chair.

Seconds turn into a long breathless minute.

'Well?'

The Ape eventually speaks. 'I heard something.'

'We got that part,' GG whispers. 'But what?'

The Ape relaxes his grip. 'Footsteps. They're gone now.'

'Footsteps? It'll be Johnson and the others!' GG excitedly starts for the open door but the Ape puts a huge hand on GG's delicate shoulder.

'Stupid people die first.'

GG is yanked backwards easily by the powerful Ape.

'Maybe I'll just take a peek out of the window,' GG says.

He crosses quietly to one of the tall classroom windows and takes a long look outside. Whatever he sees out there robs him of his breath.

'Oh good Goddy.'

'What?' I say, bracing myself for the worst.

GG eventually finds his voice. 'I spy with my little eye something beginning with "s".'

'Soldiers!' says the Ape excitedly. 'Is it soldiers?'

I march over to the window and look for myself.

'S is for snow,' says GG as the Ape joins us.

'Snow?' The Ape grins. 'I love snow!'

The world outside is covered in a deep blanket of snow. But the more I look the more I realise that there are no footprints. Not anywhere. No one has walked in this snow.

'It's empty,' I whisper. 'Outside is empty.'

'Where are we?' GG asks. 'Are we back?'

I haven't a clue, but I've still got my charger in my pocket and I plug my phone into the nearest wall.

'This is no time to charge your phone,' GG says.

'I need to make a call.'

'I hope it's to the council; they should be out there gritting.' The joke is weak, but GG never misses an opportunity to lighten the mood.

My phone finally lights up after what feels like an excruciating wait and I scroll to Johnson's number in as calm and orderly a fashion as I can. I press dial and say a silent prayer.

Please, God, please let the phone work here like last time. Please let Johnson pick up.

The phone burbles with a muffled ring. It's connecting me. Which is something.

But no one picks up.

GG looks from me to the Ape and then back to me.

More unanswered rings echo through the classroom.

It rings and rings.

Please God.

Please.

GG slips a hand on my arm as if to say, *Let it go.*

The Ape studies the snow. 'There's no footprints.'

Always a moment behind everyone else.

'No one home,' he says.

40

I look at the phone and will Johnson to answer.

Come on.

Please.

GG's finger hovers over the END CALL button. 'We're not in the right place. But there'll be another light. We'll wait for it, Rev.'

'Rev?'

The calm tone that echoes out of my phone is unmistakable.

'Johnson?' I can barely speak because it feels like my thumping heart is rising up and filling my mouth.

'Where have you been?' he asks.

My knees almost buckle as I try to stay calm. 'Long story. Where are you?'

'In town. How are you calling me? Are you back?' Johnson sounds as amazed as a Johnson ever could.

'Yeah, I think so. I'm with GG and the Ape.'

'It's Dazza!' the Ape bellows across the room.

Johnson takes a moment. 'When did you get back?'

'Just now.' I'm so excited I can't get a grip of my thoughts. 'And just to check, you know, make sure ... Is it snowing where you are?'

'Yeah ... Yeah it is.'

Oh. My. God. We are back in the empty world.

I can't find any words. I open and close my mouth as the thought of seeing Johnson again renders me speechless.

'We're in the classroom,' GG calls out, unable to stop smiling. 'We went back for extra lessons.'

'We were shifted to the wrong world, but we escaped. We're here again,' I tell Johnson.

'I blame British transport. But don't tell my dad that,' GG adds.

'Is it – is it really you?' I still won't let myself quite believe it. I don't even know if Johnson can hear the whisper I squeeze past my numb lips.

'Yeah. Well. Sort of.'

I don't know what he means, but I don't care. The sound of his voice is wrapping round me.

'Tell me exactly where you are. We're coming now,' I tell him.

'Right now?' Johnson asks.

'Of course.'

'Oh.'

'Oh?' Something jabs at my heart.

'I mean – about time,' says Johnson, and it's only now I hear the tension hidden way back in his voice. There's something not quite right. He's become too neutral too quickly, almost indifferent. It's like he's only playing at being glad to hear from me.

My heart starts to sink. 'Is everything OK, Johnson? Has something happened? To Billie? To the Moth?'

'Just come see us.'

I hesitate. 'What about the others? The usses, the bad versions. Is it safe?'

'They've gone.'

I immediately think of Other-Johnson. 'All of them?'

'Haven't seen them.'

My spider sense tickles in my shoulders. Not dramatically, but enough to put me on edge.

'You sure everything's OK?'

'I guess things have changed a little, Rev.' His words spear into me.

'Changed? I don't understand.' But I'm starting to guess,

because when we left it was the end of summer and now there's thick snow outside.

Johnson turns my fear into a reality. 'It's been five months since we heard from you. How can things not have changed?'

SNOW ANGELS AND A BROKEN HEART

We're outside in the thick snow, in the school car park. It's utterly freezing.

Outside and in.

GG is shaking as the biting air swarms around us. We've abandoned our sunglasses, because who would wear them in the middle of winter. 'Look at that,' he says, pointing.

From our high vantage point we can see that most of the town is covered in snow.

'It's like a big Christmas card.' GG has been jabbering away since we left the classroom and I'm pretty sure it's to keep me sane, to ward off the horrendous thought that almost half a year has swept by in the blink of an eye. If time has passed that much here when it was only a few hours in the 'alien' world, then how much time have we missed at home?

My mum will have given up hope: she could've held a memorial for me, or just filed me alongside my dad as another person who went missing from her life. It'll hurt her beyond belief which makes me more determined than ever to get home.

44

'I don't understand.' My breath is almost solid from the cold and I'm having difficulty trudging through the virgin snow. It's deeper than I first thought and even though we are heading downhill we are making very slow progress.

'This means I missed my birthday.' GG blows into his cupped hands. 'I love birthdays. I get to buy new clothes and eat cake all day long'

My insides are colder than the snow. There was something in Johnson's voice that I didn't recognise. And I didn't like it.

'Outta my way!'

The Ape bellows and when we turn he is hurtling towards us on a large wooden tray he must have pilfered from the school dining hall. He is sitting on his knees, crouched as low as he can to build up the maximum speed. We have to scramble to get out of his way and as he shoots between us he tosses a couple of trays at us.

'Sledge!' he yells, then on he shoots, picking up speed as his makeshift sledge bounces across the firmly packed snow.

GG quickly grabs the trays before they end up sliding after the Ape.

'Doubt we'll find a taxi in this weather.' GG tosses a tray to me then climbs aboard his. 'See you at the bottom.'

As I grab the tray I catch a glimpse of what I think are footprints leading from a side entrance to the school. There are a few concealed brick steps that lead down to a pavement then up towards a metal walkway that takes you to a music block opposite.

But these footsteps didn't take the walkway, they turned left and headed in another direction.

Back into town.

'GG, wait—'

'Apeman, I'm a-coming!' GG shoves off.

I watch GG picking up speed and he has to grip the edge of the tray as tight as he can because the hill is incredibly steep.

If there are footprints, someone else was in the school recently. The Ape was right: he did hear footsteps.

I don't know who it could have been, but what if one of the evil world inhabitants somehow come back with us and then escaped into town?

The thought fills me with dread, but if it's true then I need to warn the Ape and GG. They are hurtling down the hill and there's only one way that I can reach them.

I also can't forget that I am on a mission, that I made a promise to my non-mum, that amazing woman who took on an entire town to save us, and I will not let her down. Violent, death-dealing, footprint-leaving alien or not.

I'm already beginning to lose sight of GG and the Ape, so I take a snow-impeded run, build up as much speed as I can and throw my body flat onto the tray. I land hard but my momentum and the steepness of the hill carry me onwards. The hill is probably half a mile long and even though the cold is biting into my fingers I grip the edge of the tray tight, lying as low as I possibly can, streamlining myself so that I turn into a human bullet and shoot down the hill.

They've had a big head start but the Ape is larger and heavier than me and he's also sitting upright, just as GG is, and I am already catching them because they aren't as aerodynamic. I can also use my feet as rudders to steer better and as a tight bend looms I take it far better than either of them did. I close in on GG and he must sense me because he turns back and sees me hurtling towards him. He laughs and trails his hand in the snow so he can grab enough to make a snowball. As I close on him he starts throwing snowball after snowball at me.

'Back! Back I say!' he yells.

'I saw footprints,' I yell at him.

'Back!'

'No, listen—' A snowball hits me in the mouth and I swallow half of it.

GG is appalled. 'Rev, sorry! I've never snowballed a girl in my life! Where has all this violence come from?'

'GG, listen to me,' I shout. But GG hits another bend and loses control of his tray and tips over, going into a tumbling roll.

I shoot past him. 'Meet me at that bottom!' I yell. 'Don't do anything till we talk!'

I hope he has heard me as he sprawls face down in the snow.

I've got the Ape in my sights now and even though he is only a few metres from hitting the snow-covered main road that runs through the town I know I can catch him.

My makeshift sledge carries me faster and faster and for a second I think back to my dad and how I used to sit in the cradle of his lap on a sledge on snowy days like this. He'd made a wooden sledge but would only ever take me down what he called 'safer slopes' but I didn't care because he was wrapped round me, cocooning me, and no matter how cold it was I never felt any of it because of him.

'Ape!' I yell.

He turns his massive head and sees me heading straight for him. He starts using his bear-like hands and arms to paddle himself faster, probably determined not to be beaten by a girl. But with his extra weight I know he can't outpace me and I draw alongside him just before we hit the road.

'I saw footprints so we need to be ultra careful!' I yell at him.

'What?'

'I said there was someone at the school.'

The Ape suddenly leaps from his tray and lands on top of me. I feel his massive weight crush the breath from me and I go into a total pancake state and lose control.

'What the hell??'

I've been carrying all manner of cuts and bruises, and with him on top of me every single one of them screams.

'Get off me!' I shriek.

The Ape laughs as we veer insanely over the road and straight into a deserted car park.

I have walked through this car park a million times and I know there are steep concrete steps awaiting us.

'Ape, jump off!'

We're travelling so fast we hit the steep steps and fly out over them before he can move a muscle. We dip dramatically, landing hard some three metres below. He goes one way and I roll the other. I shoot straight for the tiny frozen river that flows in front of the ancient church.

I have no way of stopping and start to tip and roll and slip towards the iced-over river.

'Ape ... !' I'm hoping that the ice is really thick, that this cold snap has been here for weeks, as I am thrown out onto it.

I spin and spiral along the ice and can see the far bank rearing up in front of me. *I'm going to be all right*, I think, *I'm going to make it across*.

The ice cracks like a distant gunshot and just as I reach the bank it shatters underneath me and I am plunged into water that feels like it has to be at least a hundred degrees below freezing.

I SWEAR I'VE DONE SOMETHING SIMILAR BEFORE

I'm sure the river isn't usually this deep. Normally it's little more than a metre at most. I should be able to stand up in it.

Why's it so deep? Everything in this world is practically identical to my own, so why is something like the depth of the river different?

I can't work it out. But I can't seem to work anything out.

My brain is moving so slowly.

It must be the cold.

I need to do something, but I can't remember what. Something about hitting the bottom and pushing off again.

But where's the bottom?

Where are my feet?

I can't feel them.

If I shout for help will anyone hear me?

It's so cold down here.

Cold and silent.

The water fills my nose and mouth.

Numbness is crawling all over me and I'm not sure but I think my heart just shut down.

All I wanted was to see Johnson, for good or bad I wanted to lay eyes on him and have him tell me everything is OK. But the second I get within touching distance he's snatched away from me.

God it's cold.

So cold that I can't even feel it.

A memory comes to me, labouring through my frozen thoughts.

I'm back in my father's lap as we slide down a gentle slope on a sledge he built himself. Mum's already at the bottom taking photos of us. She's laughing, Dad's laughing and I just feel warm all over. Dad's here and I'm safe.

Where did you disappear to?

Where are you when I need you . . . ?

A hand grabs my hair and yanks hard.

That I do feel, because it hurts like hell, but because I can't actually command my arms to do anything other than hang limply, I have to endure the agony.

Either the arm tugging on me is very strong or I've lost a lot of weight recently. I break the surface and gasp for air but even though I can breathe again, apart from my painful arm, the rest of my body is numb.

Someone lifts me clean out of the river and into their arms, mumbling something I don't quite catch.

I try to speak but my lips and tongue are swollen with cold. The wind whips around me as I try to open my eyes but I didn't know that if you get too cold you can't actually see. My eyelids are frozen shut.

But I'm alive.

I'm breathing.

Reva Marsalis lives.

The person swings me up into their arms with indecent ease. 'This isn't a day to go swimming.'

Even through my frozen haze I recognise the voice. Johnson.

I feel a door kicked open and because we've only gone a few paces and the nearest building to the river is the fourteenth-century church then that's where I've been taken. Though kicking the door open isn't exactly holy behaviour.

Johnson's saved me again. Once from burning to death, now from drowning. What's next, a hurricane?

He lays me down on the stone floor. 'Hold still.'

'Johnson . . .' My voice is barely above a whisper. 'It's really you . . .'

'In a way.'

'Thank God—'

But just when I'm starting to feel safe, I hear the now all too familiar sound of a talon released from a fingertip.

I try to move. To kick. 'No,' I say. 'No!' I lash out with my slow-moving pathetic arms. But it's more like a weak flap. I try and kick with my leaden legs. 'Get off me!'

Hands pin me down. Strong hands. Inhuman hands. This isn't Johnson at all. My mind has played a trick on me.

Why did I charge blindly down here on a school tray of all things? Haven't I learned anything?

I saw footprints, I sensed danger, and still I didn't heed any of it.

I kick again but my legs just won't respond.

'I said lie still,' the voice soothes. But it comes out as sinister.

I heard the talon; I know what it means. The fear pumping through my blood is starting to warm me. I'm getting some feeling back. I try to curl my fingers into a fist. But they still won't co-operate.

'Please let me go!'

'Easy now.'

'You'd love that.' I try with all my might to wriggle away but the monster has me in a fierce grip and even if I wasn't frozen half to death I still wouldn't stand a chance. They're so much more powerful than us.

'Look at me, Rev.'

I open my eyes. The light stings and I blink rapidly, trying to see something more than a blur.

As soon as they focus I can see a statue of Jesus peering down at me. His kind but reproachful face is telling me I'm an idiot. No one sledges into a lion's den. No one. They move quietly, with stealth and cunning. They don't yell 'yippee' and hurtle down a hill.

I deserve this, I think. *I'm too stupid to warrant further existence.*

But no matter how stupid I am, Reva Marsalis does not die easily.

I have shaken off enough numbness to fight. Thanks to my wet slippery skin I slither free of the inhuman grip and try to swing a punch but a fast-moving hand grabs my wrist again. As it does I catch sight of a glint of metal.

The metal that is the shiny horror of the doppelgangers' hideous teeth.

Where the hell are the Ape and GG? They should be crashing in here to rescue me. The Ape can kill them. He can kill anything!

Hands curl round my wrists and push my arms back. The monster holding them looms into my eyeline.

The monster is Johnson.

I don't know what has happened to him but the boy I fell in love with is about to gut me.

ALL KINDS OF RELIGION

Johnson's face slips into view. I finally – finally, finally – get to look into his eyes gain.

Johnson usually has blazing blue eyes. These are coal black. This is Other-Johnson. But Johnson said he hadn't seen the others for a while ... had I been speaking to Other-Johnson without realising it? Was it all a hideous trick?

'I'm trying to cut you out of those clothes,' he says quietly. 'I don't want to cut you though.'

My teeth are chattering and my chin is twitching violently from the cold. 'I don't believe you.'

'I don't care. You need to get warm.'

Other-Johnson starts slicing at my soaking, freezing clothes. 'Need you out of these.'

The first time I spoke to the real Johnson was when I was here last time and he saved me from burning to death in the supermarket and, just like then, this version of him is trying to get me out of my clothes.

But the clothes are clinging to me, sticking to my skin like glue, and he can't peel them off.

'You're turning blue.'

'Blue?'

'This is not looking good, Rev.'

I would panic but my brain is moving way too slow for that.

'Listen, uh . . . Before I die, kiss me . . .' I cough again and can taste river water dribbling between my lips.

'You're not going to die.'

I can't help but think about when Other-Johnson kissed me. I always thought my heart only lay with my Johnson, but that moment changed everything. Metal teeth or not, Other-Johnson turned my heart inside out.

'Kiss me. Like last time. Remember how you said it meant we would always be together. Well, we are, I promise you. We absolutely are. There's no denying that. I came back for you. And we'll kiss and love each other every day, always, for ever. Just do it before I die.'

Other-Johnson hesitates. He peers closer, his black eyes searching mine. The tiniest sliver of pain crosses his face.

'It's me, Rev. Remember I swapped bodies? That other version of me, he put me in his body.'

My fuzzy mind takes an age to process this.

'Johnson?'

He nods. And looking closely, his eyes, black as they are, reveal a very human hurt.

'Yeah. That's me. I'm Johnson,' he says, more matter-of-fact this time.

He tugs at my sliced dress but it still won't come off. It's plastered to my soaking skin, shrink-fitting round me.

'Ow!' He yanks too hard and almost dislocates my elbow.

'Don't know my own strength.' Johnson sits back, trying to think of another solution.

But he is hurting more than any dislocated elbow would. He looks back at me and something has died in him.

'I ... I ...' I can't control my chattering teeth and twitching chin. 'I didn't ... I mean, I thought you were ...'

'I know what you thought.'

Why did my stupid frozen brain put those words in my mouth? All I wanted was to see Johnson again and when I did I said that!

'Billie?' I mumble, trying my best to deftly steer the conversation elsewhere.

As soon as I mention her name Johnson looks away, his eyes finding the floor. My heart staggers. Or wobbles. Or does something that makes it bounce hard off my ribs.

'Oh no.'

He looks back at me quickly. 'No. It's not that. Billie's OK.'

'Is she hurt?' I ask.

'No.'

'Missing?'

'No.'

What then? What the hell else can be wrong with her for him to look so – well – pained?

'I need to get you warm.' His voice is quiet.

There is something he doesn't want to share with me and it is not filling me with much in the way of hope.

'Tell me about Billie,' I say, pushing him.

'Let's worry about you first.'

'And the Moth,' I add. 'Where's the Moth? You texted. You said he was with you.' Johnson's text was sent earlier today when I was still in this world. But I didn't read it till I got to the alien world. But somehow it's not today any more. It's about a hundred and fifty days later so I doubt if Johnson will even remember sending that text.

'He's around.'

Around? How can he be so casual? There could be evil versions of us lurking in this town, and Johnson, the boy who kept us all alive, left a paraplegic, who doesn't even have a wheelchair, to somehow crawl around out there? And in the snow?

It takes all my strength to put a frozen hand on his forearm. 'Talk to me.'

'Later, Rev.' He still won't meet my eye.

'What is it? What's wrong? What's happened?' I ask him.

'It's been a long time. We need to get to know each other again.' He tries to evoke some of that easy ironic tone of his, but he's not pulling it off.

And there it is: the resentment that five months ago I abandoned him. I left him for dead, or at least that's what it must have looked like. I honestly had no idea. I thought he was right there beside me in the town square. How could I possibly know that Other-Johnson had swapped bodies with him? They are identical.

'I thought you were dead,' I tell him. 'The other Rev took your life, I mean, his life, the other you. I wouldn't have left you—'

'It doesn't matter.' His voice is neutral, giving little away, but by giving so little away he is telling me everything. He still can't believe I abandoned him.

'And GG punched me,' I add desperately. 'He knocked me out, next thing I knew I was in the classroom.'

'GG punched you?' Which when you say it out loud is the most unbelievable thing ever. Evil GG might be the very definition of evil, but our GG is the sweetest person you'll ever meet.

My words are bouncing off his alien skin. Nothing is penetrating. Right now all he knows is that I kissed Other-Johnson and in doing so I gave my heart and soul to him.

'Anyway,' he says but doesn't finish. Instead he gives me the cursory glance to end all cursory glances and disappears.

I try my best to move, to go after him.

'Wait,' I croak. I need to tell him I didn't mean that about Other-Johnson. It was panic and fear. They were the words of a desperate fool.

But nothing is working. I can't move and my limbs might as well belong to someone else.

A cupboard door opens at the back of the church and a creaky hinge screeches.

'Johnson?' I cough.

The creaky cupboard door closes and he heads back towards me. Maybe he's forgiven me, maybe when they swapped he got Other-Johnson's telepathic power and can read my mind and heart.

Johnson sinks down to the floor of the altar area with me. He has decided not to strip me and instead wraps me in a priest's thick billowing black cassock.

'Wrap this round you.'

I'm shaking and trembling with cold. He tries to rub my hands but nothing is working.

'Johnson,' I try again.

He quietly climbs inside the great billowing cassock with me. 'Body warmth,' he whispers, and then wraps himself round me and holds me tighter than tight.

'C'mon. Close as you can get. Tight. Tighter.'

I still can't move my stupid arms properly and Johnson has to do it for me, wrapping me into him, entwining my soaking, frozen body with his. Our faces are level with each other, we are nose to nose, and I think, *This is the way it should be, the way it should always be between us*. We could lie like this for ever and I'd live and die happy. Well. Once I find the Ape and GG and get reunited with Billie and the Moth and then get us all home and ... *Damn it, can't I just lie here for a few minutes?*

'How can it be five months?' My teeth are chattering so hard they're going to break.

He holds me as tight as he can, rubbing me with his hands, blowing warm breath on my exposed skin. Johnson moves his hand up my back, rubbing it in slow circles. I can feel the denim of his skinny jeans rubbing against the freezing skin of my exposed legs. As feeling returns to my body, I notice my right foot has lost a boot somewhere.

'Listen to me,' I tell him.

'Later.'

'You don't understand, Johnson. We were only gone for an an hour or so.'

He stops rubbing my back. It might be the first time I have ever seen Johnson look speechless.

REALITY IS A HALF-EATEN SANDWICH

Johnson keeps me crushed into him and I can feel his taut thin body pulling me as close as he can. His dark curly hair falls forward, covering his eyes for a moment. I wonder how come his hair isn't longer if he's been here for five months. Has someone been cutting it for him? I want to brush it away but my arms refuse to obey my brain.

'An hour?' he asks.

'Maybe a few minutes longer.'

'Seriously?' His eyes search mine, as if trying to work out whether or not to believe me.

'I swear to you. As soon as we find GG and the Ape they'll tell you the same thing.'

'Wow,' Johnson whispers. 'That's, uh ... That's ...' He loses his way and doesn't bother finishing his sentence. 'I don't understand.'

Suddenly the church doors are flung open and footsteps hurry towards me.

'OhmyGod!'

I recognise the voice immediately. It's Billie.

Johnson tenses and quickly removes his arms from round me, almost as if he's embarrassed.

'I've done what I can,' Johnson says and starts to wriggle free of the cassock. I try desperately to hold on to him but my numb hands and fingers just won't respond.

'Don't go,' I say.

'What are you doing?' Billie asks him.

'Body warmth,' he replies. 'She fell in the river.'

'What the hell, Rev?' Billie hurries over. 'I mean, my God. It's really you!'

Johnson eases himself out of the cassock, slipping free of me, and I have this terrible feeling that I will never be this close to him again. Something has shifted between us.

A thick blanket is draped over the cassock. 'Sit up,' Billie orders me.

I try to do as she tells me, but I still don't have the strength. She helps and there's a quiet sinewy strength to her that I didn't know she possessed.

She gets me upright. 'Twit,' she says and then hugs me tight. 'Only you could fall into a frozen river.' But rather than being comforting, the hug is almost too tight, and crushes me a little, squeezing the breath from me.

'Billie,' I croak.

'Where have you been?' she asks.

The hug is going to break a rib if she doesn't let me go.

'Uh ... Billie, listen ...'

'You found a way home, right? That's why you came back, isn't it? You've finally found a way.'

'No ...' A bone is about to snap, I know it.

'No?'

'Billie, you're crushing me.' I can't take in any air.

Finally she releases me and I suck in air, gulping it down. That hug was borderline fatal. But at least she's pleased to see me.

'You left us here for months,' she says. 'We thought you'd gone for ever.'

'Billie, I think there's been a weird shift in time.'

'What are you talking about?'

Johnson looks on in silence. He wants answers as well.

Billie keeps staring at me. 'Rev, what d'you mean?'

I get a proper look at her face and see that after five months the deep gouges from Non-Lucas's attack have healed but left faint scars down her right cheek. Non-Lucas, the double of our Lucas, who the Ape and I found hanging from his kitchen ceiling, was the first doppelganger we met. He lashed out at Billie and in many ways he started what turned into a war between human and alien. If he'd been a little less aggressive and a lot more understanding we could have probably all have got along. Maybe.

'I haven't been gone five months,' I tell Billie.

'Uh, yeah, you have.'

'Billie, I haven't.'

And that's when the movement comes.

Out of the corner of my eye Billie's arm slips protectively round Johnson's waist. A familiar and easy movement that stops my heart.

'Are you hearing this?' she asks him.

I wondered what they'd been doing for five months here. Alone. And the closeness of the gesture gives me my answer.

'We really thought you'd gone for good,' she says quietly to me. 'That you weren't coming back.'

But I'm not listening because all I can do is look at her arm wrapped round Johnson's waist.

I think back to the river and realise that however frozen and numb the water made me, it's nothing compared to how dead I feel now. He saved me when I was burning, and he saved me when I was drowning, and all of it has been for nothing.

Johnson darts a quick look at me then looks down at his hand. My eyes follow his and I can see he still has a few strands of my wet electric-pink hair stuck to his palm from where he yanked me out of the freezing river. He studies it for a second and then gently picks it from his palm and lets the hair – my hair – fall lightly to the stone floor.

GUTTED, OF NOWHERE IN PARTICULAR

A whirring noise breaks the quiet hush of the church. I look up and see the Moth in a new electric wheelchair caked in snow. The tiny engine that powers it has been working overtime to battle through the rotten weather and it smells of burning oil.

'Rev!' he calls out.

'Moth.'

I don't care how cold I am – I struggle to my feet, throwing off the blankets and head straight for him.

It's not as easy as you'd think hugging someone in a wheelchair, but I do the best I can and hug him tight. His face gets buried in my chest but I'm sure he can live with that. I hug him tightly, not Billie tight but tight enough, like he's a rock I'm clinging to. Which at this moment he is.

'Couldn't believe my eyes when Johnson texted me,' he says.

I'm aware of Billie and Johnson watching us but I focus my attention on the Moth. 'Did you see GG or the Ape out there?'

'They came back with you?' he asks excitedly.

'Only just. You wouldn't believe how close it was, Moth.

We ended up in the wrong world. Their world, the doppels. There was a whole town of them.'

I draw away from him. His glasses have slipped from his flat boneless nose and I push them back on for him. He is grinning, still in shock at seeing me again. 'I knew you'd come back for us. I kept thinking, the Rev I know wouldn't leave us here. Can't believe you survived all that time in their world. But you would, Rev. You always find a way.'

He sees a doubt flicker across my face.

'What?' he asks.

'It wasn't five months,' I tell him.

'Rev said they've only been gone an hour,' Johnson says.

The Moth's brow furrows.

I nod. 'It was, I swear. GG'll tell you.'

Wherever he is.

'An hour?' The Moth's voice is caught way back in his throat. He gulps. 'That's ... that's impossible.' The Moth scrutinises me. 'I don't understand.'

Join the club, I think.

Because I certainly don't understand how time has passed so differently here. I just assumed we'd come back to the same world we left. I glance at Billie and Johnson. Even after being wrapped up in blankets and a cassock I am still frozen. It can't be this way; it's not how these things turn out.

Girl meets boy.

Girl gets boy.

Not girl meets boy and then girl's best friend gets boy while first girl is stuck in an alien world. I knew she really liked Johnson but I didn't know he liked her in return. To be honest, and I sound like I'm boasting, but I really thought it was me he was interested in. Other-Johnson certainly was, but I guess I

65

had this Johnson wrong all along. The only good thing is they're all safe and now we're back together we can work on a way of getting home again. If Johnson wants Billie, then who am I to stand in the way of that? Which is a lot more understanding and mature than I actually feel underneath.

The church door bursts open and GG and the Ape walk in, GG huddling from the cold while the Ape crushes a snowball on top of his head.

'Not the hair!' GG wails.

GG sees the Moth and then Johnson and Billie. He can't help himself and sprints towards them. 'We saw the wheelchair tracks! And it is you. It really is!'

He hugs them all in turn, kissing them on their cheeks. I'm sure he lingers when it comes to Johnson. 'Oh that feels good.'

The Ape stands to one side and watches in silence. He isn't sure what to do or how to behave. He's always been the outsider of our group and it's never been so apparent as now. The others look at him and his hesitation mirrors their own.

Until Johnson bunches his fist and stretches an arm out to the Ape. 'Good to see you.'

The Ape looks at the bunched fist and then bounces his own fist against it. 'J-Man.' The Ape then turns to the Moth. 'You didn't get squashed.'

He's referring to the hotel that fell on us.

The Moth grins again. 'Not me, Dazza. Way too tough for that.'

The Ape bumps knuckles with the Moth too. 'Sweet.'

Billie is the only one who isn't smiling. She stares coldly at the Ape. The last time she set eyes on him she was drunk and said some truly awful things to him. So much so that he lumbered away and nearly didn't come back. I don't know why she can't give him a break, but the chances of her ever warming to him are slim. To his credit he nods at her. 'Want to see my snowman?'

Billie is stunned. 'You were making a snowman?'

Ape nods. 'I make the best snowmen ever.'

Billie turns away and I see her try to control her temper. 'A snowman,' she mumbles to herself. 'He made a snowman.'

The Ape shrugs and wanders further into the church. 'Always wondered what was in here.'

At least we're back together again. Well. What's left of the original eight of us who were in detention. We might still be stuck in this empty world, but we've got each other again and that's something.

The Moth wheels towards me. 'I want to hear everything about the world you ended up in.'

I glance at Johnson who is still holding hands with Billie. I wonder if they've ostracised the Moth a little, turning him into a three's-a-crowd gooseberry. The Moth has always been overlooked, but he seriously seems glad to have someone to talk to now.

We spend the next hour or so talking and debating what to do next. It seems that there has definitely been no sign of the doppels, for months now, so on that score we can count ourselves safe. It's about the only bit of good news we have though. It seems that in the last five months not even the super brain of the Moth has worked out a way to go home.

'We had your dad's papers but they got lost in the smashed hotel,' the Moth tells us. 'Then we tried to find your dad—'

'If it was your dad,' Billie adds.

'But he was gone along with the others,' the Moth finishes.

My dad – or Rev Two's dad – was burned in a weird fire as

he tried to get through to this world. Their version of Billie is a healer and the last I knew she was trying to bring him back to life.

In my heart I thought it definitely was my father. I had held what was left of his hand, and I swear I felt a connection with him.

But if they've taken him with them then I guess he wasn't my dad after all.

The Ape can't seem to settle or take an interest in anything. I'm not sure but I think he's on high alert and he is roaming the church. Something, some deep-rooted instinct, is making him edgy. That, or he's looking for a toilet.

'When you say you saw footprints outside the school . . . ?' Billie asks.

'They were heading into town,' I reply as calmly as I can.

'Leading away from the school?' she presses.

The Moth considers this. 'Were there any going up to the school?'

'None that I saw.'

'We haven't been up there in months. The footprints would imply that someone else was at the school and then left just before you,' the Moth decides.

Someone else was at the school. That is not a sentence I like the sound of.

'Told you I heard someone,' the Ape calls from the shadowy recesses of the church. So he is listening. 'I've got great ears.'

'Must be one of the doppels,' I tell them. 'They must have been in the school. They were fresh prints, I know it.'

'Told you,' the Ape calls out again, reminding us even though we don't need reminding.

'But they've disappeared. We haven't seen anyone else in all the time we've been here,' the Moth says, looking confused.

'Not even Other-Johnson,' Billie adds, directly looking at me.

So that's two Johnsons definitely gone in the space of an hour or so. I'm not doing so well on the romance front.

Johnson is leaning back on a pew with his long legs stretched out in front of him. He is usually laid-back and calm but now there is a quiet, maybe resigned, stillness to him. He doesn't even react at the mention of Other-Johnson. He doesn't bat an eyelid.

He'd looked so hurt when my stupid frozen-brain declared some kind of love for Other-Johnson that I thought he must still have a residue of feeling for me. But if there was I completely extinguished it with my frozen woeful declaration. Johnson is so over me.

'You must have have brought someone back with you,' Johnson says. 'From the alien world.'

I don't like his accusing tone.

'But we'd have seen them,' I say. 'They would have been in the classroom with us. And they were all about to attack us, so if they'd come through they'd have carried on attacking.' I'm sure of it. 'Wouldn't they?'

No one has an answer.

'Was everyone violent there?' the Moth asks. 'What was it like?'

GG shudders. 'You'd rather go to Margate.'

The Moth is seeing hope though. 'There's positives in this.' He strokes his flat nose in thought. 'We can still move from world to world. That's a big, big positive.'

'But we don't know how to go where we really want,' I tell him.

'That's something I can work on. And the time thing. I read something once about how chronology isn't universal. Time happens how and when it wants to. And there's this other amazing theory.' He's getting animated now. Finally, after five months, he has something concrete to put his mind to. 'Since the universe began with the Big Bang it's been accelerating and moving forward, but there's this thought that it's on the equivalent of an elastic band. And when it reaches as far as it possibly can it'll start pinging back, racing all the way towards the Big Bang again.'

'You lost me on "elastic",' GG quips.

But our ignorance, doesn't dampen the Moth's excitement. 'All of this'll happen again one day. The Big Bang will start again, and it'll reach its furthest point and then twang back. And it'll do it over and over. Back and forth for billions and billions of endless years. We'll all meet again and again and again. So if it happens in our universe then it's probably happening in all universes. But that's where the time shifts. It's not exact. It's not identical.' He rubs his thighs now, excited. 'There's going to be universes that don't move as quickly as ours, and others that move at a thousand times the speed.'

It takes a moment to digest, and even after that moment I'm not quite sure what the Moth is talking about. But he has latched onto a theory that satisfies his naturally questioning mind.

'We'll do this all again?' Billie glances at Johnson and she is clearly keen for that to happen.

'Love never dies,' the Moth adds. 'Nothing does.'

'I wondered why I got déjà vu.' GG smiles. 'I've been here before. What a lucky, lucky universe. GG lives for ever.'

The Moth sits back, dreaming of twanging eternities, but Billie delivers a more sombre tone. 'That's great thinking, Moth, but shouldn't we concentrate on the timeline we're in? Only the alien world knows everything.' She sits up straighter. 'They know we're here and your dad, Rev, wrote it all down like a map. They just need to find his papers and they'll have someone who'll work it all out from there.' Billie looks anxious and Johnson immediately slips a reassuring arm round her waist.

GG loses his momentary joy at immortality. 'What are you saying, Billie?'

'What if they start coming here? Maybe they already have, judging from the footsteps.'

Billie's blunt statement hits home because everyone falls silent at the dreadfulness of this idea.

GG covers his face in his hands. 'Margate doesn't sound so bad now. We should maybe pack up and go there.' He looks and sounds tired.

This is becoming too much. We are lost, we are alone – almost – and everything that could go wrong has gone wrong. We should have come up with a plan or a positive line of thought before finding the others. Instead we can't even offer a single shred of hope.

The Moth whirrs his wheelchair back and forth in tiny agitated movements, still thinking. 'I suppose that's possible.'

'Possible or probable?' asks Johnson.

'Probable,' the Moth answers.

'Only if they find the papers in their world,' I counter.

'Which they definitely will.' Billie is convinced.

I have never heard four more frightening words. They linger in the musty church air and everyone stops breathing. We fall silent again, hoping someone will break the ominous and dark atmosphere.

The Moth is first to gather himself, but he doesn't look his usual positive self. 'If they know about this world, then they'll, uh ... they'll ...' The Moth's space brain is overloading with thoughts and rapid connections. 'Yes. Of course ... There's a million good reasons to come here.'

Billie glances at me.

She and Johnson have probably been very happy here, going about their lives. It's by no means perfect but at least they were finally out of danger. And what do we do? Come back and ruin everything.

Billie unfolds her long supermodel limbs. She is a lot taller than I am, and her mixed-race grace and slender legs have always made her stand out. I spent our friendship feeling like I had to fight to be noticed when I was with her and there was always the nagging sense that she quietly enjoyed that.

'Rev, what have you done?' She says it quietly and with care and concern, but I'm sure there's the faintest hint of condemnation there as well.

'It's so obvious,' the Moth says, bewildered. 'They're going to pour through.'

GG pulls a quiet grimace. 'Could you stop sounding so certain about that?'

'Think about it, GG,' says the Moth. 'This world is full of resources. Double the oil and gas and water that they already have. Or it could even be a place to live, and their world would be less crowded and – well – there's a thousand benefits I can think of.' The Moth is almost sorry to say any more. 'So, yeah, I'd come here if I were them, and I'd get rid of anything I didn't need – or like.'

Billie pulls a cowed and vulnerable look and Johnson draws her closer so she can rest her head on his chest. She's got the damsel-in-distress act down to a tee.

'But then again they know there's another parallel world now – well, two, in fact, ours and this one,' says the Moth, 'so it could actually be even worse.'

'There's a worse?' GG asks quietly.

'They could go to our world.'

The Moth's wheelchair is edging back and forth, over and over, and he doesn't seem to know he is doing it. It's a subconscious movement but the whine of the oil-dry motor is starting to get to me.

'OMG.' GG spells it out slowly. 'They'd overrun us. It'd be like an alien invasion.'

The thought chills my newly warmed body and I drop at least twenty degrees.

'He's right. They attacked us – why not attack an entire world?' Billie's eyes widen in fear. 'It's what they do.'

My mouth dries in under a second. The Moth's wheelchair is screeching in my ears and I yell at him. 'For God's sakes stop going backwards and forwards!'

The Moth brakes hard. All eyes are upon me. Accusing. Shocked.

I try to calm down. 'That that might not happen.' I'm almost pleading. 'Why would they come here?'

'Your dad – if it was him – did.'

Johnson's words hit the hardest. They fill the church until they are squashing down on me, suffocating me, leaving me breathless.

The Moth starts whirring back and forth again.

GG tries to take some of the blame. 'I was there too. I'm responsible as well. Me and the Ape.'

'It's Dazza.' The Ape is now leaping up at one of the large stained-glass windows to try and see out of it. I have no idea

73

why. Does he sense something out there? Or is he just checking on his beloved snowman?

'All they'll have to do is find your dad's papers.' The Moth whirrs. I wish he wouldn't, because everything he says adds another layer of black. 'Yeah,' he says, working it round and round in his mind, 'someone will read them and make sense of them and that's it, game over. Not just for us, but maybe for everyone.'

'Moth, please.' GG has been experiencing the same dread and doesn't want to hear any more either.

'Any ideas, Rev?' Johnson's laser-black eyes take me by surprise and I almost, but not quite, catch my breath.

Billie tightens a little. She can see Johnson is looking straight into my eyes.

And in that moment I feel a sliver of hope that I might not have lost him completely, despite the last five months and all the loving Billie could muster.

'I guess we close the portal,' I offer.

The Moth stops whirring.

'To do that we still need your dad's papers, Rev. I never got to fully take in everything he'd written, but if I was to go over it again . . . Well, he came through to this world so he must know how to switch the portals on and off.'

'Only not very well, considering he was fried to a crisp,' Billie snaps, then quickly avoids my accusing look. 'Sorry, Rev, that slipped out. Pressure of the moment.'

'So just like before, we need the papers,' Johnson declares.

The Moth nods. 'With them I could get us home and close the whole multiverse thing down. Well . . . in theory.'

GG puts his hand in the air. 'I vote for that. I'll even cheerlead if you want. Closing portals down. Well, ra-ra-ra to that.' GG has brightened again. You can never keep a boy like him down for long.

'So if the papers would help then let's go get them.' At last I can see something positive. A sort-of plan is better than nothing.

'Yeah, let's do that,' Billie says, sarcasm dripping from her voice. 'Know anyone who can lift mega-megatons of hotel rubble? Because that's where the papers are buried.'

I wish I was outside making a snowman. I wish I was a little kid on a sledge with her dad wrapped round her, keeping her warm and safe. I wish for anything but this.

'We need to go back to London.' I'm not even really sure who says it, but I think it's Johnson. I'm not really listening because I'm caught up in my sad wishful thinking.

'We have time,' the Moth says, 'if you think about it. Five months passed here but only an hour passed in their world. Which means we could have months, maybe a year, to dig around in that smashed hotel before the doppelgangers start pouring through. We've got a chance. The papers were in my room and I was on the ground floor. I can still remember the number of the room.'

Billie stares deeply at the Moth and shakes her head. 'Hawkings, I used to think you were clever.'

'It's Hawking,' he responds for the millionth time.

GG and the Ape are down by the river trying to hook my lost boot out of the icy waters. It would probably be quicker 'shopping' for a new pair from any of a dozen shops in the town, but GG assured me that the boots were 'so, so you, Rev', and trudged outside with the Ape.

GG and the Ape's voices drift in from outside the church.

'It's been five months. An hour for us but five months for them,' explains GG. 'It was summer when we left.'

'Still is,' the Ape replies.

'How can you say that? It's winter now. Look at all the snow.' GG's voice rises an octave.

'You snow nothing!'

Their voices carry easily. That's the beauty of an empty world, a silent world. When you take away the humming drum of human existence it's amazing how acute your hearing becomes.

Sound travels, I think, *it really does travel*. But I wonder if that's a good thing. Because someone else left footprints in the snow, which means there's someone here with us. We are definitely not alone.

I have been lying stretched out along a pew, wrapped up in a sleeping bag, and my core temperature has risen to a level that means I'm probably alive, but it still doesn't feel like life. Not where it really counts.

Thanks to Johnson and Billie my heart is deader than the dead lying in the ancient frozen graves that surround the church.

'Got it!' the Ape shouts.

'That's not Rev's boot.'

'Yeah it is.'

'That's a ghastly wellington, and it's at least a size twelve. Now throw it back. Honestly.'

The voices should be a comfort to me but all I can think is why didn't I get back here earlier? As in straight away. As in maybe not ever leaving in the first place.

But more than anything: why did Johnson forget me?

Isn't it an undeniable and universal rule that romantic heroes wait in rain and storms and watch the seasons passing until their loved one returns? Carrie used to write the worst romantic poetry in the universe and if she was me right now she'd be writing things about undying sentries of the heart standing guard until the future arrives.

'How are you doing, Rev?'

The Moth whirrs up to me in his wheelchair. His nose is scarred from all the things he's been through in this world, but because he has a body that is already pretty much broken it is hard to tell if he's been damaged any further. Then I think wouldn't it be ironic if he'd actually been battered into a better shape by having a hotel land on him.

'It's not your fault. You didn't cause this,' he says gently.

I'm grateful for his concern.

'I don't understand how you escaped,' I tell him. 'A hotel fell on top of you.'

The Moth tries to draw alongside me, reversing his wheelchair, then going forward, then reversing some more. He parks like my mum parks. Sometimes a shopping trip to Asda can last days because she spends so long parking.

'Johnson was switched into that other version of himself, the stronger one, and he moved so quickly ... Well, quicker than we could, and he found us and got us out. Me and Billie anyway. I begged him to go back for Carrie ...' He falters at the memory. 'But the hotel was coming down around our ears. Can you believe someone could do that? With a punch? Anyway, it was coming down and Johnson dragged us away.'

Poor Carrie. By the time the hotel fell, she was already gone, sliced apart by Evil-GG. He too will be buried under all of that rubble and my only regret is that that monster is sharing a tomb with Carrie. She and I weren't exactly friends but she doesn't deserve that.

'What happens if we find her as well?' he asks me, but with a faraway look.

I can't answer that. Only the Moth can.

I give him a moment to allow the lump to leave his throat.

'I was thinking,' I tell him. 'We should go to the class-room, maybe I'm the reason the white light happens. It could be connected to me, because Rev Two came here as well. Maybe it's linked to my dad and there's something special about us.'

The Moth weighs the thought for a moment. 'It's possible.' Then he becomes more animated. 'We put up a tent and camped in the classroom for the first month, hoping the light would happen again. But it never did. So perhaps you're right: you could be the key.'

'You'd been living up there?'

'Didn't you notice?'

'I wasn't really taking anything in when we came through,' I tell him. But when I replay arriving back in the classroom I swear there was no sign of people having been living there. But we were only there for a few minutes and we were so keen to escape. I wasn't really going to notice too much. Not even a tent, it seems.

The Moth nods to himself. 'If you are the key then that could give us an edge.' He whirrs away. The battery of his chair must be dying because he crawls along at about one mile an hour.

I watch him go, then feel Johnson's eyes on me. When I

look away my empty stomach rumbles loudly in the least appealing and ladylike manner. What timing.

I immediately blush. 'Haven't eaten for ages,' I offer weakly. 'Actually what have you been living off?' I ask Johnson, trying to distract him from my loud stomach. But Billie answers before he can.

'All the fresh stuff has perished so it's mainly tinned food now. We have tons of it in our room. Don't we, Johnson?'

Our room.

Johnson releases a metal talon from his fingertip. 'Great can openers.'

'Your room?' I hardly dare ask.

'We moved into that hotel down the side street with the cobblestones outside. The Sun. Which is pretty ironic considering all the snow.'

Billie attempts a grin and I've got to admit, it's great to see her smile again.

'The Moth is in the room next to ours,' she adds.

'We've got the whole bar and dining room to ourselves,' Johnson says.

'Want to see?' Billie is almost too keen to show me. 'Our room and that?'

It still pierces my heart to think of them together but suck it up. *Rev, you're not a factor any more.*

'Maybe later,' I say.

Billie lowers her voice. 'It took a while for Johnson to get used to his new body,' she whispers to me. 'I tried to help him adjust though. Took some time but we got there.'

We.

The word turns my stomach inside out.

Johnson gets to his feet. 'We need food and warmth. I vote

we grab what we can then head to The Sun. I'll go find GG and the Ape and we'll get some supplies.'

'I'll come with you,' I offer.

'You crazy? You'll die of cold out there,' Billie says and I'm sure she emphasises the word 'die'. 'Leave it to us.' She definitely emphasises 'us', hanging on to the word for as long as she can until I swear she sounds like a hissing snake.

Johnson nods to me. 'Any requests?'

'Just make it warm.'

Johnson nods again, his eyes lingering on me for a moment too long.

'Don't get burned out there,' I add, hoping Johnson might remember what he said to me once.

'I'll try not to.' Johnson responds with his customary salute. It's a small thing in the face of 'we' and 'ours', but I'll take it.

He heads for the door and Billie hangs back for a second and she is about to say something to me. But whatever it is she decides against it and turns to catch up with Johnson.

'Coming, lover.' She leaves the words to echo around the church. I guess she said what she wanted to after all.

Half an hour passes before the Ape arrives with some sort of metal hiking pole with him. He kicks the huge wooden door open and lets every drop of heat escape.

'What's with the pole?' the Moth asks.

'It's got a sharp point.'

'I can see that, but why have you got it?'

'Watch this.' The Ape looks around, spots the statue of Jesus and gives a demonstration. 'Come on then!' He jabs and pokes and stabs in the general direction of Jesus, which is unutterably blasphemous.

81

The Moth looks equally at a loss. He turns to me. 'Where does it all come from? All these violent oafy thoughts? He's got an endless supply of them.'

'Got to have a weapon,' the Ape boasts. Then he starts sparring at the statue again. 'Come on, if you think you're hard enough.'

GG stumbles in, covered in snow and bright red in the face. 'He *had* to roll me in the snow, just had to.'

GG slips a mountaineer's rucksack off his back and slides it across to me.

'New jeans, new boots, new look.'

I look inside the rucksack and pull out black jeans and black leather boots. There's a thin red cardigan to go with it.

GG blows into his frozen red hands. 'Warmest thing I could find. It's still the summer sales here.'

Another thirty minutes pass and Johnson and Billie still haven't returned. I sit up, dressed in my new clothes, draw my knees into my chest and stare at the church door, willing it to open. Johnson and Billie should have definitely done their supply run by now, so where are they? Has whatever came back with us found them? Or worse, have they detoured to *their room* ...?

'They tend to go off a lot these days.' The Moth can seemingly read my thoughts. It can't be difficult because my worries must be plastered all over my face.

I look up to the ceiling and try to gather my thoughts. A giant chandelier made of glass and shimmering silver dominates the church and for a second I think it quivers. Just the tiniest amount.

'Did you see that?'

The Moth and GG look up at the ceiling. The Ape looks anywhere but.

The chandelier trembles again.

'It's just the wind,' the Moth says and wheels over to the church door and closes it.

The chandelier moves again. The tremble is a shudder now.

GG looks around. 'There must be a draught.'

The chandelier shakes.

'OK, maybe not a draught.'

The chandelier swings now and I fccl a trcmble run from the floor and up through my toes. GG feels it as well.

The Moth might be cushioned in his wheelchair but he knows something is very wrong.

'Earthquake?' I say.

The Ape has fallen silent and still. His senses are on high alert.

'Told you,' he says. 'Told you I heard someone.'

The chandelier rocks above us and we watch until it settles. Nothing moves.

The world breathes a sigh of relief and relaxes. The tremor has passed.

I breathe out. 'OK. OK. Panic over.'

'You think?' the Ape asks and as soon as the words leave his lips the chandelier starts shaking back and forth, swinging wildly above our heads.

The Ape is right.

Something is coming.

CHURCH OF THE BROKEN SOUL

The shaking stops.

The chandelier eventually comes to a rest.

Everything falls silent again.

It had to be an earth tremor; we had one once, a few years ago, and people got excited because that sort of thing never happens in this town. They got excited until some of them realised their roofs had collapsed.

Something hits the side of the church with a hard thud. For a moment I think I'm just imagining it but another harder thud hits the church. Then another.

We instinctively fall silent. We have learned the hard way that quiet is best.

'What is that?' GG whispers.

There are six stained-glass windows running through the church walls and I slip as quietly as I can from the pew and tiptoe towards the nearest one.

Another harder thud impacts the outside wall.

The stained-glass window is too high for me too see out of so GG helps me push a pew under it. We do it as soundlessly and delicately as possible as the thuds get progressively harder and harder. The chandelier continues to rock back and forth above us.

The Moth hasn't budged and he looks worried. The Ape must be able to sense his fear because he places a large hand on his shoulder, probably not even realising he's done it.

GG and I climb onto the pew and try and peer out of one of the giant windows without being seen.

'Oh my Goddy God!' GG's words ride the quiet breath that escapes him. 'It had to be *him*.'

Standing outside making snowballs is Non-Ape.

The giant version of our Ape. Correction. The giant, unstoppable version. He must have seen all of our footprints and worked out that there are people to be found in this church. One of them, not mentioning any names – you fool, Ape! – also built a huge snowman, which is the equivalent of sending up a flare.

GG gasps quietly. 'He's back.'

Non-Ape scoops up a huge shovelful of snow, compacts it until it's as hard as ice and then hurls the resultant snowball at the church. I have no idea why he is attacking the church.

Until he bellows.

'JOHNSON!'

A snowball fizzes straight towards the window and we have to duck quickly as it smashes straight through the stained glass, showering us in broken images of Mary and Jesus.

'JOHNSON!'

Another snowball hurtles through the broken window and GG and I drop to the floor, landing in the shards of stained glass. At the speed he's throwing them, if one of those snowballs hits us it would take our heads off.

The Moth, as tough as he has to have been recently, looks worried and the Ape tightens his grip on his shoulder.

'I got this,' he tells the Moth.

GG and I scurry back to them, bewildered, disbelieving. 'What the hell? I thought you said the aliens had gone?' GG whispers.

The Moth has fallen silent. His mouth opens and closes but no words emerge.

'JOHNSON!!'

The bellow is ear-splitting.

'Did he come back with us? He's huge, how could we have missed him at the school?' GG whispers heatedly.

'What if he never went back?' I say. 'Maybe they left him here.' Although I can't work out how the others haven't seen him for five months. He's not exactly the shy retiring type.

A snowball crashes through another window.

'Fair point, Rev. Would you take him back home with you?' GG hunkers down as snowballs missile into the church. 'I don't mean to sound like a bitchy-bitch type but I'd definitely think twice about it.'

'HEY, JOHNSON!'

'Keep your voices down.' The Moth finally manages to speak. He knows only too well what's coming if we don't stay totally silent.

Another snowball pounds the church wall.

'Someone made this snowman!' Non-Ape yells.

I immediately look accusingly at our Ape but he shrugs. 'Snow is snow, you gotta build a snowman.'

'I KNOW YOU'RE IN THERE, JOHNSON!'

Which is completely wrong and I have a good mind to go out there and tell him he's wasting his time. *Yeah, that would so work, Rev.*

A snowball flies like an Exocet through another stained-glass window, shattering it. The window is roughly three metres tall and a metre wide, a feat of great artistry and reverence that's probably been in the building for decades. The snowball shatters it in a heartbeat.

'YOU'RE COMING OUT OR I'M COMING IN!' he roars.

The Ape's large snowman flies straight through another window and lands on a row of pews, covering them in snow and scattering the small pebbles that the Ape had used for its coat buttons. A strangely fresh-looking carrot lands at my feet. Shards of stained glass fly off in all directions and as snow explodes around us there is no way that we can stay here. Non-Ape will quickly grow bored of hurling snow so we've probably got less than a minute to find an exit.

'Is there a back way out of here?' I whisper to the Moth.

'Got to be.'

He engages drive on his electric wheelchair and tries to move away. But the second he does the wheelchair emits a low excruciating whine and the battery dies. He jabs repeatedly at the controls but that heavy wheelchair isn't going anywhere soon. Moth's batteries have a knack of running down at the worst possible moment.

'Rev,' he says, for some reason thinking I'll have an answer. His frightened eyes plead with me. 'Get us out of here.'

Me? I think. *Why me?*

'There's got to be another door,' I whisper as the bombardment of snowballs stops for a minute.

The faint half-imagined echo of the last thunderous impact drifts into silence.

The chandelier stops rocking overhead.

I hold my breath.

He'll be crashing in here any second now.

The Ape is searching for something he can use as a weapon, but a weapon doesn't exist that can stop Non-Ape.

I have to think. There's got to be a back way.

But the Ape's eyes are looking all over the church until they settle on the large wooden cross standing tall at the back of the altar.

He can't use that, I think. *Can he?*

The Ape smiles.

His eyes meet mine. '*No,*' I mouth to him. '*You cannot fight him!*'

His eyes light up. '*NO!!*' I mouth again.

His eyes slide back to the large wooden cross. 'Yeah,' he purrs and lumbers towards the far end of the church.

'Go, Mothy, go!' GG says as he grabs the handles of Moth's wheelchair and shoves him past the stalls, where the choir would normally be belting out a hymn, and on towards a dark wooden door at the rear of the church. 'Wait for us; we have to grab the Ape!'

The Ape is already trying to work the heavy cross behind the altar free from its plinth.

'For God's sakes!' I whisper, coming right up behind him.

He slips his large arms round the cross and bends his knees in a back-breaking effort to wrench it free.

'You can't fight him!' I'm speaking through gritted teeth and wondering if I really just said that.

A lump of weathered stone flies through one of the already broken windows and smashes hard against the opposite wall. The Non-Ape has uprooted someone's ancient headstone and hurled it into the church. This is desecration on a horrendous scale.

'MEET THE DEAD!' he bellows from outside.

The Ape finally manages to yank the wooden cross free and all I can wonder is how did everything become so unholy so quickly.

Another long faded and nameless headstone crashes through a window. Then another and another. The Non-Ape bellows again.

'RIP!!'

One of the headstones hits a thick plaster column that helps to hold the church roof in place, and plaster and brick explode around me.

It is so time to leave.

'Go!' the Ape yells at me.

The Ape has strained every muscle in raising the heavy wooden cross and he now braces himself to use it as a weapon.

'You can't fight him,' I urge, joining him at the back of the altar. 'You can't go out there.'

'Move,' he says.

'If I run, you're running with me,' I tell him.

Another headstone explodes around us.

'I'll get him in the throat,' the Ape assures me.

'No, no you won't,' I whimper.

'I'll get them all, Rev.'

Two flying headstones lay waste to a second column and it starts to collapse. The ceiling groans and bows above us.

The Ape hefts the cross and marches for the exit.

GG is racing back towards us. 'There's a kitchen, there's a door, there's a way out!' he cries.

'Ape!' I shout, but another headstone enters the church with unbelievable force and drowns me out. 'Ape!'

The Ape has almost reached the large wooden entrance and

I charge after him, grabbing the tail of his big black coat. Another headstone decimates more of the church.

'No way,' I tell the Ape. 'You are not going after him.'

He keeps ploughing forward and I tug as hard as I can but my feet are skidding and slipping on the polished stone floor. 'No!' I yell. 'No!'

GG joins me. 'There's another door!' He grabs the Ape's coat as well. 'You hear that, big man? There's a way out.'

A headstone cuts clean through another badly damaged column and part of the roof comes down behind us. Non-Ape has some serious issues with buildings.

'JOHNSON!' he bellows again.

I don't get it. I don't know how anyone can spend five months bellowing the same thing over and over.

'Please!!' I screech at the back of the Ape's head, but even GG and I combined can't hold him back. 'Fight him another time.'

A headstone flies over the Ape's huge head, missing him by centimetres, before crashing straight through a stained-glass window on the opposite side of the church.

GG beseeches him. 'Ape, I can't carry the Moth on my own. I need your help.'

The roof creaks loudly above our heads, straining to stay upright.

The lone cog in the Ape's brain turns and he finally sets the cross down, seeing sense for once.

'Next time,' he mumbles, disappointed.

GG grabs the Ape's meaty paw in his tiny hand. 'With me.'

'No, homo!' The Ape snatches his hand away from GG, but GG grips it tight.

'Oh you'd be so lucky,' GG quips, ignoring the insult.

Together we run through the dangerously unstable church.

The mighty oak doors are punched clean off their hinges. I don't have to turn round to know there's a giant monstrous boy standing in the doorway, looking to kill what he believes to be the Other-Johnson.

The Non-Ape laughs. 'SAY YOUR PRAYERS!'

We duck out through the back door as quickly as we can, and I close it behind us, hoping that the Non-Ape won't think to look for us here. I look around and see we're now in a simple nineteen-fifties kitchen area. The Moth is already at a door on the other side of the kitchen that leads to outside. He looks tired out, having obviously struggled to propel his heavy wheelchair there after GG pushed him from the church. He has a hand planted either side of the doorway as he tries to pull his dead wheelchair over the high wooden threshold. He can't get enough purchase and it keeps rolling him backwards.

'I told you to wait – you're so impatient,' admonishes GG, and he and the Ape lift the Moth's wheelchair and trudge out into the snow.

Snow that is going to leave more tracks.

'JOHNSON!' the Non-Ape bellows again. His thunderous footsteps shake the church's foundations.

The Ape and GG move as fast as they can, but they'll never get away, not carrying the Moth and his wheelchair.

'Which way?' GG asks.

The Ape scans the Christmas-card town square and spots the entrance to the snooker hall. The door is open – it always seems to be in our world, and it's no different in this one.

'Snooker,' the Ape says, heading towards it.

GG tries to keep up with the Ape but his legs are shorter and his arms aren't as strong, and after a few paces he is already slipping and losing his grip on the wheelchair.

'Move it!' the Ape encourages.

'I'm coming, I'm coming,' GG responds valiantly. 'You're so bossy.'

But we won't make it. I know we won't. And even if we do Non-Ape will see our tracks.

There's no choice really. Perhaps there never was.

I turn back and head back into the church.

ONE GIANT, ONE GIRL, ONE ENDING

Non-Ape is already outside the kitchen door when I yank it open.

He is so surprised he lurches to a stop. He can't quite believe what he is seeing as he looms over me, his huge form casting a shadow all over the kitchen.

'Dazza.' I try and smile. 'Didn't know you were a churchgoer.'

He doesn't smile. He just stares down at me like he hates me with all his heart and soul.

I know I've described the pulse in my neck thrashing around like a trapped fish before but this time it's more like a school of scared fish. I have never been so terrified and that's saying something after the things I've been through recently. All I have going in my favour is my natural wit and cunning, which to be honest isn't in too plentiful a supply right now. But I'm hoping Non-Ape will think I'm the Rev from his world, and therefore he will possibly, maybe, perhaps, have a soft spot for me. Just like my Ape does.

'You've got ten seconds. Then you're dead.'

Scratch that thought.

'You hear me, Pinkhead?'

'Yeah, uh, yeah. I hear you.'

'Ten seconds.'

Which have already passed.

'For what?' I ask.

'Uh?'

'Ten seconds for what?'

I hope the others are getting away. I foolishly realise that I didn't shut the back door when I came back, so it's halfway open and I am praying, in a church no less, that it doesn't swing all the way open and reveal their footprints outside.

Non-Ape stops to collect his thoughts. He already can't seem to remember what he needs ten seconds for. He's also too busy looking at my chest. He has become so distracted by my bosom that his brain has ceased to work.

'Uh . . .' he murmurs.

I step to the side and his eyes follow my chest. I move back again and his eyes follow.

Bingo!

He is the boy to end all boys, frozen in amber by anything approaching voluptuous.

I step again and his eyes follow, glued to my cleavage.

'What you doing here?' he mumbles to them.

'Worshipping.' But my voice is tinny, without bass or treble. It's a nervous skinny voice trapped way back in my throat.

'Who?'

'Uh . . . God of course.'

Non-Ape is not only monstrously powerful but also

monstrously stupid. I heard him speaking on the phone to the Ape once and it wasn't exactly a meeting of great minds.

I step out of the kitchen and his head turns, eyes still riveted to my feminine charms.

'Where you going?'

'Uh . . . You know.' I don't know how long I can hold him in this trance. Also, I don't know how I'm going to escape. I know he isn't fast but he has reserves of stamina that would fill a town reservoir. He can keep going almost indefinitely so I know I can't outrun him. And if I did run my boobs would only bounce up and down and entrance him even more. This is not how I saw things panning out.

'This, uh, this church is ancient.' I'm babbling now. 'It's fourteenth century, I think.' I keep edging away, sticking my chest out that little bit further. I'm moving back into a building that could possibly cave in on me any second, but at least the others have got a chance.

I glimpse the destruction and I'm thinking now is the time for God to take over, to see this horrendous treatment of hallowed ground and send a bolt of lightning down. He may have to send a few but Non-Ape deserves it.

'I make that five seconds,' he says, his voice a low rumble. 'That means you've got . . .' He stops to think for a moment. 'A few more left.'

His concept of time is remarkable.

I need a plan.

Maybe I could dance in front of him, soothe his rage and calm his furrowed brow. He'd fall asleep like a mesmerised giant from mythology. I could do the Dance of the Seven Veils, whatever that is, and he would find his eyes closing and his lids getting heavier and—

'Where's Johnson?' he asks.

Maybe I won't be dancing after all. Which isn't a bad thing considering my inability to move with anything approaching rhythm or grace.

'No idea,' I tell him.

'Sure?' His eyes climb from my chest and look deeply into mine, as if he can see right through me.

'Positive. Anyway, uh . . . Thought you were in London.'

Small talk is good, I think.

'L-town was dead.'

OK. Not so good.

'No one there.'

'So you came back?'

'No.'

'No?'

The Non-Ape laughs in my face. 'Duh! Wouldn't be here if I hadn't come back.'

I laugh as if he's the funniest boy in the world. 'You kill me.' Which I immediately regret saying.

The wind whips through the smashed church windows and I know for certain that I'm eventually going to catch pneumonia. Or I would do if I get to live that long. 'The others went home. They waited for you, but the light came again and took them home.'

'What light?'

'The light in the classroom.'

'What classroom?'

'At the school. But you know what, if you went up there, I bet it'd take you home as well.'

The Non-Ape considers this for a moment. 'This is home.'

Great.

'But it's not,' I tell him.

'It's just got no people.'

'No, uh, the, uh, the Moth figured it out. This isn't home.'

The Non-Ape laughs and then lightly punches my arm. 'Ha.' It's a gentle playful punch that sends me flying backwards into a stone wall. It's a miracle my spine doesn't snap in half from the impact. I have to pretend not to be winded, or in complete agony.

'You're funny.' He laughs again.

I gingerly peel myself away from the wall. 'I'm not kidding, I swear. Something weird has happened.'

'Where's Johnson?' He's already lost interest in our conversation, his one-track mind coming back to Johnson and destruction.

'Told you, he's gone back with the others.'

'Back where?'

'Home!' I'd slap him if I could. He's even more infuriating than our Ape.

'This is home.' And so the circle of misunderstanding begins again.

'Come to the classroom with me, I'll show you.'

'Show me what?'

'The white light.'

'What white light?'

He may have the strength to crush a mountain but it's his stupidity that'll be the death of me.

'The white light that brought us here.' I can feel tears of frustration welling behind my eyes.

'Oh yeah,' he says.

I try again. 'And here isn't really here.'

'Yeah it is.'

'Look,' I say, exasperated and enduring some wretched spinal agony. 'You've been here five months, right? And you haven't seen anyone in all that time.'

'Huh?' He looks totally confused now. He frowns and I bet he could crack walnuts just from creasing up his skin.

'Look at the snow. It's winter.'

Non-Ape belches. 'Johnson shouldn't have done that to Billie.' He's gone completely off track again.

'You can tell him that when you go back,' I say.

'She liked Johnson.'

I step further into the church, one eye on the dangerously precarious roof. The chandelier now hangs by a single electrical wire.

'She cried on me,' he says, and for a moment I get this image of Another-Billie weeping in this behemoth's presence. Did he reach out to her and promise he'd make it better? I still have no idea what Other-Johnson did to their Billie but at least there is some shred of humanity in Non-Ape. If he held Another-Billie while she cried, he has a heart.

Which means I have hope.

I offer my hand to him. 'Look, uh . . . Billie still needs you.'

He looks down at my hand.

'You did what any friend would.' My tone is gentle, soothing. 'You tried to sort things but, trust me, they're sorted. There's no need for all of this anger. She's happy again.'

His eyes don't leave my hand.

'Let's go. Let's get to the classroom.'

I'll lead him up to the school, somehow lose him, then grab another dinner tray and sledge all the way back down here.

'Take my hand.'

The church creaks above my head and it's as good a reason as any to get out.

'All you've got to do is take my hand,' I repeat in case he didn't get it the first time.

His eyes are fixed on my hand. He shifts from one foot to the other. The hand seems to concern him.

I edge closer. 'It's not safe in here.' *Well, not for me.*

'Think I'm stupid?' he grunts. His temper is fraying.

'Why would you say that?'

But then I realise that I'm the stupid one. Rev Two's hand turned blue and stole Other-Johnson's life as soon as it touched his skin. Non-Ape thinks I'm trying to trick him into doing the same to him.

'No, wait . . . I wasn't trying anything, I wasn't.' I withdraw my hand as quickly as I can.

But not quickly enough.

The Non-Ape looks back at my chest. 'They're up,' he says.

'Sorry?'

The Non-Ape takes a giant step forward and grabs me by the throat. He raises me in the air until I'm level with his face.

'Your ten seconds.'

THE CURVES DON'T WORK

I try to reach for the Non-Ape, but his other hand grabs my wrists and pins my arms painfully behind my back. Both of my shoulders all but pop out.

'Wait,' I gurgle.

'I want Johnson.'

'You-you got him yesterday. I mean, five months ago ...' My words are little more than a rasp.

'Nah.'

'Yeah, he told me.'

'He got away.'

Non-Ape could snap my neck with a flick of his wrist as he brings me closer to his huge jowly face. He reeks of stale sweat, and if memory serves me right he's been wearing the same clothes since I last saw him. Ew.

'Where is Johnson?'

He presses a little harder and my throat starts to cave in on itself.

'I don't know,' I splutter.

His thick thumb moves another millimetre. My larynx is bending like a straw.

'Last chance.'

I can't speak even if I wanted to, which sort of defeats his method of interrogation. No air is getting into my airway and I'm starting to feel giddy from lack of oxygen. I know my face is turning crimson. I can feel it burning like the worst embarrassment.

'Bye, Pinkhead.' He is about to flick his thick wrist.

A voice comes from the doorway.

'Hey, Dazza.' The Non-Ape turns his monolithic head to the right and standing there is Johnson. Tall and skinny, his long dark jacket flapping around him in the onrushing wind. He is calm, abnormally so, as he stares straight at the Non-Ape. 'Let Rev go.'

The Non-Ape grins. 'Make me.'

'Careful what you wish for.'

The Non-Ape's eyes are alive at the sight of Johnson. But Johnson takes a step forward, brazen, daring.

A low guttural rumble escapes from the Non-Ape's throat.

Johnson takes another step closer. 'Let my girl go.'

The Non-Ape drops me without a care in the world and I land hard on the stone floor. I cough and retch as air tries to squeeze in past my bruised larynx.

'Johnson, no . . . I-I had it covered,' I pant.

'Looked that way.'

I get to my hands and knees but I can't seem to get upright. My head spins from the lack of oxygen and I can't tell what's floor and what's ceiling.

Johnson sets his eyes on Non-Ape. 'You want me – come get me.' He uses his super-charged body to turn and leap through one of the broken church windows.

The Non-Ape roars and runs after him, ploughing straight through the thick ancient stone wall of the church and exploding out of the other end. 'JOHNSON!'

The shattered wall was supporting part of the roof and it bows and creaks above me.

I stagger to my feet. '*Let my girl go.*' That's what he said. I may have nearly died, but it was almost worth it to hear those words.

The church keeps spinning around me and I flail out an arm to steady myself against one of the remaining supporting columns. If I could just clear my head, I could go after them. I close my eyes and count to ten.

I reach number three when Billie comes from nowhere and rugby-tackles me back to the floor.

'Why did you come back?' she screams at me. 'Why??'

Her eyes turn from blue to black as she beats at me with her fists. 'We were happy!'

I can hear Non-Ape bellowing after Johnson who I hope to God is fast enough. Billie keeps pummelling me. 'You just got him killed!'

I catch Billie's wrists to stop her battering my mega bruised body. 'Billie, please.'

But she easily twists a wrist free and beats at me again.

Through the huge hole the Non-Ape has made in the wall I can see thick snow beginning to fall.

I kick and crawl away from under Billie, but she keeps on coming. Her eyes fill with black – even the whites are black. 'I had to come back, I had to,' I tell her, crawling and scrambling backwards as fast as I can.

'But look what you've done,' she wails.

A blizzard is building now, and it's racing in through the hole in the wall. Snowflakes land but don't melt.

'Billie, I came back for you. To save you.'

But she pummels me again, and even though I put my arms up to protect myself some of her punches get through.

'Billie, please.'

Her face is within inches of mine and she is snarling now, spittle gathering on her lips. I can't believe this is my all-time best friend.

'Hey,' a deep voice calls out.

Billie turns and I don't quite know what happens but there's a blur of movement followed by a thud and suddenly Billie is spiralling away from me.

The Ape stretches a hand towards me. 'What's her problem?'

I take his giant paw-like hand and he heaves me easily to my feet.

The storm has started to rage outside as Billie glowers at the Ape. 'Did you just punch me?'

'Was a push. I don't hit girls.'

'You animal.'

But it seems like the snarling, spitting creature has disappeared and the old Billie has emerged, shoved out of her insane anger by the Ape.

'Snooker,' the Ape says and pounds towards the kitchen.

I offer my hand to Billie but she won't take it.

'I'm sorry,' I tell her. 'But Johnson will get away. He will.'

The Ape is waiting by the rear door and the snowstorm is growing stronger by the second. 'Can't see J-Man,' he says, shielding his eyes from the icy blasts.

I doubt anyone can see anything in this blizzard. I try anyway but there is no sign of him or the Non-Ape.

Billie steps alongside me. 'Rev . . .'

I can't help tensing when I hear her voice.

'Rev.' She tries again, her voice softer, her words choked. 'I'm sorry.' She can barely look me in the eye. 'I shouldn't have reacted like that. I've never been this happy before. I know it wasn't perfect but these months have been – and I know you don't want to hear this – but they've been amazing.'

'I get it, Billie, I do, and I almost wish I hadn't come back,' I say. 'But I didn't know it would be like this . . .' My words fade away.

'If it's any help, I didn't either.' She slips an arm round my bruised shoulders. 'But me and Johnson, it just happened. It just seemed right.'

The Ape crashes out into the howling storm, turning to issue more orders. 'Snooker!' He has to yell to be heard.

We don't need a second invitation and huddle behind his black-coated bulk. The snow is deeper than ever and it takes what feels like an hour of heavy trudging to reach the entrance to the snooker hall. Halfway there we draw level with the high street and I dare to glance down it, fearful of what I might see. But there is still no sign of Johnson or Non-Ape.

Billie scans the whitening world and I know she is looking for Johnson as well. Looking. And praying.

Behind us the church finally gives way and collapses. *This is awful*, I think, *this is just the worst of the worst*.

I hear a distant bellow on the wind, but I don't know if it's a bellow of triumph or frustration.

If it's one of triumph then I think I might as well die here and now.

IN OFF THE RED

Snooker balls collide into each other and scatter across the brushed green baize of a full-sized snooker table. A pink ball careers into a corner pocket.

'Got one!'

The Ape has taped three snooker cues together and is using them as one large cue as he smashes balls around the table.

'Got one!'

GG watches him for a moment, then turns to the Moth who is sitting at the window peering into the gathering night. There is a moon rising overhead and some of the street lamps are spluttering and dying, their yellow sodium glow fading from existence in a jittery dance of power failure.

'The world is stopping,' the Moth says solemnly to no one in particular. 'It's turning itself off. It was only a matter of time.'

I wait for more but the Moth disappears inside his head.

'What does he mean by that?' GG whispers to me. 'Moth?' The Moth doesn't hear him so GG waves at him. 'Timothy? Tiny Tim?'

The Moth breaks from his reflections. 'I didn't want to make it any worse.'

'There's worse than this?'

'Who's manning the nuclear reactors? Only they'll eventually fail and the world'll go kaboom.'

GG pulls a sad clown face. 'Why did I even ask? Why did I do that?'

'Then there's all the satellites in space, some of them'll miss their commands, then crash into each other and fall out of orbit. No one'll be around to spot and shoot approaching comets either. That's how the dinosaurs died out. A comet hit the earth. There's so much reliant on computers that the minute they fail – well, who knows what that'll do?'

I can't even respond. It's so mind-blowing that it's impossible to accept.

'How long have we got before the kaboom?' GG asks.

The Moth shrugs. 'It hasn't happened yet but it can't be long.'

The lights in the square flicker again, just in case we needed proof.

'How will Johnson know where we are?' Billie asks. Her eyes are back to normal now and she has taken the liberty of going behind the bar and helping herself to a vodka and tonic. She didn't ask anyone else if they wanted anything so I hand out beers to the others.

The Ape drinks his in two seconds flat then scatters more snooker balls with this triple-cue. 'Got one!'

The increasingly violent snowstorm has made hearing the Non-Ape's bellows impossible and we now have no idea what has happened to Johnson.

'We need to send up a little smoke signal for him,' GG offers. 'Or put a sign in the window.'

The Ape smashes more balls as hard as he can. The white ball races into a pocket. 'Got one!'

'Moth?' I approach the window. 'Any ideas?'

The Moth scans the night for a long moment.

But if he has got a great idea he's keeping it to himself for now.

Billie gets to her feet. 'We've been here an hour now. I'm going to go find him.'

The Moth is immediately worried. 'You can't do that, Billie.'

'You going to stop me? How? By wheeling yourself over my toes? By giving me a slight limp?' Billie drains her glass. 'That's my boyfriend out there.'

'You've been drinking alcohol. It'll make you feel ten times colder.'

'Someone needs to find him,' she says and slumps on one of the faded green-leather banquettes that run along one side of the wall.

The snooker balls crash around the table again. 'Got one!'

'C'mon, Moth,' says GG. 'Get that brain working.' GG adopts an authoritative Scottish brogue. 'What are we paying you for, man?'

The Moth stares down into the blizzard-hit square. The lamp posts continue to fizz and flicker.

'Moth?' I press.

The Moth thinks for an agonisingly long moment but remains slumped

'Sorry. I haven't one single idea.'

YOU ARE KIDDING, RIGHT?

The Non-Ape's bellows in the distance. The roar is the loudest one yet. It reminds me of that moment in *Jurassic Park* when they first hear the T rex roar, only this is way louder.

Billie has numbed her worry with more vodka and is now only half awake as she stretches her long lithe body along the green banquette.

GG is lying on one of the snooker tables staring at the overhead light. He is dancing slowly with his fingers, humming some slow tempo tune to himself.

The Moth has remained silent. Staring into the black night.

The Ape is behind the bar rummaging for more crisps. He sees me and tosses a packet at me.

'Dinner.' His warning comes too late and they hit me in the face.

He starts emptying an entire bag down the back of his throat. Half of them spill over his face. 'Crisp shower!'

I watch him and wonder how none of this ever seems to affect him.

He wipes his face. 'Want me to go find Johnson?'

It's a kind offer, but I know we're all trapped here till this storm blows over.

'I'm a great tracker,' he says.

Which surprises me.

'I followed a teacher home and he never knew I was there.'

'That's not really the same thing,' I tell him.

'At least, not until the feds showed up he didn't know I was there.'

'Forget it. It's too dangerous. You'd freeze to death out there.' The words are out before I can stop them and the pronouncement brings tears to my eyes. If the Ape can freeze so can Johnson.

The Ape knows I'm upset but he doesn't know how to deal with it so he throws another packet of crisps at me. 'More dinner.'

They bounce off me.

I wipe my eyes. But tears replace the tears.

'I could find him easy,' the Ape boasts.

I so wish you could, I think.

'Go on then, go out there in the cold and the dark and bring him back.' Billie has stirred but her words are slurred. She raises her glass to the Ape. 'I'll drink to that amazing idea.'

The Ape doesn't flinch but GG sneaks a knowing look at me from his snooker table and whispers, 'Is Carrie back? Could've sworn I heard her voice.'

Carrie was the arch queen of bitchiness and has held that title for as long as I can remember. But Billie is proving to be a rival for that crown now.

The Ape puffs out his chest. 'I'll find him, no problemo.'

'I'll close the door after you.' Billie has never had any love for the Ape and, despite trying to numb the pain of losing

Johnson with booze, her venom is rising and finding an all too easy target.

'Billie,' I say, warning her.

But she gets up on her elbows. Across the hall GG has stopped his finger dance.

'Go on then.' Billie stares hard at the Ape.

'I'm a great tracker,' he repeats.

He felt the full force of Billie's anti-Ape rage before and it hurt him more than he would ever let on. But he's standing his ground, unafraid.

'So make some tracks,' she slurs.

'I will.'

'So do it.'

'I'm going.'

'Good.'

'Ape . . .' I start to say.

'It's Dazza.'

'Dazza . . .'

He emerges from behind the bar and pulls on his great black coat.

'Ten minutes.'

'Ten?' Billie says bitterly. 'That's soooo slow.'

The Ape picks up his triple-cue weapon and Billie spits out a laugh. 'My God.'

'Billie,' I try again but she is sitting upright now, eager to goad the Ape.

'If you manage it, you can have another bag of crisps. Deal?'

GG sits up. He's as concerned as I am. 'Dazza, it's dark out there. It's cold. It's better if you stay indoors, banging balls around.'

The Ape buttons his coat and ignores GG. Only looking at Billie. 'Deal.'

'It's pitch-black.' The Moth twists in his seat. 'Tell him, Rev!'

'I've got good eyes,' the Ape responds.

GG is now moving over to the Ape. 'You'll be snow-blind in seconds.'

'Ten minutes,' he repeats.

The Ape takes a moment and then presses a stubby index finger against my cheek. He scoops up a tear and shows it to me.

He then turns and heads downstairs and trudges out into the Siberian night.

It happens before either GG or myself can really react. One second the Ape is there, the next he's gone.

I make to go after him but GG stops me. 'You can't, Rev. We need you here.'

Billie laughs but it's hollow. 'He actually went out there? I was teasing him. I was. Tell him to come back, Moth. Shout out the window.'

We all know that Billie meant every word and again I'm reminded that sometimes she seems a million miles away from being my best friend.

'Moth, shout to him!' Billie gets to her tipsy drunken feet and reels towards the window. She cups her hands and tries to peer out. 'Where is he? I can't see him.'

She bangs on the window but it's more of a futile rap than anything.

There is no response and just like that the Ape has gone.

DYING IS EASY

I check the clock on the wall. It has been seven minutes since the Ape stepped out to put his perfect eyesight and innate tracking skills to the ultimate test.

GG has watched every second tick by with me. He has fallen unusually silent and even he can find no humour in this moment. We've both come to love the Ape in our own way.

The Moth continues to keep vigil at the window while Billie tries not to look too ashamed of herself.

I should be so much angrier at her, but deep down I know the Ape went out because of me. He didn't like me crying, and even if they weren't big tears, he still wanted to stop them.

For nine minutes we have been talking idly, chatting about anything but what might be happening outside, namely the freezing to death of an Ape and a Johnson.

The Moth is trying to work out why GG, the Ape and me could shift back here and yet when he, Billie and Johnson had gone to the classroom nothing had happened. No white light had appeared for them.

'I think you were right, Rev. It's you,' the Moth declares. 'You're the missing link.'

'That makes two Neanderthals then.' Billie's joke doesn't exactly lighten the mood.

'I'm trying to think of an answer,' he says to her. 'I don't need your stupid comments.' The Moth surprises me with his curt reaction. But I guess five months of being stuck in an empty alien world changes a person.

'You've tried for months and come up with zilch.' There's spite in Billie and a tautness surrounds that spite. Everyone seems to annoy her at some level. Everyone bar Johnson.

She's definitely not the same person she was and, unlike the Moth, I don't think it's just because she's been stuck here for months. I'm worried that the scars she received from the evil version of Lucas haven't only distorted her appearance but have also altered her personality. When we were on the train to London when we were here the first time she had a weird fit and her eyes turned black. That happened a few more times and when I think back to how nasty she was to the Ape during the dinner we had at the hotel in London (before the punching incident of course), I don't think it was just the huge amount of alcohol talking. Something about her has changed. It's not her fault and I feel desperately worried for her, but that growing meanness is a worry. Who is she? What is she becoming?

'You've been useless, Hawkings.' She arrows a look at the Moth. 'Your body doesn't work and now your brain doesn't either.'

'That's nice, thank you.' The Moth just about remains level-headed and calm. 'And for the millionth time his name is Hawking, Stephen Hawking. No "S". How many times do I have to tell you that?'

Billie spots my silent disapproval and softens a little. 'All I'm saying is, you need to justify what you're saying,' she tells the Moth. 'You can't just say things and not back them up.'

'He's working on it, Billie,' GG says, walking over to the window and looking out into the freezing night, desperate for a sign. 'So we'll wait for the Ape and Johnson and then head back to the school. See if the theory about Rev is right,' he adds.

Billie is scornful. 'You don't even know where we'll be taken to. You went to the wrong world, remember? There could be hundreds of worlds and we could end up never finding our way home. Or worse, we could fall into the burning world, the one Rev's dad came through from. That'll be fun. Burning to death.'

Billie drains her vodka and throws the glass at the bar where it smashes.

Fifty-five seconds. That's all the Ape's got left to keep his ten-minute promise.

There haven't been any more T rex-style roars, which could mean the Non-Ape has gone or that he's definitely found Johnson and done whatever it is he wanted to do to him.

Fifty seconds.

The Moth has already declared that ten minutes would be the maximum survivable time outside. I don't know where the figure came from, but in his expert opinion unless the Ape found shelter he probably wouldn't make it back, as in ever.

Which leaves forty seconds.

'Tick-tock,' GG says quietly, his eyes glued to the clock.

Thirty-five seconds.

What will I do if he dies?

Thirty seconds.

And I mean that about both of them. Johnson and the Ape. What if I never see either of them again?

Twenty-five seconds.

GG lets out a long extended sigh. His eyes meet mine. 'And then there were four,' he says. 'We're not very good at this are we?'

Twenty seconds.

They're both dead. They must be.

Fifteen seconds.

Why did my dad do this to me? Or was it *her* dad? Rev Two's dad. Why would he bring us here? I know in my heart of hearts that my guess about me being the catalyst is right. He made it happen. I just wish I knew why. The obvious reason is he wanted to see me again. After twelve years of searching he had a breakthrough and did something that caused me to come here. The others got unlucky and were dragged along with me. But did he get confused? Did he bring both Revs here – because he wasn't sure which one was his daughter? How could he not know?

Ten seconds.

Despite everything I secretly hope that my non-mum has been reunited with both her Rev and her husband. That would make some of this at least partially acceptable. A small piece of good in a horrendous sequence of events.

Five seconds.

The second hand on the clock pushes past the ten-minute cut-off point and the empty world dies a little bit more.

GG looks away from the clock. The Moth slowly hangs his head. Billie swallows hard and buries her face in her hands. I want to say something profound or rousing, like we're still here and if Johnson and the Ape were here they'd tell us to keep going, to keep trying, to save the world.

'Yowza!'

The Ape bundles in, his black coat covered in snow, a beefy arm thrown round Johnson who leans into him, using the triple-cue as a makeshift crutch.

GG bounds over to them. 'He did it! The Ape found Johnson!'

'I'm a great tracker.'

The Ape's face is red raw from the biting wind and it looks like his fingers are close to being frostbitten, but he went out and he found Johnson. I have no idea how he did that. I'm totally speechless.

'I'm glad it was this Ape.' Johnson raises a feeble smile and he and the Ape share a high five.

All I manage is: 'Johnson.'

The Moth looks at them in shock and wonder and Billie shoves past me to throw her arms round Johnson's neck and kiss his face and lips in between words.

'Johnson.' Kiss. 'You're alive.' Kiss. 'I was so scared.' Kiss. 'Never be apart again.' Kiss.

GG leaps up and kisses the Ape on his frozen, stinging red cheek. 'You, sir, are the best person ever, ever, ever, ever!'

The Ape brushes away from GG and catches my eye. At this point a true hero would wink in a cool way. He belches. 'Where are my crisps?'

'The-the Non-Ape? What happened to him?' I ask.

'No idea. Didn't see him.'

But I'm really asking Johnson who is being smothered by Billie as she slips his long wet coat off him.

'Rev, get the kettle on,' Billie orders me. 'He needs a hot drink.'

'Did you lie low or something?' I press, but Johnson can't see me past Billie.

'Rev, stop dawdling, he's freezing.'

'Where were you?'

'Rev, c'mon, move it!' she barks at me, so off I dutifully go to the staff room to make hot coffee.

I watch the machine percolating and think, *I hate coffee. I hate it. Why am I making it if I hate it so much?*

But nevertheless I make two piping hot cups.

The Ape doesn't want his and so Billie takes it instead, and as I reach over to Johnson, she takes that cup from me as well and presses it into his hands.

She smiles encouragingly to him. 'I made you this,' she lies.

'I never, uh, I never got to thank you for saving me from the other Ape—' I try.

'Rev, can you give us a minute?' Billie turns to me and her eyes flick to black for a moment. 'Please.'

I utter a meek, 'sorry, sorry,' and back away. As I do Johnson finally looks at me.

It's not the look I was hoping for.

I thought he might do that lazy one-fingered salute but instead he just nods once very quickly. It's a non-gesture. A way of not really committing to anything. Or not committing to me. Instead he turns to Billie and brushes some hair from her eyes and takes her in for a long steady moment.

'How's my girl?'

I'M WITH STUPID

There's something amiss. Something very wrong. I don't know what it is but it seems almost insane for the Ape to have found Johnson in ten minutes. *Exactly* ten minutes. Practically on the dot. There was no way he could have done that in a blizzard. And yet he did. And not only that, he did it without Non-Ape seeing them. It's just too incredible.

Obviously I am thrilled and beyond relieved that they are both safe, but did that really just happen?

It feels like someone is playing games. They're twisting the truth, or at least plucking at it and making it bend in some freaky misshapen way. Or am I just saying this because I really can't believe that Billie and Johnson are together? It makes perfect sense: they were trapped here for five months and of course something would happen between them. He's amazing, Billie's gorgeous – why wouldn't they reach out to each other? Apart from the Moth there was no one else in this world. And even if the Moth is lovely, smart and wise, he also loved Carrie. She was always the girl for him.

So maybe I should just get on and accept that I was torn

between two Johnsons, but never actually managed to make up my mind. Yet Billie did. It's as simple as that. She went for it while I dragged my heels. That's what self-confidence does for you.

Anyway, there's so much more to figure out than my silly redundant feelings. We need a way home. Because this world isn't safe. In some ways, it's perfect: neatly parked cars to drive, our pick of clothes, food and all the things we could ever want, all of it for free. But it's also appallingly violent. The gruesome deaths, the horror and heartbreak – and now the new revelation that a nuclear meltdown is imminent – tends to diminish the thought of this being some kind of secret nirvana.

For a while I'd thought that the empty roads and clear railway tracks had meant that someone – or something – had planned everything, right down to the warm steak bakes that were sitting in the Greggs window. When we first came here it felt like a true motherworld and its mothering nature was taking care of us. To be truthful, it was exactly the place any father would want for his daughter. I don't know how the laws of the multiverse work, but this used to be a world with a welcome mat. It certainly isn't that any more.

Which is why, while everyone else has settled down to sleep, I've been formulating another plan to get us out of here. I don't know why I didn't think of it before. It is so blindingly obvious but I think I can be excused by the fact that I have almost died twice since I got back here. Three times if you count how I felt when Billie slipped her arm round Johnson's waist.

There was a bus parked in the street the first time I was here. I heard voices coming from it and when I went to check the door slammed shut in my face. I didn't know what was really going on then and didn't give it any more thought, but I'm pretty sure they were the same voices I heard when my father – or Rev Two's father – came through from the burning world to try and find me. So that must be another escape route. It has to be. Another portal that could mean we don't have to go to London and find some near impossible way of stopping the doppelgangers pouring through. We'll just escape. They can show up but we won't be here.

I've checked the weather and the snowstorm has died away. The town is covered in white but it's a gentle white, a cottony, cushiony layer of snow that almost seems inviting. There has been no sign of Non-Ape so I'm guessing he's probably found somewhere to sleep before renewing his relentless search for Johnson. I'm half hoping he's in the Sun Hotel where their room is.

Getting Johnson away from Non-Ape is also the reason I'm going to find the bus. I need to do it now so that we are ready to leave first thing before Non-Ape is even awake. I think the bus is about half a mile away, if that. Rather than get everyone's hopes up, I'll do it now and when the winter sun comes up in the morning I can wake everyone up and deliver the good news. I'll be a sort of hero. Maybe. And Johnson'll see that I've saved him and maybe, just maybe, he'll see I'm still trying my best. That I'm not just the fool that caused this mess, or if I am, I'm also the genius who can fix everything. This could even be a way of grabbing back some ground in our *friendship*. That's right. Our *friendship*. Which is the best I can hope for now. But that's better than nothing.

I pull my new boots on as darkness blankets the snooker hall.

The Ape farts loudly in his sleep and I'm scared it'll wake

everyone so I grab GG's *WAR(M)* jacket and tiptoe as fast as I can towards the stairs that lead down to the street. There's one lone lamp with a low wattage bulb casting pale orange into the snooker hall and it allows me to look back at my sleeping friends. The Ape sleeps face down on a snooker table and GG and the Moth are sleeping head to toe on the table next to the Ape's. The Ape lifted the Moth there and GG found green plastic sheets that are used to cover the snooker tables at night and fashioned them into makeshift blankets. I should leave a note in case someone wakes and wonders where I am but the sight of Billie and Johnson asleep in each other's arms on the banquette pushes me fast towards the door. The less time I dawdle here the better.

The door creaks – obviously – and GG suddenly sits up in his sleep. He looks around and I duck quickly behind a snooker table. I see him cast his eyes into the dying orange gloom and listen for a moment. The old GG probably wouldn't have stirred but he's like me now, on high alert for anything. The night wind rattles a window and this seems to placate him and he settles down again. I'm impressed that he is so alert to any sign of danger or intrusion. Without knowing it, this world has changed us all. Probably for ever. God alone knows what sort of mental scars we'll end up carrying around with us.

When I get outside I realise I truly am a child of summer and the sun. The cold is appallingly brutal. The wind chill lowers the temperature further and if it wasn't for an almost full moon glittering on the white snow I wouldn't have a clue where to head for. But there's enough illumination for me to make out the beginnings of the empty town square. The bus was parked on the side of a steep hill not too far from the centre of town, so I bunch my arms tight round me and pray that I find it soon. I'm imagining I'll be gone twenty minutes at the most.

The snow has deepened and it's hard going ploughing through it. It saps my strength in minutes and I'm panting by the time I'm halfway down the high street. It is empty apart from banks of snow piling up against the buildings and shop fronts. There are cars but they're buried under deep snow and it would take an eternity to dig them free. I just need to get my bearings.

Snowflakes hit my face and with increasing regularity I have to spit them out of my mouth. I'm forced to shield my face and lower my head as a fresh snowstorm gathers. But I keep trudging because it's only half a mile, and that's nothing.

I read somewhere that if you happen to be walking anywhere near the North Pole, say you've gone for a stroll and for some inexplicable reason you've ended up near the top of the world, then apparently you need to eat something like five thousand calories a day just to replace the energy you'll expend trying to keep warm. Only now do I realise what it must feel like not to be replacing any of those lost calories. Despite the cold, I am sweating from exertion. The snow is piling higher and higher and every step is becoming a laboured breathy conquest as I creep forward, bending ever lower to stop the snowflakes stinging my eyes and face.

The blizzard is draining me of energy and I'm starting to feel giddy, nauseous. My stomach feels empty and my heart and lungs are working overtime as I gulp in air. But the air is really just a mass of snowflakes and I'm drinking it rather than breathing it. I can feel the freezing flakes melt and then slip down the back of my throat, bringing horrendous stabs of brain freeze. As soon as one unearthly pain stops, another one takes its place.

I try to breathe through my nose but I can't take in enough air and so I cover my mouth with a frozen hand. My skin looks mortuary blue under the moonlight. I stop swallowing snowflakes but my hand is now stinging and tingling with a thousand tiny pinpricks. God it's cold. This was stupid. Another stupid idea in a long line of stupid ideas. I need to go back and try again in the morning. I need to get to the snooker hall before my body shuts down.

I made this reckless decision because the truth is I can't face Johnson and Billie being an item. But it's not really a selfless act to rescue us. It's a mean, envious thing. I don't want them to be together. I want him to choose me. Jealousy is a horrible sneaky thing that you often don't even know is there until it's too late.

What is wrong with me? Don't I want my best friend to be happy?

Maybe I won't answer that.

Or maybe I just did.

I'm already shivering inside and out and I can't see a thing thanks to the increasingly violent snowstorm swirling around me. I have no idea where to turn next. I can't even retrace my footsteps because the cascade of snow has already obliterated the trail that leads back to the snooker hall. I try and get my bearings, looking for a familiar shop or a landmark. I think I'm still somewhere in the high street but I have no idea in which direction I'm travelling. I spin round, hoping I'll see something that looks familiar. But the layers of snow change everything, and the moonlight distorts it further, throwing long shadows and giving rise to new mutated shapes that replace the world I know.

I need to find shelter. Any shelter. Forget finding the snooker hall, I need to get out of this freezing hell. After everything I've been through I can adapt and change my plans on a whim, it's the sign of a survivor.

I think.

I hope.

I stumble and slip towards the only door I can make out. I think it's the old Woolworths entrance. It's now an oversized clothes shop. And that's oversized clothes, not an oversized shop.

My mind is spinning off at tangents. I can feel logic and sanity leaking away, retreating from the biting vicious cold. But oversized clothes sound so good right now. I start dreaming of huge thick coats and massive woollen jerseys. My blue-tinged hand reaches for the door handle and thank God it's unlocked. But it moves about half an inch before the snowdrift piled a metre high against it prevents further progress.

What the hell? I yank as hard as I can but the door won't budge. I use both hands, desperate to get inside. Whatever strength I have left goes into getting that door open far enough for me to slide through. I yank and I yank, but it just won't move.

I think I let out a wail but I don't know if the noise actually makes it past my bitterly chilled lips. Even my voice doesn't want to take one step outside my mouth, thank you very much. I wish I'd thought this through. I really wish GG had spotted me leaving and talked me into not being such a lovelorn fool.

I give up on the door to the shop. But when I try to take my hands off the metal handle I realise they are stuck. The cold has welded my skin to the door. I wrench as hard as I can, but I'm superglued to the handle. The snow is building around me and I have this crazed image of being found in the morning, a human shape under thirty centimetres of snow, looking like some over-desperate shopper who got up early to beat the rush. Only she stupidly got caught in a blizzard and now she'll never know if that dress she spotted in the window will ever look good on her.

No one should die like this. *I can't*, I think, *I can't die outside a shop my gran thinks is the height of fashion.*

Come on, Rev.

I wrench hard. I strain every sinew in my trembling, aching arms and get my left hand free. But the skin tears off and this time I definitely do howl. Like a wolf with a sore throat. Tears spring to my eyes and I swear they become icicles even before they reach my cheeks. I yank hard again and leave more skin on the frozen door handle as my right hand releases and I stumble backwards, landing face up in the snow. My mouth tastes of iron and I think I've bitten my tongue. I jam my agonised hands into the snow hoping for some relief or at least a numbing of the searing rawness. It's the only good thing the snow has done for me as I feel my bloodied hands cauterised by the insane cold.

I climb labouredly to my knees, breathing hard again, but at least I have a reference point now. The shop is at the far end of the high street and it's on the north side. And I know the church is two streets behind on the south side. But what now? My brain is refusing to offer any coherent thoughts. It's simple though. It's got to be simple. I'm north and I need to go two streets south.

South is south of north.

I think.

I climb to my feet and dredge up a memory. The Moth was down an alleyway when we found him a few days ago.

125

I remember him calling out to us from the alley that doubles as a short cut to the next street. It runs between a shoe shop and a gift and card shop. Those shops are almost opposite the oversized clothes shop.

I trudge across the high street, knowing for certain that the alleyway will take me one street closer to the church.

The Moth had been trapped in his motorised wheelchair after the battery had died and the alleyway was right here ...

Only it's not.

There is no alleyway. There is no shoe shop or gift shop. There is only snow banked high against the buildings. Too high to see what those buildings are.

I don't know what to do now. I'm out of ideas. That was my only plan.

And even that wasn't the right plan. Why was I heading for the church anyway? Everyone is safe and warm in the snooker hall, *not* the church.

This isn't good. I'm starting to feel the first waves of panic. I can't even scream for help because my voice would never rise above the gale that is whipping around me. It would grab my words and hurl them into a snowdrift, muffling them and silencing me.

But ... what if that's what it wants?

What if this world, this perfect welcome-mat world doesn't want me in it after all?

I didn't drown in the river. The Non-Ape didn't finish the job either, so the world is rolling up its sleeves with a deep sigh. If you want someone killed, then you may as well do it yourself.

Wait. My phone. I can call for help. You don't get me that easy!

My fingers are so numb and frostbitten and skinless that it's like using flippers to unzip GG's jacket and fumble for the phone.

I don't give in though. I need that phone and I will get it.

Every time I grab it, it slips out of my numb fingers. Time and again I almost have it until eventually, after blowing as hard as I can on my hands, I manage to get hold of it.

Yes. Yes, yes, yes, yes!

I'm a phone call away from rescue.

But the phone is dead.

It doesn't light up. It doesn't do anything except reveal the drops of dank river water trapped behind the screen. The one thing you can't do with a mobile phone is get it wet, and guess who fell in a river earlier?

I let the useless phone slip from my hands.

I can feel the panic rising again and try to squash it back down with the only thought that could ever keep me from giving up entirely.

That my mum would never forgive me if I died. I can't leave her to spend the rest of her life not knowing where I disappeared to.

I cling to this thought because there is nothing else in my frozen head.

Don't die.

Over and over I repeat the thoughts.

Don't die. Make Mum happy.

They fall into harmony with my steps.

Do not die.

That's one step.

Make sure Mum isn't alone.

That's another step.

Live.

That's yet another step.

I'm gaining some sort of momentum.

Live.

Be.

Exist.

I reach the end of the high street.

Don't ... Uh ...

I turn what I think is south.

Die.

I take another turn, which probably isn't south but might be.

See Mum again.

I can hear an engine.

I stop, which I shouldn't do because I'll lose the momentum and the mantra.

I move towards the sound.

Live, you idiot!

I trudge faster.

Live. And faster.

Live, live, live.

'Hey, Rev.'

My overworked heart skips a beat.

'Johnson?'

BOY ON A MOTORBIKE

My brain has finally had enough of me. My blood has started to freeze internally and somewhere inside my brain there is a voice that sounds like Johnson and it is being dangled in front of me like a hypnotist's pocket watch. *You failed*, it's saying. *There is no fixing this. So why don't you give up and let the cold claim you?*

I have stopped walking.

But worse I have stopped trying.

My knees give out first as I sink into the whiteness.

'*Rev.*'

'I know what you're doing,' I tell the voice in my head.

'*Get up.*'

'I can't move.'

The engine stops. Or rather the noise stops. It was a figment of my imagination.

'C'mon,' Johnson says.

I'm sinking further into the snow. The world is claiming me and I can't stop it. Why did I think I could win?

'Get up.'

129

It's taunting me now. It's offering me hope and salvation but only so it can snatch it away.

What a rotten cruel world.

Mother Nature is a Mean Girl.

A hand reaches for me through the snowstorm. A dry warm hand.

Yeah right, I think. *You want me to take that hand because you know it'll drag me under*.

'Rev.'

'Go away.'

'I only just got here.'

'Go,' I tell the hand.

'Rev.'

'I know what you're trying to do to me.'

'You think?' he asks. And then he grabs me and hoicks me to my feet. 'C'mon.' He drags me forward and I stumble through the snow.

'Don't,' I tell the apparition. Because that's what this is. An apparition, a mirage, a deadly trick of the mind.

'I don't do don't,' he says and yanks me as hard as he can.

And a moment later Johnson stands before me.

'Hardly the weather for a stroll.'

'Johnson?'

Johnson grins. 'You remembered me. That's a start.' Then he takes my hand and pulls me towards him. 'C'mon.'

Johnson drags me away from the snowstorm.

I can feel tarmac under my sodden feet and snowflakes are already melting around me, creating a puddle. I'm standing in a perfectly dry and warm summer night.

Which means I'm dead. I have to be.

'No you're not.'

Johnson stands in front of a motorbike, a large one like I've seen Hells Angels driving around on. Not in person, but in films. I think it's a Harley-Davidson and it gleams in the moonlight.

'*Climb on.*'

His lips aren't moving but his voice is inside my head.

It's not Johnson.

It's Other-Johnson.

But that's not possible.

He grins. '*Believe it.*'

Other-Johnson helps me move my frozen inflexible body onto the back of the motorbike. He slides on in front of me and kick-starts the engine. '*Hold on tight.*'

'I-I-I can't,' I shudder.

He reaches behind him and pulls my arms tight round his waist. He sees my skinless palms in the moonlight. 'I'll find you something for that,' he says, speaking out loud at last.

Other-Johnson kicks the bike off its stand and revs the engine. 'Bend with me.'

'What?'

'Lean with me. You'll feel like you want to bend the other way but you can't do that. Not on a motorbike. We'll be taking corners fast, so when I lean into one, come along with me. OK?'

I nod vaguely, not knowing what on earth is happening.

'You were dead and now I am too. Right? This is how we get to heaven. On a motorbike.'

'Heaven,' he grins, 'that's us.'

He pulls the clutch in and flicks the bike into first gear.

'Where are we going?' I ask him.

'Just hold on tight.'

He twists the accelerator and we quicken into the moonlit night. There is no snow, there is no freezing wind and when I look back the winter storm has come to an abrupt stop on the edge of town.

Which is clearly impossible.

Other-Johnson obviously knows what I'm thinking because he yells over the roar of the speeding bike. 'I'm glad I'm not the only one who thinks that.'

I instinctively hold on tighter to him, leaning my face into his shoulder. The warm night air whips my plastered-wet pink hair around my face and I lean closer into Other-Johnson's back to try and avoid the stings.

I have a thousand questions for him.

'I know you have,' he tells me. 'But I don't have a thousand answers.'

He reaches down and pats my arms, which wrap tightly round his skinny midriff.

'You were dead,' I tell him.

Last time I saw him he was lying in the town square with grey skin, drained of every shred of life by Rev Two's existence-sucking power.

'I fall, I bounce.' He is grinning in my mind. 'Corner coming up.'

He leans into the corner and he's right – I do want to lean the opposite way. He knows this.

'Trust me,' he says and against all of my better instincts I lean with him. But I grip him tighter just in case.

The large Harley takes the corner and for a second I think I'm going to slide off, but Other-Johnson's command of motorbike physics is spot on and as we come out of the corner the bike straightens to the vertical and I straighten with it.

'Get you,' he says proudly. 'A natural biker. We could go miles together.'

NIGHT SCHOOL

'*This isn't going to be easy to get your head around.*' Other-Johnson's voice comes into my head again. It seems that he's heading to the school, heading to the classroom where it all began. '*So it's better showing than telling.*'

Even though the freak storm continues to hover around the town centre it is becoming pretty clear that everywhere else is still experiencing late summer. The roads are slippery and clogged with deep snow but that doesn't stop Other-Johnson coaxing the powerful motorbike up the hill that leads to the school.

I stood at the top of the same hill about seven hours earlier and swear I saw the winter stretching in every direction.

'*You saw what you were meant to see.*' I can't hide a single thought from Other-Johnson. '*Don't know how or why but someone's been playing games with you.*'

'*Someone came back with us,*' I transmit to him. '*Any idea who can make it snow like this?*'

'*Wish I did. Power like that is on a whole new scale. It's not one I've ever heard about. Even in my world.*'

The motorbike struggles, despite its power, and we slip, gain some grip and then slip again. At one point I think we're going to skid all the way back down the hill but Other-Johnson knows how to get the best out of the bike and he cajoles it forward with flicks of his boot and seamless twists of his wrist. Even when the rear wheel threatens to go from under us he shifts his weight easily and takes command of the huge bike again.

We park in the small staff car park that sits in front of a sports field. He kicks the stand down and within seconds we are heading into school.

'Prepare yourself,' Johnson whispers.

The climb to the top floor where the classroom sits exhausts me but only because I am near to the point of physical collapse. At least the hike upwards gets my blood pumping. Other-Johnson is aware of my fatigue and takes my hand and pulls me up the last flight.

He holds my hand all the way along the hallway to the classroom door. Which is shut now.

Other-Johnson stops outside the door. 'You won't see any tents in here,' he tells me.

'Tents?'

Other-Johnson enters my head and rifles through it, plucking images and snatches of conversation from my memory. He's like a computer operator sifting through webpages until he finds the right one. He shows me the Moth telling me how they camped out in the classroom for a month or so.

He then turns the door handle only to find that the door is locked. Which surprises both of us. He tries it again but the door won't open.

'Someone's locked it,' he says, even though I can see that for myself.

He tries it again, then backs up a few paces and kicks the door as hard as he can with the flat of his boot. It doesn't budge an inch. He kicks it again but the door remains closed.

'OK,' he says. 'What are we dealing with here?' He keeps kicking it, but there is no getting through that door.

'Why are we here anyway?' I ask.

Other-Johnson isn't happy about the door but lets it go for now. 'No one camped in there. Total lie,' Other-Johnson tells me, not bothering to finesse or ease the way. 'Never happened.'

'Why would the Moth lie?'

'The Moth didn't know he was lying. He believed it.'

I take a moment as Other-Johnson kicks the door again as hard as he can. It just won't open. Which is not good. His black desert boots leave scuff marks on it.

Other-Johnson's eyes meet mine. 'You ready for this?'

I nod, but don't know why.

'You haven't been gone five months. It was only an hour or so, just like you thought it was.'

I have seen and heard the most incredible things these past few days but this might be the most astonishing one of all.

'Say that again.' The words flop in slow motion from my lips.

'It was an hour in both worlds.'

I look to the floor as if there's going to be answers down there. I know I'm frowning and that my mouth is hanging open but I'm not sure I know much more than that. 'That can't be.'

'Like winter can't be winter? It's still summer, Rev.'

I feel like I've just been slapped in the face.

'An hour? Are you sure? But the others said . . .' I trail off, my thoughts scattering and reforming like someone's just turned a leaf blower on them. 'They said ... Johnson, Billie, the Moth, they all believe they've been here for months.'

'I think someone's playing with their heads.' Other-Johnson kicks the door as hard as he can again but it still refuses to yield.

The world spins for a moment before settling. 'I need to tell them.'

'There's one other thing you should see first.'

'There's more?' I'm not sure I'm in any fit state to take anything else on board.

'There's always more.'

TWELVE LONG AND SHORT YEARS

We spend another few minutes trying to get into the classroom but it's firmly sealed shut.

'This is not good,' Other-Johnson tells me.

'Look on the bright side – if we can't get in, then people won't be able to get out either,' I tell him, dredging up what I think is a smart observation.

Other-Johnson frowns though. 'Rev, the door being jammed isn't an accident. Someone doesn't want us to leave. They're keeping us from escaping.'

'Who would do that?'

'If I knew I'd tell you.'

The moonlight streams in through the window at the far end of the corridor. It casts a pale glow over Other-Johnson's face. It makes him look gaunt and tense.

'I have no idea, Rev.'

Other-Johnson heads down the hallway. 'C'mon.'

I hurry to catch up with him. 'There were footsteps in the snow,' I tell him. 'We think someone came from your world with us. Can you sense them?'

Other-Johnson heads down the stairs.

'Do a scan,' I tell him. 'Do that mind thing you do.'

Other-Johnson takes a moment and I imagine he is doing his mind thing, but if he is it doesn't provide any answers. 'There's nothing, Rev. At least no one I can find.'

Which scares me more than anything.

It means we have no way of knowing who's out there, or what they want with us.

The motorbike approaches a roundabout which offers four destinations: the way we just came, left into a more industrial area, straight ahead to the edge of town and the railway station or right towards the posh tree-lined avenues of desirable living.

The snow hasn't reached this far out of town, which comes as a great relief to my shivering soul.

We take the sweeping right, Other-Johnson leaning the bike impossibly low, less than forty-five degrees to the horizontal as he takes the roundabout.

'*Really thought I'd never you see again,*' he beams into my mind as we head away from the roundabout. '*I wasn't even scanning the waves for you.*'

Other-Johnson's mind thing meant he could talk to me from miles away, over a secret telepathic link.

'*You don't get rid of me that easy,*' I quip, but I'm kind of low on killer lines.

'*I must have sensed you were in danger, because you were suddenly in my head again.*'

Which could mean we're eternally bonded now.

'*You aren't lying, are you? About the five months? How did you even know?*'

139

'*It's still summer for one thing. And I saw what was in your head. Sorry about Johnson and Billie.*'

There's a sense of sorrow in his tone, but if I could see his face I bet he'd be smiling right now.

He kicks through the gears as we start to climb another of the extremely steep hills that populate this town.

Other-Johnson surfs through more of my memories. He winces at the lynch mob in the town square of his world. '*Sorry about that.*'

All of this feels so typical of the way our up-and-down luck has been running. Get shifted out of this world by the light: tick. End up in the world full of evil aliens, instead of ours: cross. Escape unharmed from the alien world: tick. Bring something awful with us: big red cross. And whatever the something awful is, it looks like it has the power to create winter in a matter of minutes and cram five fictional months into the heads of three people. Huge, enormous red cross.

'*I need to get back to the others.*'

'*Hold that thought.*' He slows at a junction and takes another right.

'*They could be in danger, or awake and looking for me.*'

'*They're not,*' he says with conviction. He must be able to see them in his head. '*They're sleeping like babies.*'

Other-Johnson accelerates, taking me further and further away from the others.

'*This thing that came back with us . . .*' I tell him. '*If we want to go home, we'll have to fight it, won't we?*' Meaning kill it. '*It's going to come down to that, right? It's not someone playing for fun.*'

But he doesn't answer as the bike roars deeper into the

night. I guess he doesn't know. Or worse, he can't bring himself to tell me.

I never knew there was a private hospital. I've lived in an exact copy of this town my whole life and didn't know it existed. It's hidden behind a mass of trees and the entrance is easy to miss because of the foliage growing around it. It's not an area of town I frequent. It's the posh part, the tree-lined, doctor-dwelling area. I have no friends up here.

'If the Ape's still roaming around he'll have heard the bike,' Other-Johnson whispers. 'So we might not have long.'

He cuts the engine and the motorbike drifts in silence.

'Billie healed me here,' his voice says in my mind. Even that is a whisper, as if he's afraid to disturb the silence.

The Harley glides to a stop. The building is surprisingly modern, with a small tarmac car park and automatic doors at the entrance. It looks clean and antiseptic. The security lights are on, lighting most of the frontage. The car park wraps around the small hospital and I can see the edge of a grassy field beyond it.

Johnson is on edge, wary. *'Not a sound.'*

I'm still freezing cold but a thought has just lit a small fire in me. Johnson and Billie are together, but in a way they're not, because what they think they're feeling isn't real! Other-Johnson takes my absolute delight at this well.

'Whoever it is, knows where to stick the knives,' he tells me quietly. 'Which means they may know you, or know my Rev.' And then he adds for good measure: 'And hate her.'

He kicks the stand down and turns to help me off the bike.

His arms are sinewy and taut as he slips them round me and pulls me to him. He doesn't care that my clothes are still damp from my snow expedition and when we pull apart he has a wet stain spreading all over his T-shirt. It clings to his tight torso. He moves my plastered hair away from my forehead and there's enough light pooling in the car park to pick out the brilliant blue of his eyes.

He's in Johnson's body but behind the eyes he's entirely Other-Johnson. I can tell from the brazen way he looks at me.

The automatic doors slide open in silence and we step into the small hospital. The reception area is all polished floor and shining wood veneer. The lights are on but set to a low night-time glow.

Again, Other-Johnson slips his hand into mine. It surprises me but makes me feel braver somehow.

'*Stay close.*' He squeezes my hand and then lets go.

We move down the empty silent corridor, passing doors to offices with nameplates on them. Doctors and surgeons would usually hold consultations behind them but in this world no one is around to be ill. Or in need of a tummy tuck.

Other-Johnson doesn't say a word. His quiet breathing is all I can hear as we round a corridor that leads to a stairway. Again it is clean and sterile, but as we pass a window that looks out onto the field beyond the hospital I get the first tingle in my shoulders.

'Wait,' I whisper.

Other-Johnson stops, sees my concern. 'Don't stop, you have to see this.'

'Where are the others?'

'Others?'

'They're here, aren't they? Your Billie and Rev.'

'Don't worry about them.'

'They're in this hospital, aren't they?'

Other-Johnson keeps heading quietly up the stairs. 'Forget them.'

'I'm not taking another step,' I tell him.

But I do take another step. Which I don't understand. Then I take another. I'm walking but it's not me who's walking.

Other-Johnson glances back down at me. 'We don't have much time.'

He's in my head. He's taken control of me. There's nothing I can do but follow him. I want to shout at him but he won't even allow me to do that. The barely lit stairwell rises above me and Other-Johnson has already faded into the shadows.

I feel myself propelled forward, damp feet in squelchy boots, and GG's sodden jacket feeling twice as heavy as when I first put it on. I'm almost glad we're going to a hospital because my hands are throbbing and I really need to put something on them. Johnson treated my burns with special creams after I almost went up in flames so he'll know what to do when I show him my red raw hands.

I hate to admit it but I can't stop feeling relieved that Johnson and Billie aren't really together. It means I can go back to sitting on the fence about which Johnson I really like. Strangely enough my crippling indecision almost brings a comfort.

A door opens on the third floor.

Other-Johnson waits for me.

'*Let go of me*,' I whisper heatedly over the airwaves, worried that I've been too trusting. What if everything he's told me is a lie? What if he just wanted to lure me here?

'Brace yourself,' he commands.

143

I don't know what is behind the door but there is nothing I can do to stop Other-Johnson manoeuvring me through it.

We come out into another dimly lit corridor and Other-Johnson puts a finger to his lips. 'I want you to be brave.'

My eyes widen. This *is* a trap.

The hallway is warm, too warm to be comfortable, and the steady thrum of a heater makes the hall feel stuffy.

I should be glad of the heat after being cold for so long, but it's a sleep-inducing heat, which mixed with my strung-out and sleep-deprived brain and body is making me want to close my eyes.

I try to shake the fatigue away but Other-Johnson owns my every muscle.

'*Let me go!*' I mentally plead.

'*Stop fighting me.*'

Fighting is all I know how to do now. It has become my first reaction to everything.

'*Get the hell out of me!*' But my struggle is in vain.

'*We're here,*' he responds.

We're in front of the last door at the end of the corridor. The temperature is rising, and even through the door I can sense the increased warmth in the room behind it.

He looks at me for a moment, then lets go of the control he has over me. I almost drop to the floor.

'Quietly and quickly,' he warns.

He pushes open the door and switches the light on.

Inside is a bed, a rumbling heater and a person.

The person is my father.

DAD, IT'S ME, LOOK HOW I'VE GROWN

My dad is lying unconscious in bed. His weak breaths lift and lower his chest and there are red blotches on his skin from where he was burned, but the rest of him is intact as far as I can see. The last time I saw him was in a supermarket in town and he'd been badly burned by the same strange heat that almost killed me. But, I assume with the help from the healing powers of Another-Billie, aside from the marks on his body, he almost looks normal – most of his hair is even back now.

He looks older than I remember, but the twelve years since I've properly seen him haven't aged him as badly as they aged my mum. He has the same dark hair and the same face, but with a few more wrinkles. To be honest, I can't really remember him well. I was four when he left us. I had a dream about him that seemed very real but this is a different person to the one I saw in my mind. He's less immaculate and more human because of that.

And that's the question, isn't it? That's the question I have to answer. *Is* he human like I am? Is this my father or Rev Two's?

'*Billie drained herself bringing him back*.' Other-Johnson's

145

voice is in my head again. *'She's in the room next door. Recovering.'*

'And your Rev?'

'Asleep downstairs. Waiting to see who he really is.'

I step over to the bed and reach for my dad's hand. It was a molten lump of seared flesh the last time I did this in the supermarket. I'm trembling and I want to cry but I'm also looking at his hand because I need to know if it has talons.

I can't see any but that doesn't mean they're not sheathed. He's out cold after all. 'Take a proper look,' Other-Johnson quietly urges.

If it's really my dad I'm going to cry, I know I am. I'm going to bawl my eyes out.

I lean closer to his face. He's still handsome, with high cheekbones and a strong chin.

'Dad?' I whisper, even though I know he's not aware of me. 'Where did you go?'

It seems like such a stupid question and I have a million more that are probably just as stupid.

'Mum ... Mum's still waiting for you. Can you believe that?' I wipe my eyes of tears I didn't know I was crying. 'I wasn't. I didn't tell her, but I'd written you off. You can understand that though – right?'

'Rev.' Other-Johnson is in my head again. *'You need to look.'*

He knows I'm stalling, that I don't want the truth. I'm scared it won't be my dad and I'm scared it will be.

But I have to check his teeth. Like I'm some sort of dentist, or, worse, a horse trader. My hand hovers over my dad's mouth. If his teeth are steel then there is no hope. He won't love me and he won't want to take me home; he'll take Rev Two instead.

146

But if he is my dad, how will I send Rev Two home? How will I keep that promise to her mum?

This is not how I ever pictured a reunion with my father. 'Hi, Dad, mind if I see your teeth?' probably doesn't rate too high on the list of things to say to a long-lost parent.

Other-Johnson comes over to the bed and does it for me. He's keen to make this a short visit. 'Look,' he says to me.

I don't want to.

But he does that mind-control thing again and my head turns and I have no choice but to look.

My breath stalls in my throat.

'He's your dad, Rev.'

There is no glint of steel in my dad's teeth. Just a set of pearly whites.

'Dad!' I fall to my knees at his bedside. 'Dad, it's me. Reva. Dad, I'm here. I've found you.'

'Not so loud.'

I grip my dad's hand tightly, squeezing it in both hands. 'You're going to wake up, you are, and I'm going to be here.'

'We need to go,' Other-Johnson says, looking around.

'What?'

'We can't hang around here.'

'I'm not leaving him. Not when I've just found him.'

'He's in a coma. He's not going anywhere.'

'Then neither am I. And don't try any of that mind-controlling making-me-walk-away stuff. Do that and I'll never forgive you.' I flash a warning look at Other-Johnson but he isn't fazed.

'You can't do anything for him. It's a matter of waiting it out,' he tells me.

'So I'll wait.'

'And when the other Rev finds you? What then?'

I don't have an answer to that but I also know I'm not leaving my dad.

'He'll know how to send us all home. He can end this,' I tell Other-Johnson.

'You stole her boyfriend.' Our eyes meet at this. 'You did, Rev, you stole his heart.' He's talking about himself. 'And she will kill you for that. She's not the sharing kind.'

'I didn't ask you to kiss me.'

'You didn't stop me either,' he responds, talking in a low whisper now.

'I've seen inside you. I know you.'

He pulls me closer. I already know what's coming. I should fight it, twist away.

'Rev—'

'Don't.'

His lips find mine.

'No,' I murmur, but even I know that I don't really mean it.

The kiss devours me. It pulls me onto my tiptoes and then presses me back against the far wall. I push back and try to twist away, but bang into the electric heater and have to steady myself, and then Other-Johnson is pushing against me, releasing me, then pinning me again to the wall. We can't find separation; we're bonded and breathless and fresh tears are running from my eyes because this is too much and yet not enough. I wrap myself tight round him and my momentum turns him so I'm kissing him now. I'm taking charge and he's the Johnson I want.

'What the hell?'

The voice snaps between us, prising us apart. We turn simultaneously and Another-Billie is standing, pale and weary in the doorway. My chest is heaving and I think I'm panting.

I don't know if she knows which Rev I am, but Other-Johnson knows immediately what she's thinking.

'Don't touch her,' he warns.

Despite her weakened state Another-Billie's talons slide out and she reveals her glinting metal teeth.

'You going to stop me?' she snarls.

I need a weapon but the private hospital room is sparse. There's just the heater, a small bedside cabinet and a lamp.

Other-Johnson tries to get between us. 'Billie,' he says. He raises a hand, warding her off.

But he won't be able to stop her, not when he's in the wrong body. He's a puny human just like me. I grab the lamp and rip the cord from it, revealing live wires that could send a ton of volts straight through Another-Billie.

'Don't forget you've got metal inside you,' I warn her. 'And metal is a great conductor!' Which is the worst tough-guy line ever spoken. It's not even bad enough to be funny.

Other-Johnson now raises his hand to me. 'Back off. Both of you.'

Neither of us is prepared to back down. Another-Billie edges forward and I mirror her move, eyes locked on her.

'If Rev knew you were here,' she threatens.

'*I'm Rev,*' I respond.

'All I've got to do is call out to her.'

'Try calling with a thousand volts in you.' Which I think is a much better tough-guy line.

Other-Johnson moves closer to Another-Billie. 'If you kill her and her dad finds out then he'll never take us home.'

'That's her dad?' Another-Billie falters. 'No. It can't be. It's not possible.'

'Check his teeth,' Other-Johnson tells her.

I really hope my dad can't hear this. Another-Billie is thrown. Despite her Irish-Indian colouring she is nearly white from her healing exertions. She takes a long moment to process the information.

'I all but killed myself bringing the wrong person back?'

'My dad's a good man—' I begin.

'You don't know that,' she snaps.

'Of course he is.'

'You don't even know him!' she hisses. 'Maybe he left you and your mum because he hated you.'

Turns out she doesn't need her talons to gut me.

'I mean, why else would he up and leave you?'

The horror of that notion hits like a rock. She knows she has hurt me and I know she enjoyed it. She shares a few of Billie's less than kind attributes.

'My dad came to find me,' I eventually counter. 'He climbed through fire to reach me. I know he did.' I stare hard at Another-Billie. 'So he'll help us. He'll wake up and he will know what to do.' I turn back to Other-Johnson. 'So I'm staying put.'

'You think?' Another-Billie responds. 'Wait till Rev knows you two were kissing. No one'll get home then.'

I know from experience that Rev Two is both fearsome and lethal. And if Non-Ape was concerned about her touching him then she must be far more powerful than I ever imagined.

Other-Johnson reaches out to Another-Billie and puts a hand on her arm. 'Billie.'

But she shakes it off. 'Don't even think about playing your mind games with me.'

'Never,' he responds.

150

'Stay out of my head, Johnson,' she warns. 'Do not ever come near me again. You listening? I don't want you inside me.'

But it's not her head he's inside; it's her heart. I can tell from the way she can't stop looking at him. When I saw her and Rev Two together before it was pretty clear they were good friends so whatever Other-Johnson did with Another-Billie has remained a secret. So far.

'I'm sorry,' he says, his eyes meeting hers full on. 'I never got the chance to tell you that. But I am.'

'You led me on, Johnson. You said you were bored of Rev and I believed you.'

Other-Johnson doesn't have to be a mind reader to know I am staring hard at him now.

'It was one of those things,' he says in his defence. He's talking to her but he's also talking to me.

'One of those things? You said you loved me.'

Other-Johnson remains as calm as he can. But inside I'm starting to boil over. Is he just a player?

'*No, Rev,*' he tells me over our mind-link. '*You're different. Special.*'

His words are soothing like honey and he sounds so deeply honest.

He turns to Another-Billie. 'I do love you, Billie. Just not in the way you wanted me to.'

Another-Billie flushes despite her pale appearance. 'Don't go there, Johnson. Do. Not. Go. There.' She is really hurting inside. 'Love is love, and you ... You have no idea what you do to girls. But then again, if you do then you're the worst of the worst.'

Other-Johnson steps closer to Another-Billie. 'You could've

151

left me for dead,' he adds, his voice soft. 'But you didn't, you healed me. And I need you to heal me again.'

She shifts uncomfortably on the balls of her feet. 'I only healed you for Rev,' she says.

But even I know that's only a half-truth. She is still captivated by Other-Johnson, despite what she says. Apparently whatever world he's from a Johnson will create havoc between me and Billie.

She bows her head a little, just like my Billie does when she's embarrassed. 'None of this has been for you, Johnson.'

Other-Johnson reaches again for her arm and this time she allows him to touch her. 'How long till he wakes up?'

I'm still holding the thin cable from the lamp and don't know what to do with it now. Do I just drop it, or could I maybe give my dad a few volts to wake him up? I need to speak to him, to hear his voice telling me that everything's going to be OK.

Another-Billie glances at my comatose father. 'I don't know that he will wake up. I've done everything I can but this is as far as it goes. He was in such a bad way. It could be tomorrow, it could be a week, a month, it could be never.'

Sounds like I definitely need to shock him then.

'We haven't got that long,' I offer.

I can feel Other-Johnson invade my mind, searching and shifting through my recent thoughts. He sees hordes of his kind charging through the town looking for blood.

He sucks in his breath. 'She's right.'

My hope that an hour there equals five months has vanished. We are running out of time.

He turns to Another-Billie. 'We can't go home. Someone's locked us out of the classroom. And not just with a key.'

'Well, that's just peachy,' Another-Billie tells him. 'That's wonderful news. Who is it?'

'I have no idea,' he tells her.

'And the news keeps getting better.'

I glance at my dad and still can't take in how well he looks. He was little more than a seared lump of flesh.

'The bus!' I exclaim too loudly. Then remember that Rev Two is sleeping close by. I lower my voice but my heart's hammering. 'My dad came here another way, through a different portal to us. And there was another one, inside a bus. I'm sure he was trying to get through there as well.'

Another-Billie scowls at me. 'So?'

'Those portals could be open. I tried the lorry and got burned, but the bus ... Whoever is out there might not know about the bus.'

I'm breathing faster now, giddy with the sheer force of my hope. 'We can all escape that way.'

'Brilliant,' Other-Johnson says. 'How does it work?'

And in typical Reva Marsalis fashion my 'genius' comes undone, unravelling horribly. They both look at me, waiting for an answer.

'I don't ... I don't know.' And then I get inspired again. 'But my dad can tell us.'

'If he wakes up.' Another-Billie's hopes are already falling.

'Yeah, but ...' *What, Rev? What? Think.*

Other-Johnson steps in and rescues the moment. 'They've got a Moth. And there are papers in London that he will understand.'

'Yes, he worked some of this out before,' I add, heart starting to beat faster again. 'If we get the Moth to the papers, he'll work out a way for all of us to get home. I'm sure he will.'

153

Which pretty much makes my spectacular plan to become a hero and usher everyone to safety through the bus redundant. We have to go to London. Maybe there was never any getting away from that. This world isn't just a copy, it's starting to repeat itself.

Another-Billie hesitates as if she has something she doesn't want to say.

'Look,' she finally offers, 'I'll do whatever I can here but if I can't bring your dad back, then you need to find those papers – and be quick, because I want to go home and forget any of this happened.' She looks at my dad. 'I just wish he'd turned out to be one of us. He'd have been tougher, stronger. He'd have got better quicker.' But then her eyes brighten. 'Go grab those papers.'

Other-Johnson pulls a face. 'That's not so easy. Not unless you know someone who can lift a thousand tons of rubble.'

As soon as the words have left his mouth he wishes he could yank them back.

The answer's obvious. And Another-Billie stares at him, not needing to say it out loud.

'No,' he whispers.

She's staring harder at him now.

'C'mon, Billie – really?' It's the first time I've ever seen Other-Johnson look faintly lost.

Another-Billie knows she has the upper hand and enjoys it. 'You owe me that much.'

But before he can respond Other-Johnson grabs us and drags us down to the floor with him. 'Get down!'

Other-Johnson's motorbike crashes through the window and lands in a mangled heap, missing us by inches.

'JOHNSON!'

Oh, great.

'Get him away from here! He'll bring down the whole hospital around us!' Another-Billie hisses. 'I can't repair Rev's dad again, I don't have the strength.'

But I'm already worrying about what's inside the small hospital as much as what waits for us outside. Rev Two will have woken up. No one could sleep through that.

I grab Other-Johnson's wrist. 'He must've heard your motorbike and homed in on it. We've got to lead him away.'

I turn to Another-Billie. 'Don't, whatever you do, let Rev know that he's my dad,' I warn her. I don't want Rev Two anywhere near my dad. There is no telling what she would do to him if she found out he was mine and not hers. 'He's still our best hope for getting home. *And that's all of us.*'

Another-Billie understands but she doesn't like being told what to do. 'Get out of here,' she snarls.

'C'mon.' I tug on Other-Johnson's arm.

But Another-Billie grabs his other wrist and he's now stuck between us.

'If you really want forgiveness, Johnson, then you can do two things for me. One is difficult – make sure I get home. The other is impossible – you need to make friends with the Ape.'

'GOING TO KILL YOU!' the monster outside screams as if on cue.

Other-Johnson hesitates. He lowers his voice. Something else is worrying him. 'She's on the floor below.'

'What?'

'Rev. And she's coming straight here.'

A car door flies through the window. Non-Ape is nothing if not predictably predictable in his destructive habits. The car door short-circuits the electrics in the room and plunges it into darkness.

Another-Billie wheels my dad's bed towards the corridor as Other-Johnson edges over to the shattered window and peers out. I don't know what he's planning but we can't have much time.

'I'm coming out,' he calls down to Non-Ape. 'There's a door at the back. I'll meet you there.'

'You better be there, Johnson.'

I can hear Non-Ape's lumbering footsteps crunching towards the rear of the hospital.

Other-Johnson ushers me towards the window. 'Jump.'

'What?'

'Rev's right outside.'

I peer out of the window and it's got to be at least a six-metre drop. 'I'll be squished.'

'Aim for those bushes.'

'Stop her, do your mind thingy.'

Other-Johnson grabs me and shoves me out of the shattered window. Even as I'm falling I can hear him turning on his charm with Rev Two. 'Hey, guess who's awake?'

I land hard in a bush and even though the foliage is thick and the small branches cushion my drop I still plunge straight through it and hit earth. The branches and twigs tear at my clothes and skin and I get scratched and cut everywhere. But Other-Johnson's aim was good enough and I somehow survive the fall.

Other-Johnson and Rev Two's voices reach me from the window.

'Billie healed you? When?' she asks, dazed and elated. She has my voice, only it sounds like when you hear yourself on a recording or a home movie. You are a little surprised that you sound so different from the voice you hear in your head.

'About a minute ago,' he lies.

'My God.' Her voice sounds muffled and I wonder if she's hugging him. 'I'm so sorry. I didn't mean to touch you like that.' Meaning: I didn't mean to drain the life from you and kill you.

'Well . . . these things happen. Look, I've got to go.'

'What?'

'Ape's out there,' he replies, and I imagine him slipping her arms from round him.

'And *I'm* here,' she tells him, without the slightest trace of fear in her voice. Rev Two knows how to handle Non-Ape and I realise that back in the church he was definitely worried that I – or she – was going to kill him.

'Rev, protect your dad,' Other-Johnson tells her. We need to get going and there is urgency in his voice.

'He's my dad?'

'You were right all along.' He's able to lie almost too easily to Rev Two's face. I know it's because he's protecting my dad but he's still very good at it. 'But he's not well enough yet.' He doesn't miss a beat. God knows what she'll do to him when she finds out the truth.

'I'll be back as soon as I lose the Ape,' he promises her.

'No! I'm coming with you. I can stop him.'

'Rev – listen to me – your dad can take us home. He's the priority. Protect him. There's someone in the town who doesn't like us very much.'

'Like who?'

'I don't know but they've turned the world to winter.'

I imagine him taking her hands in his and looking deep into her eyes.

'I can't let them get you,' he tells her. 'So stay hidden and I'll come back for you.'

'Promise?' she asks.

'Cross my dark heart.' Which I'm sure he says with a smile.

'JOHNSON!' Non-Ape bellows from somewhere round the back of the hospital.

Before Rev Two can respond he kisses her. I just know he does because the silence goes on too long. 'I love you,' he whispers and I wonder if he's worried that I'll hear him. But I get it. I get why he has to say that to her. It's all part of his master plan.

Isn't it?

'I'll be back as soon as I can.'

There's another longer silence and I know for sure they're kissing again.

'JOHNSON!'

'Go,' she tells him.

But damn me if there isn't another silent pause.

He seems incapable of keeping his hands off her.

Other-Johnson probably thinks I've scurried into the night but he suddenly clicks into my head. '*I've got to make it look good,*' he reassures me.

Well, you certainly did that, I think.

It makes perfect sense now. Johnson's hair wouldn't have grown and Non-Ape wouldn't have changed his clothes. Not if we'd only been gone an hour.

It's weird the thoughts that come to you when you're running for your life.

Rather than emerging from the back door Other-Johnson kicked open an emergency exit door, which set off a wailing alarm. He called to me telepathically and I met him in the car park.

'*Stay put, I'm going to draw him away.*'

Other-Johnson races around and starts hitting cars, banging on their roofs and bonnets, setting off alarms to get Non-Ape's attention. 'Here! Hey! Here!'

It takes all of ten seconds for Non-Ape to stomp round to the side of the hospital and find Other-Johnson.

'We need to talk, Ape,' Other-Johnson tells him. 'Stop all this running around and fighting.'

A car comes flying straight towards Other-Johnson and he has to hurl himself to the ground.

'Dazza, c'mon, let's be civil.'

There is no civility in Non-Ape as he looms over Other-Johnson, standing at his full massive height.

Other-Johnson stays calm as he gets to his feet. 'I need your help, D-Man. Seriously, there's no one else I'd ask.'

Non-Ape hesitates.

'I know we've hit a rocky patch ...' Other-Johnson can't help himself. He has to put a little ironic spin on his words, and I wish he wouldn't because he's badly underestimating Non-Ape. 'But all of the best friendships do.'

If Non-Ape was a dog his hackles would be rising now. I'm hiding behind a car, hoping desperately that Non-Ape doesn't see me. If he does, he'll think that he's been led into some sort of trap.

'So how d'you fancy a trip to London?' Other-Johnson is too confident for his own good. I know he can't read Non-Ape's mind because there's probably nothing in it, but he's also failing to read the look in his eyes. The car-park lights are picking it out all too clearly for me though – he can sense that Other-Johnson is teasing him.

'The old L-Town,' Other-Johnson adds. 'Up for that?'

Non-Ape's chest gently swells and deflates with great chunks of air – he could inhale a small room's worth in one breath.

He takes a step towards Other-Johnson who thinks this is a good sign and smiles. 'See, good things happen when we talk.'

Non-Ape moves, but I move quicker and charge out from behind the car and push Other-Johnson out of the way of a swinging right hook that would have knocked him all the way to the next town.

I grab Other-Johnson's hand and drag him towards the darkened woods that surround the hospital.

'That should've worked,' he says half to himself, a little bewildered that his nuanced charm failed so abysmally.

'JOHNSON!'

I'm getting so tired of hearing that. It's *OTHER*-JOHNSON! I want to yell back at him.

The woods aren't large, they're more of a copse, but at least they're dense and turn the night pitch-black as a result.

Other-Johnson labours behind me, still not used to being in Johnson's human body. He can't run as fast, he's not as strong as in his own body and his skin is vulnerable to cuts and scratches. To his credit he plunges onwards, ignoring his limitations.

Non-Ape's large body isn't built to move easily between the sturdy trees of the small wood and he keeps stopping to push them apart, like Samson between the pillars, so he can squeeze through. We're actually drawing away from him but the copse won't last for ever and all that lies ahead of us is the large open field. We'll be sitting ducks out there.

Other-Johnson is breathing hard. 'Rev.'

'Ycah?'

'Got any ideas?'

We hear the crack and groan of a tree as it is brutally shouldered to one side.

'Doesn't he ever stop?'

'Rev, focus, we need an idea.'

'And you're looking at me?'

'I'm always looking at you.'

'That's not creepy.'

We duck under a large overhanging branch and then squeeze between two oak trees that have probably spent millennia getting up close and personal with each other.

'What sort of idea?' I ask as he follows me between the oaks.

'A good one.'

Something undignified happens to a tree some fifteen metres behind us and a resounding nature-killing crack pierces the night.

We are almost at the open field. If we can cross it, we can take a short cut through a new housing estate, which I think leads back towards the railway station on the edge of town. Not knowing this area means the best I can do is make an educated guess. I think we are at the far end of town now, about two miles from its centre.

'Know how to drive a train?' I ask, hoping we could make it to the station and find the train GG left there.

'Sorry. I'm a biker boy.'

Behind us a tree is punched. 'Timber!' Non-Ape shouts.

'Plan B, Rev?'

The open expanse affords no cover or protection. And in a cruel trick of nature the full moon seems to be hovering directly above it and has lit it up like a football stadium. This world is determined to get me.

But I'm determined not to let it.

'Send a message,' I tell Other-Johnson.

'To who?'

'To Billie.'

'Billie?'

'My Billie. You can do that, right?'

'What do I tell her?'

Non-Ape tears the smooching oak trees apart.

'I've got her a date.'

NON-APE WUZ HERE

We have to run; there is no other choice. Non-Ape is bearing down on us and we have to cross that wide-open field.

Other-Johnson lets go of my hand. He's perspiring and looks like he would cough if he didn't know it would lead Non-Ape straight to us.

'Does your Johnson smoke?' he pants.

'Um, yes. Sorry.'

'I should swap with him now. Leave this bit to him. That'll teach him to poison his lungs.'

'But at least you get to spend time with me,' I try and quip. 'Racing through dark woods for our lives. Can't beat it.'

We burst out from the small copse and race across the lush green field. I go west and Other-Johnson goes east. I don't realise he's not behind me until I've gone quite a way into the field. Non-Ape crashes out into the field and I'm expecting his heavy thunderous footfalls to be right behind us but if anything they are growing quieter and more distant. I dare to turn round and see that Other-Johnson, like the cavalier he is, has led him away from me.

'*Johnson!*' I yell through our mind-link.

'*Not now, Rev.*' Even telepathically he is wheezing.

'*We had a plan.*'

'*The plan's still on.*'

I watch Other-Johnson reach a steep dip in the field and then skid and slide down it, his long slim legs splaying like a drunken spider's. Non-Ape is about forty metres behind him but gaining all the time. He's not fast but he is relentless, and it would appear, remorseless. He must have seen that Other-Johnson broke Another-Billie's heart and is looking to make him pay.

I've already seen Other-Johnson's charms fail to bewitch Non-Ape as easily as he can a girl so I head after them as fast as my aching legs will take me. Lactic acid is building up and burning through my veins, and my poor muscles are tightening with cramp, but I cannot let Non-Ape catch Other-Johnson.

Other-Johnson has dipped out of view but I am closing on Non-Ape. He doesn't realise that there is such a sudden and severe slope in the field and takes a heavy fall, pitching forward into a neck-jarring tumble that sends him rolling head over heels.

'*Johnson!*' I transmit.

Other-Johnson is gasping for air. '*I'm done, Rev, I'm done. This body.*'

'*Send that message to Billie.*'

'*I can't get my thoughts,*' he pants.

'*Send it, Johnson!*'

I reach the crest of the hill, which is more sheer than I had counted on. It's slippery from the night dew and Non-Ape is now lying at the bottom of it, not really dazed or injured, more struggling to comprehend what just happened.

Other-Johnson is still trying to reach the housing estate but he is fast running out of puff. He looks heavy-legged and disoriented.

'*The message, Johnson, the message,*' I urge him.

'*Heard you the first and second time.*'

He won't be able to keep running. His legs will give up and tell him enough's enough. He'll never get away from Non-Ape.

'Hey, stupid!' I call down the steep slope.

Non-Ape gets to his feet. He watches Other-Johnson for a moment then turns his great head and looks back up the slippery slope towards me.

'Ha, know your name,' I say with a swagger that is entirely fake and see-through.

Non-Ape turns again to watch Other-Johnson, then his great block of cranium turns once more to me.

I think he's calculating which one of us he has a better chance of catching.

He turns his head back to Other-Johnson and I'm starting to think we could be here all night when he turns back to me and frowns.

At this rate Johnson could be in London before Non-Ape's startlingly slow attempt at mental arithmetic kicks in.

Non-Ape settles on an answer and starts back up the hill.

I'm easily the closest.

AND THEY SAID DEATH WAS NOT THE END

Non-Ape can't get any purchase on the slope and even if it's just a few seconds it still equates to a small distance in my desperate bid to make it back to the cover of the trees.

My torn, skinless hands decide that now is a good time to make their presence felt again and with the blood pumping through me, sending throbs in every direction, they come alive with pain. Where's the calming snow when I need it?

Non-Ape reaches the top of the rise and his thunderous footsteps start to pound after me.

I don't know how to tell if you're having a heart attack or not, but as my heart hammers in my chest I feel like I might be having one now. The glow from the hospital to my left is a mocking beacon of health and hope. I could get treated there. They could lay me in a bed, put me on a drip, maybe waft some oxygen my way, and then they'd let me sleep. For days. Only waking me to feed me mouthfuls of specially prepared soups. I wonder if Another-Billie would help or turn a blind eye. 'Sorry, but I'm all out of healing magic. Shame.'

166

The small wood looms before me and the moonlight casts a glow over the arboreal devastation that Non-Ape has wreaked. It makes it easier for me to cut a path back through the trees until I meet a three-metre-high wooden fence that hides who knows what behind it.

With all my might I leap and catch the top of the wooden fence before heaving myself up it. My skinned hands howl in protest. But the fence is rotten and hasn't been maintained so the panel I'm clinging to crashes forward under my weight. I go with it, toppling into an overgrown tarmac alleyway and somehow end up under the fence.

Omph! The breath is knocked from me and I don't know if I have the strength in my arms to raise the rotting soggy panel. *But you have to, Rev*, I tell myself, *you have to*.

Because Non-Ape is almost upon you.

I wriggle and kick and feel what could be a rusty nail slice deep into my thigh and then rip along it as I yank myself free. I bite down on a girlie whimper and look around me. I'm in an alleyway that seems to run the length of the field. I limp down it with no idea where I'm going. But the alleyway is so dark that I'm assuming if I can't see more than a metre in front of me then I'm guessing Non-Ape won't be able to either.

He crashes into the narrow alleyway and despite every instinct screaming at me to run – I stop.

I fall as still as I can and crouch, praying my knees don't crack, which is the only break I get so far. I go as low and small as I can. I need to get my breathing under control but my chest is heaving so I clasp a red raw hand over my mouth and try to cup the noise.

Non-Ape has also fallen silent. He has stopped to listen.

We stay that way for well over a minute.

The silence expands and again I'm amazed by how loud a packed and thriving world usually is. I've never heard so much silence.

My thigh drips blood which lands on a piece of tin foil. It's the faintest of noises.

I move my hand from my mouth and try to stop the blood, which is running more freely now, hitting the tin foil with a more regular pitter-pat. I clasp my hand to the wound but the blood seeps between my fingers and I can't stop it.

Non-Ape takes a step towards the sound.

I dare to edge backwards, away from the tin foil.

The pitter-pat stops.

Non-Ape stops with it.

Silence blossoms again.

I daren't move but blood loss is starting to make me feel dizzy. I blink a couple of times, shake my head and try to stay focused.

As I do my damp hair whips against the fence. It makes a dull cushioned slap.

In a normal world you'd never hear it. But that's not where I am.

Non-Ape takes another step in my direction.

He has heard me.

The dizziness is bringing on nausea now.

He starts to advance.

I try to sink back into the shadows, but the alleyway is so narrow that even if he can't see me he's bound to trip over me, and that's even if I flatten myself right up against the dark wooden fence.

His footsteps are slow and heavy as they close on me.

Damn it, Rev. Damn it, damn it, damn it.

HELL HATH NO FURY

Even in the dark tree-cloaked alley I can feel Non-Ape's shadow fall over me. His musty body odour is overpowering.

'Gotcha.' The words escape with his breath.

'It doesn't have to be this way,' I tell him.

'Does.'

'Listen ... You chased me for a reason.' My thigh is pumping blood now. The throb is like a beacon to all the other blood in my body. *Guys, this way, I've found an escape route. We're free!*

I try to blink away the nausea. 'You chased me because ...' *Think, Rev.* 'Because you want me as bait.'

'What's bait?'

'You don't know what bait is? They use it for fishing.'

'Why would I want to go fishing?'

'I don't mean literally.'

'Then why say it?'

I will bleed all eight pints of blood if I don't get him to see the point I want to make.

'Look. You want to get Johnson through me.' Every word is

169

laboured now. 'By telling him you'll hurt me or something. That's why you chased me. To *lure* him.'

He stays silent.

'I'm a worm!' I shout. 'OK? I'm a worm on a hook.'

Non-Ape bursts out laughing.

'What's so funny?'

He laughs again. 'Worm.'

'Not a real one.'

'Worm,' he repeats, finding it hysterical now.

'You need me to get to Johnson. This is the deal. All right? Here's what you want to do with me.'

I imagine for a second what it must be like being one of his teachers. They must teeter on the brink of a mental breakdown every time he lumbers into their classrooms.

'Why can't you understand?'

I wait for him to respond but he doesn't. He just stands there.

'Well?' I ask.

'Well what?'

'The deal.' *For God's sake, concentrate, you great oaf.* 'You want to hear it?'

'Worm!' He laughs again and even in the pitch-black I know he's pointing a big stubby finger at me.

My thigh is pumping too much blood. I need to tear my top so I can wrap something round it as a tourniquet. But first I have to get him to understand.

'OK,' I pant. 'OK. Here's what we do.'

I press back into the fence and push upwards so I'm at least standing.

'You want Johnson. And I'm going to take you right to him.'

The words take another minute to sink into his empty brain and I have no idea if he understands at all.

'I know where he's gone,' I add. 'You can find him and do whatever you like to him.'

I'm wondering if Other-Johnson is reading my mind. I hope he knows that I have no choice. I'm not going to die in this alleyway. I have to survive. There is too much at stake.

If he has heard me then he'll keep running.

Not that it'll matter.

Because in truth I'm taking Non-Ape to meet my Johnson.

I know how it sounds but I've got a plan. And it's a good plan.

'Where is he?' Non-Ape asks.

This plan is so clever I am smiling inside. All I need to do is . . .

. . . is stay conscious for long enough to make the plan work.

That's all I've got to do.

I'm going to save everyone.

Me.

Rev the hero.

Rev the . . .

Why is everything suddenly black?

Oh God I'm passing out.

WHAT ON EARTH WAS I THINKING?

White is the new black. When I open my eyes I am back in the snow-covered town square and all I can see is white. I can also smell someone's rank armpit.

Non-Ape is holding me in the crook of one of his thick hairy arms. I'm slumped there like an unwanted jersey on a hot afternoon. He has one hand wedged into his oversized jeans pocket as he stands all too casually for a teenager on a murder rampage.

It takes a few seconds to work out how I came to be in this predicament. I think there was something about leading Non-Ape to Johnson but why would I do that? I mean, what on earth was I thinking? Even if he did choose Billie instead of me, I don't want to hurt him. I don't want to hurt *any* of them.

'*Don't move.*' Other-Johnson's voice is back in my head.

'*Not a problem,*' I whisper in my head, then remember that I don't need to whisper.

'JOHNSON!' Non-Ape roars.

My eardrums shudder. If I hear that bellow one more time . . .

The faint sodium glow from the flickering lamp post in the

square reveals snow that lies on the ground, lush and calming, completely at odds with the situation I'm in. Some of the snow is pink from my blood and looks like a strawberry slushie.

I try to wriggle free of Non-Ape's arm but he feels me move and tightens the squeeze on my torso. 'Quit that,' he orders.

'I'm freezing to death.'

'JOHNSON!' he bellows again.

'*Rev?*' Other-Johnson says.

I can hardly hear him over the bellow, even if his voice is in my head.

'*Yeah?*'

'*I'm on my way.*'

'Rev?'

I manage to arc my neck and see my Johnson appear in the doorway to the snooker hall. Non-Ape's bellowing has finally woken him.

Johnson is calm. And ready. 'Put her down.'

This is the second time he's told Non-Ape to let me go and I'm losing count of the number of times he comes to my rescue. I seriously need to stop being such a damsel in distress.

I feel Non-Ape tense at the sight of him.

Then he chuckles. 'You want her back?'

'That's what I said.'

'She's all yours.'

Non-Ape unhooks his hand from his trousers, grabs me with his other hand and then hurls me straight at Johnson. I must be moving at a hundred miles an hour and the wall of a pub and nightclub situated next to the snooker hall rears up at me in a heartbeat. I'm going to be little more than a stain of bone and skin and blood laced with electric-pink hair.

I remember seeing pictures of men in white catsuits wedged into large painted cannons, crash helmets tied tight around their moustachioed faces. They were always smiling, or waving, just before a fuse was lit and they got fired towards a cushioned landing area. But if anyone asks, hurtling through the air is not as much fun as it looks.

The End.

But Johnson, in his souped-up body, leaps through the air to catch me. He curls himself round me and has just enough time to tell me to 'Go limp,' before he takes the brunt of the impact on his back.

It's a shocking smack of a sound as his rubbery head and torso are driven back into the bricks and mortar. He wraps tight round me, shielding me as best he can, sponging my momentum, as we leave a human-sized impact crater in the wall, before toppling forward and falling down into the deep snow.

Snow that saves my life as Johnson lands on top of me. He is badly winded and who knows what the impact has done to him but he is still breathing. Just.

'Ouch,' he whispers gingerly, his hands and arms still wrapped round me.

'Johnson,' I splutter through a mouthful of snow.

'Yeah?'

'You've got to run.'

Non-Ape is already crunching towards us and I feel Johnson unpeel himself from me. But he doesn't run.

'Johnson, please.' I get to my knees, worried.

Johnson steps in front of me as my Ape comes charging out of the snooker hall, his triple-cue gripped tight in his hands. GG is with him, a rock-hard snooker ball in each hand.

'Hey!' GG yells to Non-Ape. 'Over here, you – you big person you.'

The Ape doesn't bother with words and is already moving straight for Non-Ape, ploughing through the thick snow with his triple-cue raised. 'I got this!'

Non-Ape stops to watch his mini mirror-image lumbering towards him.

'No, I got this,' he replies and starts towards the Ape. The snow slows them down but it's still like watching two testosterone-fuelled bulls on the charge.

'You ain't got nothing!' the Ape yells at the Non-Ape.

'Got more than you!'

Johnson pulls me to my feet. GG is trying to keep up with the Ape.

'Duck, Dazza, I'm going throw my balls at him.' GG realises what's he just said and winces. 'Yes, I really said that.'

The Apes are on a cataclysmic collision course as Johnson coils and takes off to intercept. 'It's me he wants!' he calls to the Ape.

'It's me he's getting,' the Ape responds.

Non-Ape quickens his pace. 'Come on then!'

'I'm coming!' The Ape quickens as they clump through the deep snow.

Johnson tries to cover the wet slippery distance. But he's hurting from being slammed into a wall and his movement is pained and doesn't come fluidly.

GG throws a snooker ball at Non-Ape and, if I'm honest, it's a bit of a girlie throw. The ball doesn't even reach Non-Ape and plugs in the snow. GG looks forlorn. 'Why didn't I pay attention in games? Why, why, why?'

He's as scared as I am for the Ape but doesn't know what else to do so he gets ready to throw the second snooker ball.

'No one throws Rev at a wall.' The Ape takes Non-Ape by surprise and leaps the last few paces towards him. I can see Non-Ape's brow furrow in the split second that the Ape is flying towards him, his triple-cue driving straight for the throat.

And he's going to do it. The Ape's actually going to take Non-Ape down. He's going to beat him, just like he beats everyone.

The triple-cue is centimetres from Non-Ape's throat.

David is about to kill Goliath all over again.

Until Non-Ape bows his massive head and the triple-cue shatters and splinters against his great monolithic chin. The Ape's momentum pitches him into Non-Ape and even as the triple-cue shatters he is already letting go of it and bunching his fist. But the punch never lands because the Ape crashes into Non-Ape and bounces straight back off him.

He is thrown backwards in a spine-jarring snap, before landing in the deep snow.

Non-Ape takes a mighty step towards the Ape and laughs. 'I told you.' He raises a mighty foot to stamp down on the Ape when a snooker ball hits him smack on the forehead. It doesn't do any damage other than to Non-Ape's vanity, but it makes him stop just as GG reaches the fallen Ape.

'Get up, get up!' GG helps the Ape to his feet and then turns and brazenly adopts a hands-on-hips teapot stance right under Non-Ape's nose. 'You have really ticked me off, buster!'

Non-Ape can't fathom the sight of tiny, skinny GG standing before him with no sign of fear whatsoever.

'You hear me, big man?'

I realise what GG is doing. He's hoping Non-Ape is going to be as terrified of him as Not-Del was. He's going all Evil-GG on him.

'Well? I'm waiting.'

GG is channelling Evil-GG as best he can as the Ape gets ready to fight.

'That the best you got?' he asks Non-Ape.

'I'm handling this if you don't mind,' GG admonishes the Ape, then gets his Evil-GG on. 'Why don't you dance for me?'

Non-Ape is still totally confused by GG.

'As in dance your way down the high street.'

Johnson has joined GG and the Ape but doesn't get GG's totally bizarre behaviour either.

'What are you doing?' he whispers to him.

'Johnson – didn't you hear? I'm the worst of the worst,' GG boasts as he turns to Non-Ape. 'You still here? Thought I told you to do a little two-step. As in now!'

The three boys stand before the giant Non-Ape. He looms over them, a juggernaut of power and unrelenting stupidity.

'What's a two-step?' he finally asks.

'Duh! It's one shy of a three-step.'

The Ape still has part of the triple-cue in his large paw. Because it's shattered and broken it's a lot shorter, but it's also a lot sharper. He straightens and I can almost hear his brain whirring. Sharp point plus throat equals good.

I know he's going to try for Non-Ape's neck again.

I glance at the first-floor window to the snooker hall and the Moth's face is pressed as close as possible to it. He looks horrified. There is no sign of Billie anywhere. But I'm sure in the fuzz of my blood-drained brain she was part of my plan. But I'm still struggling to remember what that was.

I know it had something to do with Billie going on a date but that doesn't seem much of a plan in the face of a giant Ape.

Johnson weighs up Non-Ape. 'What is your problem anyway?'

'You,' he replies.

'Johnson, I'm handling this,' GG says, admonishing him, before again focusing on Non-Ape. 'Now run along, Dazza, before I get very cross. You won't like me when I'm throwing a hissy.'

It's one of the bravest bluffs of all time.

But it doesn't work.

'I don't like *you* at any time,' Non-Ape says and grabs GG and the Ape by their necks and hoists them into the air.

The movement is so sudden and swift that Johnson is caught off guard. He unsheathes his talons knowing that they'll probably be useless but he has to try something.

'Darren?'

Billie stands in the doorway to the snooker hall. She is doing her best to look natural and at ease.

'Long time no see.' She smiles at Non-Ape.

Non-Ape looks like he has been hit by a torpedo. Standing in the doorway is the love of his life. She has to be. No one would spend days punching the world to pieces if it wasn't a matter of the heart.

I have no idea why Another-Billie didn't try this herself. It looks like she could have stopped Non-Ape in his tracks back at the hospital, but then these creatures aren't like us. They're crueller and more vindictive. So maybe she was so badly hurt by Other-Johnson she felt he deserved whatever came his way. Hell hath no fury and all that.

'What you doing?' she calls out.

'Fighting.'

'You don't need to.'

'Yeah I do.'

'I'm . . . I'm OK now.'

Non-Ape takes a moment to digest this.

'You don't need to be angry any more,' she adds for good measure.

Non-Ape's slow thought processes mean that time stops around us – GG and the Ape dangle in the air while Johnson stands momentarily frozen in front of the giant beast.

'I'm good now,' she tells Non-Ape

His brow furrows. 'You sure?'

Billie smiles. 'D'you see me crying?'

Non-Ape scrutinises Billie from across the square.

'Let them go,' she adds. 'For me.'

Non-Ape looks at GG and the Ape gripped in his massive fists and then, after a moment, he sets them down.

Billie steps out into the snow. 'Things are really good,' she promises.

'Come on then!' The Ape completely destroys the moment by seizing his chance and stabbing the broken cue at Non-Ape but again it snaps. He is now left with a few inches of wood and an instantly furious Non-Ape.

There are moments in life when I truly wonder if some people should be allowed to share the planet with the rest of us.

Non-Ape's rage billows through him and he is ready to land a death punch on the Ape when Billie calls to him.

179

'Don't!'

Non-Ape's arm is drawn back and his massive fist is clenched tight.

'You want to make me cry like Johnson did?' she says, pleading with him. 'Do you?'

Non-Ape has frozen, caught between his rage and his shame.

She keeps pressing. 'That what you want?'

Non-Ape lowers his arm.

'That's it. Make me happy instead. I want to be happy.'

Non-Ape relaxes his fist as he gazes through the lamp's glow at Billie. Her smile transfixes him.

The Ape still wants to attack but thank God Johnson has witnessed the change in the Non-Ape. He lays a hand on the Ape's shoulder. 'Chill, D-man.'

The Ape is confused, not meeting violence with violence goes against every instinct that he possesses, so GG wades in too. 'You're making everything worse, big D.'

'I'm saving you,' the Ape protests. 'You're just standing there doing nothing.'

Non-Ape stares at Billie like she's the loveliest vision there ever was. All anger and rage has fled from him. But more than that he turns a bright crimson. He's embarrassed and turns shy. His great head lowers and he looks at his snow-buried feet while he tries his hardest to think of something to say.

Billie keeps walking towards him. 'I'll never forget that you cared,' she tells him, reinforcing how wonderful he is in case he didn't get it the first two times.

Non-Ape manages to lift his head but he's still red in the face, unable to meet her eye. He nervously licks his bottom lip. 'Promise?' he finally manages.

'Yeah. And listen, it's not been a good time, and I haven't been a great friend to anyone.' Billie glances at the Ape when she says this – and now he blushes and bows his great head. She looks back at Non-Ape. 'But seeing how much you care, it makes everything so much better.'

Non-Ape doesn't know whether to walk towards her or wait. He shuffles awkwardly on the spot.

'Good is good.' His voice is a low mumble and he dares to meet her eyes.

The midnight snow is beginning to melt. There's a rising warmth in the air that proves the tail end of summer is still here after all.

Billie stops and holds out a hand, just the way I did, to Non-Ape. 'We need you.'

His monolithic body rises into a near army-like stand to attention. I'm amazed he doesn't salute. Whatever effect Another-Billie has on him is as powerful as he is.

'Yeah?' His eyes shine in the reflection from the street lamp.

'We got some digging to do.'

And suddenly I get it. This isn't Billie talking. It's Other-Johnson. He's inside her, making her walk and talk.

That was the plan!

It's come back to me at last. That's what we decided to do. To use Billie to soothe the Beast. She's going to be horrified when she finds out she has to keep being nice to two Apes, but at least it'll keep both of the Johnsons alive.

But more than that I have no idea what she'll do when she learns that the last five months were pure myth. If ever I was going to be a good friend it's going to be now.

Poor Billie, I think. *She isn't going to like this one bit.*

AND HERE WE ARE AGAIN

I need to talk to Billie but she has wandered back into the snooker hall. When everything calmed down I filled them all in on the timescale issues and now Johnson is sitting alone under the blue clock in a partial daze, as he tries to come to terms with what he has just learned. He hasn't said anything and I'm imagining that all of the false memories and experiences are draining from him, falling like sheets of melting ice into one big puddle of incomprehension.

Other-Johnson came out from where he was hiding but still has a hold on Billie just to make sure she doesn't go and do anything crazy. I silently asked him to try and help her and he said he'd put good thoughts into her head if he could.

All the lights in the snooker hall are on and their glow spills down into the square where GG and the Moth are trying to explain to both Apes what has happened with the strange fluctuations in time and season. GG tried before with the Ape when they were outside the church but Non-Ape wants it spelled out in the simplest of terms. They have to comply or he'll probably punch them. It isn't going well.

'It was an hour in both worlds,' says the Moth.

'You said it wasn't,' says the Ape.

'But it was,' GG adds.

'But you said it wasn't,' repeats the Ape.

'I know, but I think I get it now – and it definitely was an hour.'

'So why say it wasn't?' The Ape can't let it go.

'Because it felt like it wasn't. Even though it was,' the Moth says.

'So it was an hour?' Non-Ape chips in with his deep gruff voice.

GG nods. 'Yes.'

'That lasted five months.' The Ape looks pleased; he's got it now.

'No, it was an hour that lasted an hour,' GG clarifies.

'So how come it was Christmas?' Non-Ape asks.

'It wasn't.'

'Was. I made a snowman,' the Ape tells them.

'Was a great snowman.' Non-Ape's eyes light up, impressed.

'Best one ever.' The Ape is deeply proud.

'You got skills.'

They knock knuckles together at this. One large slab of hand banging into an even larger slab of hand.

'Skills.' The Ape lets the word roll off his tongue, savouring it.

'Skilllllls,' Non-Ape repeats.

'Look, it doesn't really matter now. Main thing is we know it wasn't real.' The Moth's voice has gone a little more whiney with exasperation.

'Was real,' the Ape responds.

'Can't build a snowman out of not real.' Non-Ape jabs the air in the front of the Moth's eyes, pointing with each word.

'It's rude to point.' GG lays a hand on Non-Ape's pointing finger, pushing it gently down. 'But nothing was really real.'

'The snow was real. I made a snowman,' the Ape repeats. 'Skilllllls.'

'OK, look at it this way, someone made us believe that time had passed and they also created all manner of things to help make us believe it.' The Moth looks increasingly tired and drawn.

'It was real then.' Non-Ape punches the air. 'We win!'

'No. No, no, no.'

'What else can they make?' the Ape asks.

'What?' GG says.

'Can they make a zoo?' Non-Ape's eyes brighten like a child's.

'A zoo?'

'Can they?'

'I don't know. We don't even know who made the snow.'

'What about Disneyland?' Non-Ape grins.

'Like I said—'

'Thunder Mountain!' Ape yells.

'I don't think they were doing it to make us happy. They wanted to hurt us,' GG says. The Moth has fallen silent: he has given up trying.

'Snow doesn't hurt,' Non-Ape reasons.

The Moth breaks his silence. 'You were throwing snowballs at a million miles an hour!'

'Anyway, great chat. That's pretty much explained everything.' GG makes to walk away.

But the Ape stops him. 'So how long have we been here?'

GG groans. 'What!?'

'Is it an hour or not?'

'Feels longer,' Non-Ape says.

'Well, it's longer now. It's more like eight hours.' GG has a please-hang-me-now look.

'So it's not an hour?'

'Not any more it's not!' the Moth whispers through clenched, desperate teeth.

'So why say it was an hour?' the Non-Ape asks.

'Ha, you lose!' the Ape punches the air again.

'They know nothing,' Non-Ape tells him and adds a satisfied belch.

Ape dredges his own louder belch and a belch-war starts between the Apes. It could almost be called a mating ritual because I have never seen two people click as quickly – and, well, lovingly – as the Ape and Non-Ape. They are a match made in heaven. All hate and rage has bled away from Non-Ape and I am praying that they can stay friends long cnough to help get us out of here because we could use them both.

GG walks slowly away, his hands covering his face. 'I've never wanted to die before, never saw it as a healthy option, but after that conversation I'm not so sure.'

With the snow melting and the winter crawling away before our eyes GG decides that we should all go to the train station and start heading for London and the smashed hotel. There is still the chance that the alien world will find a way to break through to this world and no one wants to be around when that happens. If one of them is already here, messing with our perceptions, and changing the weather, then it is no time to dawdle. We need to get as far away as we can from whoever is doing these things because recent experience tells me it's only going to get worse.

Non-Ape hoists the Moth and his wheelchair with indecent ease onto one of his broad shoulders. 'Let's go.'

His mind – if he has one – should be overloading with questions. Like, why is the Moth in a wheelchair and why are there two Johnsons? But he hasn't said a thing yet, though I'm pretty sure that time is bound to come. It takes an age for any thought to strike an Ape and he still hasn't questioned why there's a smaller version of himself.

'I'll get Billie,' I tell the others. Other-Johnson has been looking after her; after taking over her mind he knows she has to be treated delicately.

I head past Johnson at the clock who looks up and he raises his finger to his temple and cocks it my way.

'That was weird.' He's trying to sound calm but there's something in his voice, an edge or a subtle twang of the vocal chords, which tells me he is suffering. I want to stop and say something that'll help but I'm saving it all for Billie.

'Weird but not wonderful,' he adds, and a chill runs through him as more of the fake five months slip away.

I find Billie sitting on a snooker table, her legs dangling as she cups her chin in her hands. Other-Johnson doesn't need to read my mind to know I want some alone time with her. A simple nod and he's gone.

I've known Billie since we were four years old and when I first laid eyes on her she was sitting in the exact same way. She was troubled, so I went over and we became best friends from that moment on. She's seriously troubled now so I do the same.

'Billie?'

186

Billie's facial scars are back, deep gouges down one cheek caused by Non-Lucas's talons. That was a horrible trick to play on her. Making her believe they were healing. The Manipulator who created the fake months has a deeply cruel streak and the sooner we escape the better.

'Hey, Rev.' Billie offers me a smile but it fails.

'We, uh, we need to get going.'

'I thought maybe I could stay here.' Billie's eyes are filling with tears.

'Hey. No. No way. We go together. Like always.'

'I don't think I can . . .' She stops, then starts again. 'I don't think I can be around Johnson.' Her eyes meet mine. 'Rev, I feel like such a fool.'

I step closer and lay my forehead against hers, our eyes level. 'You were tricked. We all were.'

'But I love him. That's what's inside me now. That is still there.'

I want to tell her it's not real, that it's all just residue.

'Billie, we can figure this out. You and me. We'll look back and . . . And . . .'

'Laugh? Only that's the last thing I'm thinking about right now. I've got these feelings, Rev. Whether they're real or not, I've got them.'

I slip my hand into hers and squeeze. 'I'm not leaving you behind. And I know it's tough but I'm right here, just like always.'

'I keep running it round in my head. Every single bit of it was as real as, well, real gets. We watched the seasons change. We saw the end of summer, then the autumn came, and I've got to tell you, Rev, it was so romantic. The leaves were turning gold, the sun was dipping lower. We went for long walks – you know that field where the bull lives? What was his name?'

'Napoleon.' He's a massive beast, like Non-Ape on all fours, but he always ambled over if you stood at the fence long enough.

'We went there. Napoleon wasn't around of course, but we walked all over the fields.'

That's one thing about this world. No animals. Which makes me wonder where the steak bakes come from. This is a world that operates on rules I truly can't comprehend. The Moth could spend a lifetime working out what makes this parallel world tick. And he probably will. If we ever get home to safety.

'Me and Johnson. Just walking. The Moth wasn't interested.' She smiles at the memory. 'Even the rain was like something from a film. We got caught in it once and had to shelter under an ancient oak tree. We huddled there watching the rain and every now and then I got a drip on the back of my neck. It felt real, it made me shiver! And Johnson ... slipped an arm round me.'

But he didn't, I want to tell her. *He didn't do any of that.* Billie covers her face with her hands and then shudders, as if trying to shake the memories away. 'I guess we didn't have a room in the hotel either.'

She sits up straighter and takes a deep breath She looks up at me and a small familiar light switches on behind her eyes. 'This is still all your fault.'

I offer half a smile. 'Give me a thousand lines. I must not take people to another universe.'

Billie smiles, then she rubs her eyes. 'OK.' She breathes out. 'I can do this. I think. Let's go.'

*

188

As soon as we get outside Non-Ape is waiting at the entrance with the Moth and his wheelchair still perched on his shoulder. The Moth has a resigned look on his face.

'Don't let him see you're upset,' I whisper to her.

'You OK, Billie?' Non-Ape asks.

Billie's been wrenched this way and that over the last few hours. I know what it feels like to have Johnson slip away from you and even though I can still feel a weird distance between us no one wants to see this sort of heartbreak in their best friend.

Billie sniffles.

Non-Ape looms. He looks worried. Ready to blow.

'Billie?'

Answer him.

Billie stares at Johnson who is still seated outside. She breathes deeply and then to her credit she dredges a white-toothed smile for Non-Ape. 'I'm OK,' she says.

'You sure?'

I can see Other-Johnson and GG returning from the nearest shop with food and drinks for our journey. The Ape is with them but all he carries are cans of beer.

She nods. 'Yeah. Just need a second. Lot to take in.'

I breathe out. 'OK, let's get going.'

'Why haven't you fixed your scars?' Non-Ape asks Billie staring at her gouged cheek.

She swallows. 'Uh.'

Non-Ape thinks Billie should heal herself. I'm surprised he's even noticed, but that only reinforces the notion of his deep infatuation with her.

Billie struggles to think of a response and the silence comes with a death knell as I wait and pray for Billie to think of an answer.

'Uh ... Yeah. I, uh ... I'm a bit low on power right now. Need to, uh, to recharge.'

Non-Ape thinks for a long moment and then nods. 'You'd know.'

He sets off, carrying the Moth who wobbles a little with the movement. Non-Ape isn't unhappy but he isn't altogether happy either. I get the feeling he is like a savage animal that we can only hope is part domesticated. I don't for a minute think we'll fool him for ever and I don't think anyone feels particularly comfortable around him.

Johnson joins us and shares a quiet look with Billie. I know he feels as embarrassed as she does, but neither seems to know what to say to each other.

'Billie, listen ...'

'It's all right, I'm OK.' She nods. 'Are you?'

Johnson reaches for her and before they know it they are hugging. 'Yeah. Well. I will be,' he whispers, care and concern in his voice.

'Me too,' she says. 'Me too.'

They stay that way for a moment. Enveloped in a quiet sadness.

Johnson is the first to break from the hug. Billie feels the wrench but hides it as best she can.

'We'll always have Napoleon,' Johnson tells her with a small smile.

She nods and I can't help but be impressed by how strong she's being.

GG leads the way to the train station. 'London, here we come.'

My hands throb, my burns burn and my stabbed thigh aches, but at least it's stopped bleeding. The melting snow is little more than sludge and disappearing fast as we splash through huge puddles.

I still can't believe someone could create this. They're practically God-like. Under different circumstances it would have been worth hanging around to see what else they can do, but today isn't the day to find out.

'*Rev?*' Other-Johnson is walking about ten metres behind me. '*Great plan.*'

'*Thanks,*' I reply.

'*Impressed,*' he replies. I can almost feel him smile inside my head.

'*We're getting out of this,*' I tell him, determined.

'*We'll need to talk about that, you know, when the time comes.*'

'*About what?*'

'*I've only just got you back, and the moment'll come when I have to let you go again. Probably for ever.*'

I've been ignoring the fact that sooner or later we're going to have to go to our own worlds. The thought sends a quiet shiver through me. '*You've got your Rev.*'

'*And, like I said, she isn't you. Isn't even close.*'

Which I think is probably a lie. He is very good at lying. Or maybe not if I know it's a lie. I wish he wasn't like that. I promised myself I'd never forgive him for lying to me but I'm just too tired to pull him up on that.

'*If we find those papers or get your dad fixed, then it's the end of us.*'

'*There's an us?*' I ask him.

'*Across every world you care to mention, there's always going to be an us, Rev.*'

He always says the thing that goes straight to my heart. I'm pathetic, I know but I can't help it, he makes me swoon. Every single time.

'*Maybe with my dad's or the Moth's help we can work out a way to come to each other's worlds.*'

'*Now that's what I call a long-distance relationship.*'

'*Let's just see if we can get home first.*'

'*I know you, Rev, you're going to save them all and then close the portals down. You can't have my kind coming after you in this world or yours.*'

'*Can we talk about something else?*' I'm not ready to say goodbye to anyone right now.

We fall silent for a moment.

'*I have to be with you.*'

The words lift me but only so that the realisation that follows can shove me right back down again.

'*That can't happen. We both know that.*'

'*I'll find a way.*'

I don't understand. Why, when he has Rev Two, am I so special to him?

'*I need to be with you, Rev.*'

'*Please don't.*'

'*I don't know how, but I'll make it happen.*'

He leaves my head and I walk on in silence. No one's talking but the Apes are at least matching each other step for step. They seem very comfortable in each other's company.

'Think I'm going to be sick.' The Moth is rocking like he's on the back of an elephant so Non-Ape stops and sets him down.

'Go on. Chuck up.'

'I was just saying—'

'Show some chunks,' the Ape adds.

The Moth recovers. 'I'm, uh . . . I'm OK . . . Was just a bit of a bumpy ride.'

Billie draws alongside them. 'Just push him.'

Non-Ape is ready to do anything she says and places his giant hands on the back of the wheelchair.

'No, wait!' I shout.

But I'm too late and Non-Ape pushes the Moth with a mighty shove.

The Moth rockets along the high street, straight down the centre of the road. 'Nooooooooooooo!'

The heavy wheelchair grips the tarmac as it splashes through puddle after puddle, soaking the Moth with icy-cold water.

We lose sight of him after he's gone about three hundred metres.

All of us stand in a bewildered silence.

Billie stares in dismay at the great behemoth. 'Gently. I meant push him gently.'

'Oh,' is his only response.

GG quickens his pace. 'That's one way to catch your train.'

We all run after the Moth. Non-Ape feels bad now but the Ape punches his arm in a show of solidarity. 'Great push.'

Non-Ape grins, spirits buoyed. 'Skills.'

'Skiiiiiiiiiiilllllllllls!'

ALL ABOARD THE CHOO-CHOO

The train station is silent and still as we troop out onto platform one and find what's left of GG's train. There is an engine and two battered carriages.

We found the Moth buried head first in a hedge but apart from a few scratches he and his wheelchair weren't badly damaged.

'I must've been going at fifty miles an hour!' he mumbled in a daze.

Which still isn't as fast as his doppelganger Moth Two was going when I hit him with a train.

My spider sense hasn't troubled me and as the sun rises I'm wondering if we've caught the Manipulator off guard. Everyone has to sleep, and using that much power must take it out of you, so there's every chance he – or she – isn't even awake yet. Which gives us an advantage for once.

Other-Johnson and I have conveniently forgotten to mention Another-Billie and Rev Two gathered around my dad's hospital bed. I have no idea if he'll pull through, so why give Billie and the others a hope that might not be there? Finding my dad's papers is a long shot, but if my dad doesn't wake up, it might be the only chance we have. Besides, it's about all we can do while Another-Billie tries to revive him.

We fall back behind the others and Other-Johnson mentally contacts Another-Billie and Rev Two, opening the waves to let me in on their conversation.

'*The Ape is still chasing me,*' he lies.

'*Jesus, Johnson.*' Rev Two's voice still spooks me a little. '*What did you do to him?*'

'*Nothing, I swear.*' Other-Johnson is careful not to let Rev Two know anything about me or the others, but he's also secretly drawing Another-Billie in. The boy never misses a beat.

'*Billie, keep trying to make Rev's dad better.*'

'*I will.*'

'*Good girl, you're the best,*' he tells her. '*I'll check in for updates, and, uh – tell you how I'm doing.*'

'*I miss you,*' Rev Two says.

'*I miss you too. Loads.*'

'I *could do with going home,*' Another-Billie adds. It's a loaded comment.

'*That's going to happen,*' Other-Johnson assures her.

'*It'd better.*' Which comes out as a warning more than anything.

'*I'll be waiting for you,*' Rev Two says. '*So lose the Ape and get back here.*'

'*I'm trying my best. And, Rev—*'

But at that point he cuts my link so that I don't hear what he tells her. It's pretty obvious though because he avoids my look for a few moments.

Then he breaks their connection. 'I've got to keep up appearances,' he whispers to me.

'I know that,' I whisper back a little bit too tightly. 'How long do you think we have before your Rev finds out that's not her dad?'

'Let's just get to London.'

I stride on ahead to catch up with the others as they're boarding the front carriage.

The two Apes hoist the Moth and his chair into the train and I jump on behind them, just in time to see the Moth moving at speed straight down the aisle.

'Stop doing that!'

Non-Ape laughs and high-fives the Ape. Their latest game seems to be shove the Moth.

I sit down in a window seat that's part of a set of four seats with a table. Billie steps onboard and I expect her to sit with me, but instead she takes a seat a little further down. Guess we all need a bit of alone time.

Other-Johnson springs into the carriage and I put my feet up on the seat opposite me, hoping he'll get the message. He does and strolls past me to sit a few rows behind me.

GG fires up the train. And incredibly it starts first time. '*Ding dong!* All aboard!' his voice rings out of the tannoy.

It's then I realise that Johnson is missing. The doors close and I'm ready to pull the emergency cord.

'Where's Johnson?' I shout.

Whoosh! The doors open again and I look up to meet Johnson's eyes as he climbs aboard.

Unlike Other-Johnson, he isn't discouraged by my feet, walking up to me and pushing them gently off the chair so he can sit opposite me.

He holds up a bag from Boots.

'You've taken a few hits. Thought you might need some

196

TLC so I ducked into Boots when you were all chasing after the Moth.'

'Thank you,' I say.

He starts pulling out all manner of creams, ointments and plasters from the bag.

'Need to bandage your hands. You won't be able to do it on your own.'

'Look at Doctor Johnson,' I hear Other-Johnson say under his breath.

Johnson ignores Other-Johnson, acting as if he isn't there. I try to do the same. This Johnson is the one it all began with after all. I know I can trust him, whereas Other-Johnson is much less certain a proposition.

'Hands.' He pops the cap on a tube of antiseptic cream and squeezes it onto my open skinless palms. It stings to high heaven and I grimace.

Gingerly he rubs it into my palms and after a minute or so the pain starts to ease.

'Better?' he asks.

'Much,' I reply.

He starts wrapping bandages round my hands, as tight as he dares. 'Tell me if it's too tight.'

'It's fine.'

The train moves off and GG's voice comes over the tannoy again. 'We've done this before so sit back and enjoy the scenery.'

Johnson winds the bandage round and round, first one hand and then the other. He doesn't say a word but I listen to his breathing until he finishes.

'How's that?' he asks.

'Gorgeous,' I say dreamily.

'Sorry?'

I sit up, breaking from my reverie. 'Great. I meant great.'

Johnson nods, then looks down at my wounded thigh. I have stretched my leg under the table because it somehow helps the pain, but in doing so I have inadvertently touched my knee with his.

Johnson's next move is obvious. But he hesitates.

'Listen, I'm going to get you home, Rev,' he eventually says.

'We'll all get home,' I assure him.

His eyes blaze. 'And when I do . . .'

I wait.

'When I do. Look out.'

He gives me a short almost embarrassed smile, then gets up. 'I'd better check on Billie.'

He heads down the carriage as we gather speed and Other-Johnson immediately sends me a mind message. *'I'd be bandaging your thigh right now.'*

'Go away,' I tell him.

'Calls himself a doctor?'

'You called him that.'

'Let me take a look at your leg,' Other-Johnson adds.

'I'm good, thanks.'

'Rev—'

'Please,' I tell him, *'there's more to think about than my leg. So get out of my head. I need the space.'*

Other-Johnson 'leaves' my head and leaves me to sit and wonder. Just wonder and wonder about what happens next.

The last time we boarded this train to London Moth Two had turned into some sort of human–animal hybrid and chased us down the track. I'm still not proud of what happened, but mainly thanks to me he ended up decapitated and very dead.

Johnson now sits across the aisle from Billie but she is looking anywhere but at him. She still can't face him.

'When's this going to end, Rev?' she asks.

The Moth has applied his brake to his wheelchair and the Apes are standing by the door showing each other pictures they have on their phones. I'm not sure what the picture or photos are of but I'm pretty sure it has something to do with girls.

'Eight.'

'Seven.'

'Nine.'

'Yeah. She's a nine.'

'Soon,' I tell Billie. 'It's got to be soon.'

'But it *will* end, right?'

'It has to,' I say. 'One way or another.'

CRAZY TRAIN

GG is behind the wheel of the train – if there is a wheel, I don't know much about trains. He has kept up a running tour-guide commentary over the tannoy for most of the trip. We aren't moving fast, maybe forty miles an hour, and Billie has joined me now, not wanting to be too close to Johnson.

'So cruel,' she says quietly, glancing back at Johnson. 'So horribly cruel.'

'On your left you will see houses built circa the nineteen-eighties. There are small gardens and, look, some people have squeezed in a greenhouse.'

Billie cups her scarred face, her elbow placed on the table between us.

'Least whoever it was won't be on the train.' Billie tenses as a thought strikes her. 'Assuming we are on a train. This might not be real either.'

Non-Ape farts two rows down. It's a loud all-engulfing explosion. Non-Ape starts laughing and then waves the fetid stench our way. 'Eat that.'

'That's maybe too much attention to detail,' I tell Billie.

'On your right you'll notice some empty fields. Horses would usually be grazing there, so use your imaginations.' GG then whinnies to help. 'Down, boy,' he adds.

Johnson has moved to sit with the Other-Johnson but they're obviously not overly fond of each other. Any Johnson really should be a unique creature. Two just isn't right.

'Flip me back,' Johnson tells Other-Johnson.

'Maybe I can't. Maybe we're stuck like this.'

'I don't like being you.'

'Don't mind me, say it like it is.'

Other-Johnson's irony doesn't wash with Johnson. 'You left me for dead. Took my body so you could save yourself.'

'I gave you a shot at survival,' Other-Johnson counters.

'You gave yourself that shot.'

'Don't you like being strong and fast?'

Johnson leans forward and releases a talon. Other-Johnson's eyes are drawn to its gleaming tip. 'You can have these – either way.'

Johnson's quiet anger surprises me. I didn't know he had that in him. Or is being in the body of an aggressive doppelganger beginning to rub off on him? Is he subtly changing like Billie? Maybe that's what Other-Johnson is hoping for.

Another talon slides out. 'You want them or not?'

Other-Johnson reflects for a moment. Then grins. 'Let me sleep on it.'

'Coming up soon we'll be passing the cereal factory, a rather charming building – and if you happen to be a cereal addict then you've found your mecca.' GG toots the train horn as we pass the giant cereal plant. 'All hail the Weetabix God.'

'Snap!' the Ape shouts. He and Non-Ape are playing cards

now. I have no idea where the cards have come from but the game is becoming a little exuberant.

'Snap!' the Ape shouts again.

'You're too fast,' Non-Ape complains.

'You're too slow,' the Ape responds.

'You're saying I'm slow?'

'I'm saying you're not fast.'

'That's strong words.' Non-Ape's bulk takes up two seats and he looks completely awkward squeezed into the train.

'I only know strong words,' the Ape replies.

I'm imagining a fight is about to break out, but Non-Ape seems to appreciate the Ape even more now. He nods his gargantuan head at the fearless defiance, enjoying it. 'O-kay.'

They lay more cards down but Non-Ape is determined to win and pays closer attention. The cards are dealt swiftly as both Apes become more and more crouched over the table that sits between them, desperate to be the first to—

'SNAP!' Non-Ape's thick palm slams down on the deck and smashes the table.

The cards go flying as the table disintegrates. After the shock the Apes start laughing. It hits a funny bone for both of them because they cannot stop laughing. The Apes truly are in heaven. They have found their kindred spirit.

'Too quick, man.' The Ape finally manages to talk through his laughter.

'Fast is good,' Non-Ape says.

'Hey, you heard my fast song?' the Ape asks.

The Ape yanks out his phone and scrolls to a song.

Please. I've heard enough of this song to last a lifetime. The Ape once played me songs that he thinks can help you survive. It was a simple private moment that left my ears hanging off.

He turns up the volume on his phone and a band called Terrorvision's 'D'Ya Wanna Go Faster?' fills the carriage.

'Do ya wanna go faster?' the Ape starts singing.

Somehow Non-Ape knows the song – so it seems that music is something we have in common too – and starts singing with him. His voice is a good three octaves lower and the happy racket they create fills the entire train.

They start rocking in their seats. Non-Ape is now perched on his but every time he rocks he makes the train wobble.

'Dancing down the motorway,' the Ape bellows.

'In the fast lane all the way,' Non-Ape adds as they grin at each other.

GG's next announcement is practically drowned out by them. 'We're now travelling through more suburbia with its endless copies of the same house. Wave, everyone.'

I look over at the Moth who has barely said a word since we left. He's dragged himself into a seat by himself. I'm not sure what he is thinking, but I wonder if it's about what he'll do if Non-Ape clears the rubble and reveals Carrie lying there. He pretty much came close to giving up when she died. I need to make sure we all look out for him. He found the love of his life only to have her die before anything could happen between them. That would change anyone.

I briefly wonder if Another-Billie could heal him, make him walk again. Wouldn't that be something? But then imagine his parents and doctors back home wondering how such a miracle could have happened. He'd be a major celebrity and he wouldn't be able to explain any of it. But the thought lifts my spirits. Being back home with my mum and dad would be the biggest and best miracle of all.

But who would believe any of this? If we did get home, who would we tell?

'I think we should make a pact that none of us ever talks about this world,' I tell Billie.

'If we get home.'

'When we get home,' I correct her.

'Your plan to find the papers is lousy, Rev. That hotel was huge.'

'The Moth was in one of the ground-floor rooms. The hotel toppled when Non-Ape hit it, which could mean it fell away from the ground floor.'

'So?'

'So it could mean that the room is mostly still intact. And the papers could be in that room.'

'Dreamer.'

'Maybe, but it's the only plan we've got.' I say, again conveniently leaving out the plan B involving my dad.

Billie eases back in her chair. She glances at Johnson. She has been stealing looks at him for the past ten minutes. 'Forget the plan. Forget London. Europe would be better.'

I laugh, thinking she is joking, but she turns to me and her eyes switch to black for a moment.

My laugh dies away.

Billie sits straighter in her seat. 'Rev, that's where I want to go.'

Her eyes are still black and I feel like pointing it out to her but she's got enough to deal with at the moment. 'Promise me we'll go there if this plan doesn't work.'

'Europe? Why?'

She reaches out and her fingers curl round my wrist. Her

204

grip is powerful and she isn't concerned that she's squeezing my barely-healed burns.

'There are trains at St Pancras that go to Europe. The station is right next to King's Cross. We can get GG to drive one.'

'We've got a plan, Billie.'

Her grip tightens. I try not to draw attention to it because her eyes are unforgivingly black.

'Non-Ape will clear the rubble and we'll find the papers for the Moth,' I assure her. 'I promise you.'

'It's too dangerous. Rev. You said yourself the alien world could come through a portal. By the time we get back to town it could be swarming with those monsters. There's already one of them roaming around. Why take that chance when we could all run away?'

It's a fair point. But it's not the right one.

'And what if they open a portal and they get to our world? They'd be unstoppable. We've got family and friends there. My mum, your dad. We have to make sure that never happens, not hide away,' I counter.

Billie takes a long while before relaxing her grip. 'Was just thinking aloud,' she offers as her blue eyes return.

My wrist is white from lack of blood and I slip my arm under the table so that I can subtly rub the circulation back into it.

The Apes erupt with a singalong rendition of 'Run to the Hills' by Iron Maiden.

'Run for your life!' they bawl.

Which Billie would probably love to be our theme tune.

MOTHS 2,3,4,5,6,7, ETC.

I look out of the window and recognise the spot where we killed Moth Two and it's not a good memory. But I can't hear myself think because the Apes are now standing playing air guitar to the solo in 'Run to the Hills'.

GG's panicked voice erupts into the carriage. 'No! No way! That's impossible! Good Goddy God!'

I am up and out of my seat before anyone can move, heading down the carriage to the driver compartment door.

'What is it?' I ask GG as he pulls open the door. He's white as a sheet.

Johnson is behind me in a heartbeat. 'GG?'

GG clears his throat then points to the mirror attached to the side of the train. I have to get in the driver's compartment to get a proper look.

And he's right.

'Totally, totally not possible,' he says weakly.

It is impossible.

Moth Two is running behind us. Gaining with every stride.

206

The same Moth Two we decapitated and left for dead by the rail track not that far from where we are now.

'Rev?' Other-Johnson has joined Johnson and I realise I have no idea now if they have changed back or not.

'It's Moth Two ,' I tell them.

The Apes haven't noticed because they are so busy singing 'Crazy Train' by Ozzy Osbourne, banging their feet down hard on the floor of the carriage in tune to the beat. Billie and the Moth are on full alert as they remain seated, awaiting news.

Moth Two can turn into a dark panther; it's the only way I can describe it. A sleek black panther with the Moth's face. But this Moth can run way faster than a real panther.

'He was headless,' GG whimpers. 'He was definitely without a head.'

'Johnson?' I ask Other-Johnson.

They both answer. 'What?'

'Is this possible?'

Other-Johnson looks at the approaching Moth Two . 'Looks like it is.'

'But how?' I ask him.

'I dunno. But don't worry, we've got the Apes.'

Then the Moth all but screams. 'Oh my God!' He is pointing out of the window. 'That can't be. It can't!'

We pile back into the main carriage and crowd the window the Moth is sitting by. There are more Moth Twos swarming towards the train. They are charging through fields, overrunning gardens, plunging straight through greenhouses and crashing through fences as they home in on the train.

It's like a plague of giant black locusts, all of them with talons and steel teeth.

'GG, floor it!' Johnson yells.

GG scoots to the driver compartment and within seconds the train accelerates. 'Everyone hang on to something!' he yells. 'Warp speed is upon us.'

Billie is looking out of the opposite window and she speaks quietly. 'Guys . . .'

No one really hears her. We are too fixated on the Moth Two swarm.

'How tough is Non-Ape?' I ask anyone who will listen.

Billie raises her voice. 'Guys!'

When we turn we see that more Moth Twos are converging on the other side of the train. There must be at least another twenty of them. And they are going to catch up with us.

GG babbles on the tannoy. 'There's less train to pull since we lost a couple of carriages. We can go so much faster. So strap yourselves in. It's going to be a bumpy ride.'

The train continues to pick up speed.

But so do the Moth Twos. They stretch their long sinewy limbs and cover the ground at breakneck speed.

'Nothing suffocates you more than the passing of everyday human events.' It's the beginning of 'The Fight Song' by Marilyn Manson and it's booming out of the Ape's phone.

I resist the pull of the train's increased momentum and drag myself toward the Apes.

'Dazza.'

They both turn to me, blissfully unaware of the Moth Twos.

'Worm,' Non-Ape replies. He has a new name for me now. Though I think I prefer Pinkhead. Just.

'That song you're listening to—' I tell them, watching the first of the Moth Twos pulling alongside the train.

'Best song ever!' The Ape high-fives Non-Ape.

'Well, it's for real,' I say, and point outside the window to the swarming black tide. 'It's time to fight.'

No four words could ever sound better to an Ape.

Their eyes locate and lock onto the Moth Twos who are closing in on the train.

'Yowza,' the Ape says calmly.

'Worm,' Non-Ape says.

'Yeah?'

'Switch your hand on.'

I keep forgetting he thinks I'm the Rev from his world.

'Switch it on,' Non-Ape repeats and, moving with the speed of a natural-born warrior, he grabs and snaps the metal poles commuters cling to in rush hour and starts handing the broken pieces out as weapons.

'Throats!' The Ape grabs a metal pole, equally genius in the ways of war.

The first of the Moth Twos reaches the side of the train. He leaps and lands with a hard dull whump that echoes through the carriage, as he drives his talons into the side of it for purchase.

'OhmyGod,' the Moth says as another Moth Two lands on the other side of the train and he spins to watch him use his lethal talons to penetrate the metal coachwork and cling on.

The Johnsons are up and tensed, looking from one side of the train to the other.

Another Moth Two lands on the far side of the train.

Then another.

And another.

Whump, whump, whump.

Johnson looks to Other-Johnson. 'Tell me your Ape can smash them.'

209

'He can smash anything.' Other-Johnson is assured of this.

Whump.

Whump.

Whump, whump, whump.

More leaping Moth Twos are landing on the train like flies on a windscreen.

Whump, whump, whump.

They're swarming all over the outside of the carriage.

Johnson unsheathes his talons.

Whump, whump, whump.

The tips of the Moth Twos' talons pierce all along the carriage.

Billie seems to have frozen in her seat.

'They're everywhere!' GG's shrill voice booms out of the tannoy. 'Begone, you wretched creatures.'

Other-Johnson grips a metal pole, as he stands back to back with me. 'Where the hell did they come from?' he mutters.

London doesn't seem like such a good idea any more.

More Moth Twos land and attach themselves to the carriage. By the sound of it some are climbing towards the roof, scurrying fast like giant beetles along the bodywork.

The natural light in the carriage is disappearing as the Moth Twos land and blot out the windows. There is no telling how many of them there are.

GG is giving it all the speed he's got but even he knows we're lost. 'Is it too late to apologise for the business with the head?'

But even Other-Johnson has never seen the likes of this before. 'I didn't know the Moth could replicate.'

'He was dead,' I respond. 'We killed him . . .'

'You didn't kill him enough,' he replies.

'Hey! Can someone please give me a weapon?' the Moth yells.

The Ape plants a sharp metal pole in his hands.

'They'll have to come through me first,' he assures the Moth and stands ready to shield him. 'And that isn't happening.'

Marilyn Manson's plea for fighting reaches a crescendo, acting as a signal to the Moth Twos. 'Fight! Fight! Fight!'

The first window shatters and in they pour.

FIGHT

Non-Ape might be unbeatable, but there are so many Moth Twos that there's no room for his huge bulk to manoeuvre and the size of the carriage is cramping his effectiveness. He punches the life out of every Moth Two that attacks him, breaking them apart with thunderous blows, but he can't keep all of them at bay.

They snap and stab at him, slashing and biting as his ferocious power repels them. They keep coming though, focusing as many of their legion as they can entirely on him.

They crash in through the windows and above Non-Ape the ones on the roof start tearing a hole in the top of the carriage. Moth Twos only seem interested in Non-Ape and it dawns on me that anyone with a better brain than the average man in the street would do this. They'd send the first wave for the strongest one amongst us. They'll keep him royally occupied while the second wave comes for us. There's got to be about forty of them, half on the train, half running alongside, awaiting their chance.

Their assault on Non-Ape is savage and brutal and, no matter how many he smashes and hurls through the broken windows, replacements keep climbing through. He is twisting and turning, pounding or tearing them apart, but I know it's a battle ploy. I so know it.

Moth Two is just as smart as our Moth.

Splatters of black blood start to soak the inside of the carriage. Their broken bodies are even used to batter live ones and Non-Ape bellows as loud as he can as smashed Moth Twos are ejected from the carriage.

The Ape joins the fight and wields his metal pole like a samurai, stabbing and slashing, a thing of terrible beauty to anyone who wants to live through this. Namely me. He bends and arcs and moves with all the fury of a warrior born. Moth Twos keep coming and I try to copy the Ape, but almost take Johnson down as he weaves through the carriage, taking the fight to the Moth Twos.

'Rev!' He ducks and is then past me.

He has power and speed but when the Moth Twos finally tear open the roof and three of them plunge into the carriage he is swiftly taken down. I scream and charge with all the desperate fury I possess at the vicious snapping creatures. They are not getting Johnson, not now, not ever. I fight dirty and ram the metal pole into the back of their exposed necks but it only works if I drive it straight through to the other side. I slam and plunge and pound the metal pole as Johnson slices and slashes at the Moth Twos crawling over him. It's a grim and graceless assault but I didn't come here to play nice.

Souped up, Johnson throws the last Moth Two in the opposite direction to the driver's compartment and springs to his feet. Incredibly, in fact impossibly, he is unscathed and gives me the Johnson nod as another Moth Two drops into the carriage behind us.

Other-Johnson keeps forgetting that he has less than super abilities and his moves are slower than he expects and he has to keep compensating. Why didn't he swap when he had the chance? He has the upper hand only in that his kind are more savage than us. He possesses that something extra, which makes him a natural killer, and he'll be damned before he goes down. The Moth Twos come for him as Billie sinks down in her seat, her head in her hands.

So far they either haven't noticed her or they don't care. She's just a puny human to them, and there's no way she can escape them. I have a terrible thought they're saving the rest of us till after they've taken Non-Ape down.

Non-Ape crushes every Moth Two that gets in his way because he has seen how scared Billie is and he will not, not ever, let any harm befall her. Her panic and fear gives him renewed strength and he bellows again as he hurls Moth Twos from the train.

Other-Johnson is driven back towards the second carriage by a group of Moth Twos. They are cutting him off. Johnson and I are being driven in the opposite direction. They're splitting us up, carving our gathered might into smaller, more manageable pieces.

The Apes stand savage and brutal, repelling and killing every attack as our Moth sits there, unable to do anything but grip his weapon and try and avoid the sprays of black blood that continue to decorate the carriage. Non-Ape's matchless power and reserves of stamina power his massive arms and hands as he punches and snaps and crushes. But they keep on coming.

Whump, whump, whump.

Every Moth Two we take down is swiftly replaced by another.

Whump, whump, whump.

That sound is starting to eat into me. Is there no end to them?

A Moth Two leaps in through the window and onto my back and I feel the talons tear my clothes as it drags me down to the floor.

'Johnson!'

Johnson is quick but the Ape is quicker. He's on the Moth Two in a heartbeat, plunging his metal pole straight into its neck.

'Watch your back!' he tells me. Like I needed telling.

GG bursts from the driver's compartment and slams the door shut behind him.

'They're coming in the front!'

GG braces himself against the door as more Moth Twos hammer at it, their talons bursting through and nearly slicing into him until Non-Ape pushes through, drags GG out of the way and uses his back and powerful legs to keep the door closed.

'I got this.'

'God you're wonderful,' GG says and then ducks as a Moth Two swoops down for him from the torn open ceiling.

Non-Ape crushes that Moth Two's neck in an instant.

'Be still, my beating heart.' GG ducks and dodges his way to the Moth who is sitting crouched waiting to fight. GG takes the metal pole from him.

'Get under the table, go on, get under it.'

'I'm fighting,' the Moth tells him and I know he is fighting for Carrie and GG knows it as well and backs away.

'Then we fight together.'

GG stands back to back with the Ape as they struggle to keep the Moth Twos at bay.

'There's so many of them!' GG cries.

'I know.' The Ape grins in delight.

I glance at Non-Ape and I'm not sure if it's his blood or just more dark splashes from the Moth Twos but I think he's injured. I think the talons slicing through the driver's door, are hurting him and I swear I see him wince.

That is not possible. It can't be. He's our only real hope of surviving this.

Billie is crouched low under a table and Johnson has taken it upon himself to stand protectively on top of it, crouching low as he jabs hard through the smashed window at the Moth Twos clinging on outside until they lose their grip on the speeding train and fall off.

Johnson is doing all in his power to protect Billie. I want to drag her from under the table and get her to do something to help. But the Moth Twos continue to snap and snarl and lunge and I can't hold them off.

Whump, whump, whump.

More Moth Twos land and jump in through the smashed, gaping windows and Johnson sets about them, a blur of death-dealing motion.

Non-Ape is being slashed in the back over and over as he keeps the Moth Twos in the driver's compartment from breaking through.

The train is hurtling along the track and still they keep leaping and landing.

Above us the torn roof reveals Moth Twos perched round the edges of the huge hole, glaring down at us with their dead eyes and grinning mouths.

'Are they laughing?' Johnson can't believe it and climbs out through the smashed window and hauls himself outside. He

216

takes them by surprise – a second later a Moth Two is hurled from the roof, flying past the window and landing in an ugly bone-snapping pile by the track.

Another Moth Two drags me down and its teeth snap and snarl an inch from my face until Non-Ape crushes its head by slapping his hands together round it. The thick black blood spurts everywhere and I get it in my eyes and mouth.

It tastes like oil and the amount of black blood that has been spilled in this carriage could heat a school for a month. I retch from the taste, spitting and coughing.

Non-Ape turns and yanks the driver's door off its hinges. He uses it as a shield and ploughs straight into the Moth Twos filling the tiny driver's compartment.

They slash and bite him. His back is torn and bleeding and his black blood is mingling with theirs. Turns out if he's cut enough times, he's just the same as the rest of us – he bleeds.

'Ape!' I call to him but he is too intent on shoving the onrush of Moth Twos back into the driver's compartment to pay any attention to me. His idea is pure genius. He shoves them clear through the broken windows at the front of the train where they are instantly crushed under the oncoming wheels.

The train bumps and shudders from impact after impact and throws us all off balance. GG is flung towards me and I almost stab him in the face. The Ape staggers as he slams a Moth Two back towards the doors. He hits the EMERGENCY OPEN button and the beeping door opens automatically and the Moth Two flies out. But another shunt almost sends the Ape out after him and GG dives for his black coat and hangs on to it for dear life.

'Not your stop, Dazza!'

With GG's help the Ape pulls himself back into the carriage, turns and drives his pole past GG's face and into the throat of another Moth Two.

But it's no good. There's too many of them; they keep on coming. We've got a souped-up Johnson and a not-quite-invincible Ape, but it's not enough. If they can cut Non-Ape, they will cut us all.

Other-Johnson knows exactly what I'm thinking as he is pushed further into the rear carriage and Moth Twos crowd around him.

'*Can you read them?*' I pant over the airwaves. '*What do they want?*'

Other-Johnson tries to get a mental image or a thought, grabbing it from the horde of Moth Twos.

'Oh, God!' he says. 'Rev! They're after the Moth!'

He's a second too late as taloned panther arms reach in through the smashed window and wrap round the Moth's neck.

Moth barely has time to scream as he is wrenched from his seat and dragged out of the train.

'Moth!' I scream.

Johnson leaps back into the carriage in time to see the Moth's weak, spindly legs disappearing out of the window.

'They took him!' I yell. 'They took the Moth!'

Johnson doesn't hesitate and gives it all the black-eyed ferocity he can muster but as he lunges after the Moth the train runs over a fallen Moth Two and bounces him out of the window.

Even from her hiding place Billie has seen him disappear and screams. 'Johnson!!'

First the Moth, now Johnson. I clamber towards the window thinking we've lost both of them, when Johnson's hand reaches up and grabs the jagged edge of the broken window as he hangs on for dear life to the outside of the train. All around us the few Moth Twos that are left start retreating, leaping from the train, one of them almost taking Johnson with him, another barging me out of the way and knocking me into a torn and slashed seat.

When I look up Johnson is trying to pull himself back into the window, but he is battered by the black blur of escaping Moth Twos.

'Johnson!' Billie screams again.

I scrabble as quickly as I can towards him, shouldering into a Moth Two in my desperation. He turns and looks at me and grins with a full set of glinting teeth. 'You're never going home again,' he hisses spitefully.

He leaps out of the train as I finally reach Johnson and try to pull him back into the carriage. I'm so desperate to save him that I suddenly have the strength of ten teenage girls and drag him back inside before falling and landing on my back. Johnson crashes down on top of me and for a second the world stops.

His eyes find mine and there is nothing but us in the carriage. It could be a microsecond or it could be a century but we are together. He knows it. I know it.

Then out of the corner of my eye I see Billie crouching under the table, staring at us.

At me.

And there is nothing but dark there. Her eyes, her heart, her soul. It is all wrapped up in an unforgiving blackness.

Other-Johnson breaks the moment by helping to pull Johnson to his feet.

'No sleep till Hammersmith,' he tells Johnson, but he is already reaching for me and helping me to my feet.

I can't stop looking at Billie crouching on the floor, looking like an animal partially obscured by shadows. You know it's there but you don't know what it's going to do. Or if it's scared or angry. You hope scared, but you sort of know it won't make any difference if it decides to attack.

Johnson grabs GG. 'Stop the train. They've got the Moth.'

'What?' GG wails.

'Do it, GG, now!'

GG glances out of the smashed window and sees the remaining Moth Twos racing back into suburbia. One of them has our Moth but they are already fast disappearing into the distance.

I put a hand on GG's shoulder. 'GG, you have to stop the train,' I say quietly.

'We can go back and get him,' Johnson adds.

I have no idea if we can or not but that's not going to stop us at least trying.

If my dad doesn't ever wake, the Moth's our only ticket home. I don't tell anyone that but GG breaks from his panic and heads quickly down the aisle.

'Must save the Moth, must save him,' he repeats over and over.

Non-Ape emerges from the driver's compartment as GG squeezes past him. 'Coming through.'

GG notices the cuts to Non-Ape's skin and can't believe it. 'You got hurt.'

Non-Ape looks down, frowns, then shrugs. 'That's nothing.'

The train ploughs onwards, unrelenting. Wind whips in through the windows and the open door.

GG is in the driver's compartment now, but there is no sense that we are slowing down.

The Johnsons sense it as well. Billie is still hiding under the table and maybe she'll stay there for ever. Half of me wants to join her because I can't believe we've lost the Moth.

'GG!' Johnson and Other-Johnson yell at the exact same time. There is no reply from the driver's compartment and I'm already moving for it, Johnson one step behind.

'GG?' we call.

I quicken my pace, fighting the bone-rattling speed of the train as it shakes from side to side. 'GG!'

GG finally appears, standing in the doorway to the driver's compartment. He looks deathly pale and for a second I think he's been stabbed by a Moth Two who got left behind.

But it's far worse than that.

'Brakes, GG, use the brakes. What are you waiting for?' Johnson urges. 'We need to get the Moth.'

GG looks shrunken and cowed as he steps to one side to reveal crushed and twisted controls. All of them are beyond repair thanks to the fight with the Moth Twos.

'Sorry but it's all wrecked in there.' GG's voice is faint, barely audible. 'This train is a straight-through non-stopper.'

BULLET TRAIN

London is probably less than ten minutes away. King's Cross lies in wait. We are doing over ninety miles an hour and impact is imminent.

'Could jump.' The Ape is at the door he opened with the emergency switch and stares at the ground as it rushes past.

'Some of us could,' I respond, thinking of Johnson and Non-Ape.

'Some is better than none,' GG adds.

'Isn't this where you usually do your swap?' Johnson asks Other-Johnson. 'When you think you're about to die?'

Other-Johnson seems keen to make up for leaving Johnson under a collapsing hotel. 'Not me, but if you want to abandon us and get free, don't worry. I'll take my chances.' He glances my way and I know he is trying to prove something to me. Or have me all to himself – at least for the limited time left before impact.

Johnson heads down the carriage and opens the connecting door to the second carriage that trails behind us.

'GG,' he calls. 'How do you uncouple this?'

GG follows him. 'You can't. Not at this speed.'

'There's got to be a way. C'mon, think.'

GG takes a moment, pinching his thumb and forefingers together like someone in a t'ai chi class.

'Let me centre myself.' He closes his eyes and breathes out. 'Let GG see the rabbit.'

'C'mon.'

GG's eyes spring open. 'OK. The carriages are coupled using a hook and links with a turnbuckle. It's called a screw coupling. If we can reach that, we might have a chance.'

'Let's do it!'

'Teeny prob. The coupling is on the outside. Sort of under the connecting doors.'

'I can get out there.'

The train is going so fast it's rocking from side to side, and I can't see Johnson being able to hang on and even if he did would it work? Would the second carriage slow in time? What's to stop it?

'How long have we got till we hit the station?' Other Johnson asks.

'You'd need the Moth to work that out,' GG replies. 'His little space brain would do it in nanoseconds. I'd still be on one plus one when we smacked into the platform.'

Other-Johnson sees Non-Ape rest his bloodied bulk on a table.

'Forget the coupling, Ape could drag the carriages apart.'

I look at Non-Ape. He must have been bitten and stabbed a thousand times over and he looks disoriented. And worse. He looks weak.

'He's out of it,' I say.

Non-Ape hears me and gets to his feet. 'Not me.' But as soon as he stands, he staggers and he has to sit back down

223

again. Black blood is pooling at his feet. I'm worried that even if we get out of this he might be too weak to move the rubble. Everything is going spectacularly wrong.

'You know how to uncouple the train, don't you, GG?' Johnson's taking command now.

'I think so.'

'Then climb on my back.'

GG pretends to go weak at the knees. 'Johnson, I thought you'd never ask.'

'We're going out there,' Johnson explains.

Billie has climbed back into her seat but she looks horrified.

'You can't do that,' she tells Johnson. 'You'll both be killed.'

'I can use the talons like the Moth Twos did.' Johnson unsheathes his claws. 'I'll hang on to the train and GG'll hang on to me.'

'Can we get engaged after?' GG asks.

'I've already got a ring in mind,' Johnson responds and I get a glimpse of the old Johnson. The one who promised me we'd get home. He must sense that I'm looking at him because he turns to me and gives me the Johnson salute.

'All aboard,' Johnson quips. 'The rest of you get into the rear carriage,' he instructs. Non-Ape is the last one to cross through the tiny connecting doors and it takes whatever strength he has left. The Ape helps him to a seat as I watch Johnson squat so that GG can climb onto his back.

GG squeals. 'Be gentle with me.'

'Johnson, please don't go out there,' Billie pleads. There's an exhaustion to her that I don't understand. She did nothing but hide during the fight.

'Got no choice, Billie. We'll all die if we don't do something.' Johnson easily hefts the lightweight GG.

There's no time for last-minute declarations or soliloquies but a look passes between us and I know that Johnson has shaken off all residue of the fake five months and is back to who he was.

I sense Other-Johnson watching me, taking it all in and storing it away. He made clear his intention to be with me at any cost and I wonder if he is thinking that by remaining in the human body it'll make me like him more.

'*Maybe,*' he says in my head.

'*If you want to impress me, then stay out of my mind,*' I tell him. '*Don't do what I'm thinking, do what you're thinking. At least make it natural.*'

'*You only had to ask.*'

He breaks the connection.

I snapped at Other-Johnson. I don't think I'm quite the same person any more either.

'Let's get lucky,' Johnson declares, then with GG clinging on for dear life, he opens the rear carriage doors and climbs out.

'Eeek!' GG offers shrilly.

Johnson jams his talons into the side of the train carriage and inches along the coach. I can see the tips of his talons penetrating the steel bodywork but it is slow going. I have no idea how GG is hanging on when the onrushing wind must be buffeting him so hard.

I can't help myself and get the Ape to hold my hand so I can lean out of the open doors and watch. 'Don't let go.'

'Of what?'

Which is when he does let go, and for a split second I am tipping head first out of the train until he grabs my hand again and laughs. 'Gotcha!'

One day I will hit the Ape so hard.

The roaring wind thuds into my face and I have to bow my head and try to suck air in through tightened lips. Johnson is edging along the train, one talon at a time, while GG half chokes him, his legs and torso nearly prised from Johnson's back by the violent wind.

'You're choking me,' Johnson squawks.

GG changes his grip. 'But what a way to go.'

Johnson glances back down the train and sees me watching him. I don't know if it helps but he redoubles his efforts and climbs steadily along to the end of the carriage.

They are near the coupling as we flash through Finsbury Park station. That's usually a five-minute journey to King's Cross but at this speed it's probably half that.

'You need to go quicker!' I call out. As if that's a help to anyone.

The hurricane wind nearly tears my hair out at the roots and GG is losing his battle to stay with Johnson.

'I can't do it, Johnson. I can't hang on.'

GG's fingers slip and slide, numb from the strain of clinging on.

'We're there,' Johnson shouts to him. 'What now?'

'Johnson!' One of GG's hands is wrenched free of Johnson.

'GG, show me the coupling!'

'OK, OK—' GG's other hand is torn free from Johnson.

'GG!' I scream.

Johnson moves like lightning to catch him. He grabs GG's wrist. 'Whoa!'

Johnson has saved GG but they're totally stuck now. Johnson, with one hand holding GG while the other hand's talons are dug deep into the side of the train, can't move without letting GG go.

'Oh God. This was not a good plan,' I whisper.

'What is it?' Other-Johnson tries to lean out to see but the wind buffets him back.

The Ape has both hands on my wrist now and I can feel my shoulder socket starting to pop, so who knows what agony GG is enduring as the ferocious wind tries to tear him from Johnson's grasp.

Johnson doesn't know what to do.

'GG!' he yells. 'Any ideas would be good!'

'You're going to have to let me go!' GG calls out.

'Apart from that one!'

'Pull me in,' I order the Ape, who does so with a yank that makes my eyes water. I march through the ferociously rocking carriage towards Non-Ape. 'Get up.'

Non-Ape tries to get to his feet but as soon as he does he sinks back down again.

I grab him and try and pull him upright. 'We need you.'

'I'm trying.'

Even his deep rumbling voice is weak.

Other-Johnson tries to take control of Non-Ape. 'Let me in, let me see if I can move you.'

Non-Ape has no idea what Other-Johnson is talking about.

'Let me in!' Other-Johnson shouts.

I'd forgotten that Other-Johnson said it was almost impossible to get inside Non-Ape's mind.

'Can you do it?' I beg him.

'Open your mind, Ape, don't resist me.'

Non-Ape blinks his heavy eyelids and nods. 'Whatever,' he mumbles.

Other-Johnson focuses as hard as he can. 'It's like trying to cut into a bank vault with a penknife.'

I stagger back to the open door. 'Hold my hand again,' I tell the Ape and lean out.

But time is running out.

'Hold on!' I yell. 'We're going to help you!'

GG is being thrown around like a kite in a hurricane. Johnson is holding on as best he can but I can see his metal talons are starting to slide free of their mooring.

'Whatever you're going to do, Rev, do it now,' he calls back to me.

'There's no time,' GG calls, as his legs flail around in the wind like a crazed puppet. 'You're going to have to let me go!'

Johnson's talons are working loose. The relentless rattling of the train is shaking them free. 'Not your best joke, GG.'

'Let me go and then slice through the coupling; you'll have to try and just cut the thing apart.'

I look back into the carriage. Other-Johnson, nose bleeding now, has managed to get Non-Ape to his feet.

Billie watches but I'm not sure she is too aware of what is happening. She has zoned out again and looks weak and ill.

'What's the plan?' Other-Johnson calls to me.

'Get him to the connecting door and tell him to tear the carriages apart,' I say.

Other-Johnson mentally heaves and Non-Ape is turned towards the connecting carriage doors.

I look back outside but we're surely too close to King's Cross now. Johnson and GG are trapped in their ugly wind-thrashed tableau.

'Johnson!' I shout.

GG is starting to slip free of his grip.

'Johnson, hold on!'

'Move it!' I hear the Ape shout at Non-Ape; even he understands we've only got seconds to save GG.

'Listen to me, Johnson,' GG yells. 'You've got to let me go.'

'No way.'

GG knows it's the only answer. 'Johnson, we're out of time.'

'*Hurry!!*' I scream through the airwaves. But Other-Johnson's so busy struggling to move Non-Ape he can't hear me.

'Do this for little GG,' GG tells Johnson.

No.

Don't.

You can't do this.

'Time's up, Johnson.' GG starts twisting to get free of Johnson's grip.

Tears are filling my eyes.

'I'm light, I'll float.' GG is adamant. 'I will, I'll just float away.'

'Rev – update!' Johnson calls to me, desperation in his voice. He's going to be rattled free of the train any second.

'We can't lose both of us,' GG says.

And with that GG twists mightily and slips from Johnson's grip. He flies free, bangs into the end of the carriage and then he's gone, spinning through the skies before a bend in the track takes him out of sight.

THERE'S NO GG IN GOODBYE

There is no scream or panicked yell from GG; there is just the roaring wind and the beginnings of emptiness.

I look back at the Ape and can't speak. He pulls me back into the carriage. I can't look at him. I can't meet his eyes.

Other-Johnson, nose pouring blood, breaks his grip on Non-Ape, leaving him to crash to the floor, and kicks open the connecting door between the carriages.

'Can you do what GG said? Cut through the coupling?' he yells at the frozen and shocked Johnson. 'Hey! Johnson! Don't waste what GG just did.'

Johnson gathers himself and drives one set of talons into the carriage and with the other set he reaches for the coupling and slices with all his might, over and over. He uses every ounce of alien strength and speed that he possesses. But more than that he uses his absolute and total grief at what just happened. We hit the outskirts of King's Cross when the carriage comes free.

Johnson has to leap back towards us because already the momentum of the second carriage is slowing. He almost doesn't make it because he's leaping against the momentum but Other-Johnson shoots out an arm and catches him. For a second Johnson is between the carriages with only Other-Johnson holding him. I know that in that second Other-Johnson debates letting Johnson go. It would be so easy to do. Wiping out his rival.

But he hauls him inside as the first carriage roars onwards, less than half a mile from the suburban platforms. It rockets forward, creating an ever-increasing distance between us. Other-Johnson gets a thanks from Johnson but there's little any of us can say.

All we can do is wait and hope we slow in time.

The Moth has gone.

GG has gone.

I can't believe we've lost both of them.

'Rev,' the Ape says finally.

I go to him as an almighty collision between the fast-moving train and a stationary platform happens some way down the track. There's a seismic boom and I swear I can hear metal crying as it concertinas and compacts before the first carriage ends its journey mashed into the concrete and earth that used to be platform nine.

Our carriage keeps slowing – the momentum is dying – and I have my head on the Ape's shoulder and I feel his clumsy hand cup the back of my head. Tears shake from me in great heaving sobs but the Ape stands tall, allowing me to dissolve into him.

I can feel his mighty heartbeat and it slows over the minute or so it takes for the carriage to decelerate enough for Other-Johnson to get control of Non-Ape again and force him to leap out onto the adjacent rail tracks.

We're still going too fast and a dreadful impact is imminent until Non-Ape grabs hold of the train and starts dragging it back. But the momentum of the train is too much for him and as he digs his great feet into the tracks the train pulls him along.

Other-Johnson grits his teeth and redoubles his mental control over Non-Ape. 'C'mon big man, c'mon.'

It's not going to be enough; we're going to crash into what's left of the first carriage.

Johnson pushes me into a seat and then climbs into the seat beside me. He grabs me and pulls me into him, ready to protect me as best he can. 'Brace yourselves.'

The Ape sees him do this and tries to do the same with the catatonic Billie, pulling her head under his sweat-drenched armpit.

Other-Johnson screams with one last monumental effort and ignites the last remaining residue of power in Non-Ape's limbs as he is dragged alongside the train. Non-Ape responds and bringing all of his prodigious strength to bear he begins to slow the carriage. A gouged trail ripples along the track in Non-Ape's wake as he heaves and strains and begins to overpower the carriage. The momentum is bleeding away and Non-Ape roars to the heavens as he wrestles the carriage to a skidding, skewing halt. He can't stop it thudding into what's left of the front carriage and we are thrown back and forth but Non-Ape does it, he stops the train.

Other-Johnson lets go of Non-Ape and collapses to his knees, coughing blood, while outside Non-Ape staggers and reels before slamming into the wall that runs under the platform. He sinks down to his haunches and sits there, completely dazed.

Johnson rocks gently with the motion of the impact and I rock with him until we finally stop for good.

I look up and find the Ape staring dully at me.

'No homo?' he says gently.

'No,' I say quietly. 'No homo.'

Quiz question:

Eight teenagers boarded a train. The train doesn't stop at any station until it reaches its destination but only six teenagers disembarked.

Please explain how that happened. You may confer.

The Ape is standing on platform nine, staring back down the track we just came down. He looks tired and he winces every now and then from the pain in his long-ago battered ribs. But nothing hurts like the loss of GG.

He has been standing there for over five minutes, as if willing GG to come skipping down the track.

Non-Ape is lying flat out on the concourse, wracked by exhaustion and somehow looking smaller. Other-Johnson, a tissue wedged into his bleeding nose, has opened the Starbucks coffee kiosk and is gathering as much food into his arms as he can. He takes it to Non-Ape.

'*Can you hear GG?*' I transmit to him.

'*Not one camp quip,*' Other-Johnson tells me but his voice is leaden.

'*Keep scanning for him.*'

'*I'm trying, Rev. I'm trying the Moth too, but there's nothing. There's just silence.*'

I am sitting under one of two giant arrivals and departures boards, near the cashpoint machines. Johnson is seated beside me and he is as numb as I am.

Other-Johnson reaches Non-Ape, his arms crammed full of food. 'Sit up,' he tells Non-Ape.

Non-Ape is almost too weak to breathe.

'C'mon, Dazza. I got crisps.'

Non-Ape takes an eternity to pull himself to a sitting position. But as soon as he sets eyes on the pile of food Other-Johnson has brought him he manages a big wide grin.

'Fill me,' he says and opens his great mouth.

Other-Johnson starts feeding him: a father with a very hungry and very huge baby.

Billie hasn't spoken since we disembarked. I think she feels ashamed at hiding from the Moth Two onslaught but there is no shame in not wanting to be eviscerated. She makes her way to the circular open-air information kiosk and slides into one of the fake-leather swivel chairs. She lays her head in her arms and I watch her shoulders shake as she weeps gently.

I drag myself over to her. 'Billie?'

'This is getting worse and worse, Rev.'

Seeing her cry makes me want to cry and I take some deep breaths as I try and hold it together.

'I didn't think GG would do that.'

'He's braver than any of us realise.'

'Was braver, Rev. Was. Isn't any more.'

Billie buries her face again and her shoulders shake as she

weeps for GG. 'Why did he do that?' she manages to ask between sobs. 'Why?'

'He did it for us, and we have to repay that by . . .'

'Going home? That's all you ever say. Over and over. We're going home. Well, that's going to be fun, finding our way back just so we can tell his parents – who love him to bits – that their son didn't make it.'

GG is adored by his family and I have to turn away because I don't think I can face this.

'We need to run, Rev, or we're all going to die.'

'We can't run. No one else knows how to drive a train. And the Moth needs us. He's still alive.'

'You think? Honestly?' Billie's sobs stop as she looks back up at me. I can feel her eyes boring into the back of my head. 'Your plan isn't working.'

I bow my head a little.

'I hate to be the one to tell you, Rev, but speaking as your friend, maybe someone else should take over.'

I turn back and Billie's eyes are small and puffy from crying.

'I'm trying my best,' I tell her quietly.

'I know you are. But it hasn't helped a bit.'

Billie is completely right when she says this. My best has been what it's always been: useless. I'm not that bright in school, I'm not in any top sets, I can't sing, I can't dance, I don't have a talent for anything, so who the hell did I think I was trying to lead us?

I'm so sorry, GG.

Moth, the same goes to you.

I'm sorry I screwed up.

Billie stares hard at me but she's said all she needed to and

236

we stay that way for a good minute or so. It takes a good friend to tell you who you really are.

Non-Ape didn't really get what we were going through but after stopping the train, then eventually getting to his feet and clomping slowly down the track, he did start to lose it when Billie wouldn't heal his wounds.

'I can't do it,' she told him.

'I need it.'

'I'm too . . . I'm just . . . No. OK? No.'

Non-Ape looked more hurt in that moment than at any other time. I could imagine his dinosaur brain trying to understand and then cope with what must have seemed like a terrible rejection. He really likes Billie and after the savage attack by the Moth Twos, he wanted someone to reach out to him.

He saved all of us and we can't give him anything in return.

The Ape turns and looks back down the huge concourse towards us. 'I'm going to get them,' he calls out.

Johnson is already easing himself to his feet. 'Wait.'

'I found you. I can find anyone. I'm a great tracker.'

The Ape starts heading down the platform, going back in the direction of GG and all the Moths.

'Dazza,' Johnson calls out.

But the Ape is marching forth, not about to turn back.

Johnson joins me at the information kiosk and offers his hand. 'I can piggyback you.'

I feel myself lifted easily, and when Johnson spins me onto his back I see stars from the speed he moves me. I slip my arms round his shoulders as he slides his arms under my thighs, holding me tight.

'I haven't done this since … since for ever,' I tell him.

'Hold tight.'

Johnson starts marching after the Ape. 'Dazza! Wait up.'

As he calls out I spot Other-Johnson stopping mid-feed. He doesn't need to be a telepath to tell me what he's thinking. He doesn't like the sight of me being carried by Johnson.

Johnson can't help but rub it in. 'Should've swapped,' he tells him.

But I know Other-Johnson wants to be human so that he can come back with me. He's willing to sacrifice his entire life and world for me, and there's not many boys who would do that.

'*We'll be back, so don't move from here,*' I tell him telepathically. But he doesn't respond. He just watches.

Johnson's easy smooth gait coupled with the loose steel in his sinews makes me feel like I'm gliding. We're closing on the Ape already.

'Fill me!' Non-Ape grabs Other-Johnson's hand and pulls even more food into his huge gullet.

The Ape is powering onwards, as determined as ever, and it takes at least a minute for us to draw alongside him.

'It's got to be about four or five miles,' Johnson tells him.

'I'm a great tracker.'

The Ape ploughs on and as I ride piggyback on Johnson he reaches up and pats one of my hands.

'We'll find them, Rev,' he promises.

His hand stays on mine and without realising I feel my fingers lace with his and I'm so glad I've got him to hold on to.

THE TRACKS OF OUR TEARS

Mum and I had a dog once. Rufus. A hairy ginger hound who kept running away. But when I eventually got him back on the lead and walked him home it was usually miles from home. Based on that experience I reckon I can walk two miles in an hour. The Ape is moving quicker than that and super-powered Johnson easily keeps up with him. I need to make him let me go because even with his new strength I'm soon going to weigh him down. After an hour we have probably managed three miles. Pretty close to the spot we lost GG.

Every step has been in silence.

I have no idea what's going on in the Ape's head but for the first time since we were transported here he looks sad. His eyes are smaller and every now and then he sucks in a deep breath. I don't think he's talking because he's worried we might hear the sad choke in his voice.

Johnson breaks the silence. 'GG could have floated . . .' But his voice trails off. He takes a moment and tries again. 'It's that sort of world. Crazy things happen.'

But not good crazy, I think. This is a world that kills.

239

'I didn't see him land.' Johnson talks quietly. 'Could be stuck halfway up a tree. He'd hate that. It'd mess up his hair.'

The Ape thrusts his hands deep into his big black coat pockets. He's scanning the area, desperate for any sign of GG or the Moth.

We keep walking, hoping for a sign – any sign – of either of our friends.

'I should've known, Rev,' Johnson tells me quietly.

'Known what?'

'The five months. Should've sensed it wasn't real.'

'It wasn't your fault. Someone was playing mind games with you.'

'But me and Billie? Seriously? She's great and that, but how come I didn't know any better?'

'You weren't allowed to.'

He squeezes my hand. 'It's lucky we had the other Johnson to put us right.'

Mentioning Other-Johnson isn't an accident. Johnson knows what he is doing.

'Listen, about him,' I start, but the Ape comes to a sudden stop and Johnson almost walks into him.

He's quicker now and sidesteps him easily. 'What is it?' Johnson asks.

I'm waiting for my shoulders to start screaming danger but there's nothing.

The Ape scans the world. Suburbia to one side, a field that usually has horses in it on the other.

'It was here.'

The track and everything around it is silent and empty.

'He fell here.'

'You sure?' Johnson asks.

The Ape points a thick finger towards a lone shoe lying on the track about twenty-five metres away. Even from here I can tell that it's one of GG's and the sight of it lying there, alone and abandoned, brings a sudden rush of tears that I can't hold back.

Johnson stays silent for a moment but I can hear the Ape crunching along the track, his big heavy shoes scraping through the grey shale scattered between the sleepers.

'He might be OK.' Johnson speaks as if his voice is trapped way back in his throat.

I talk through my tears. 'GG would never be seen with only one shoe,' I blubber. 'Can you imagine the shame?'

Johnson takes a moment to bring his sadness and shock under control.

'I never spoke to him before at school. You know, before detention.'

'No?'

'Not really. Wish I had.'

In truth, apart from Billie, I didn't really know the others. I knew of them of course, but they weren't in my circle. I certainly wasn't in the Ape's. In fact, I don't actually know who was in his circle, maybe his scrawny pal Del, but apart from that none of us had any connection before this.

'He was the best,' the Ape says quietly.

And never in a million worlds would any Ape have ever said that about any GG. Which shows how far we've come and how much we've changed. Johnson knows it too because at one time he was the coolest of the cool who lived by his own code and did things his way. A lone wolf who has found out that he doesn't mind company after all.

I blink my eyes a few times, then wipe them with the back of my free hand.

The Ape has picked up GG's shoe and is staring at it. I know he won't cry but standing there gripping that shoe in his lion-sized paw says everything. He quietly flattens the shoe as best he can and slips it into one of his coat pockets.

He then starts along the track heading away from us.

'Oh, no,' I whisper.

Johnson tenses. 'He's going after them. He's going after the evil Moths.'

Johnson sets off again, covering the ground between us and the Ape with stunning ease. I run after them as fast as I can.

Johnson overtakes the Ape and gets in front of him, facing him down. 'There's too many of them,' he tells him.

But the Ape keeps walking.

'Dazza.' Johnson tries again. 'There were loads of Moth Twos.'

'Still isn't enough. Got to get our Moth back,' the Ape says boldly before brushing past us.

Johnson spins and races past the Ape to get in front of him again and puts a hand out to warn him to stop. 'We don't want to lose you too.'

'You won't.'

The Ape walks straight past Johnson who spins again and this time tries to leap over the Ape, but pitches forward as he lands before regaining his balance. He's still not used to what he has become and could have probably done with a real five months to come to terms with what he can do now.

Johnson is more adamant as the Ape approaches. 'GG did what he did so we could escape.'

The Ape marches straight past him.

Johnson isn't sure what to do next. He half turns to me and I glimpse his strong profile. 'Rev.'

I know the Ape will go to war. I know he will somehow find the Moth Twos and I know he will take them all on.

'Stop him.'

Johnson accelerates and races past the Ape. 'We need to find the papers first,' he tells him.

'What papers?'

I knew he wasn't listening when I outlined my plan. I hurry to catch up.

'I want to find the Moth as well but we need the other Johnson to do that and right now he can't find him with his mind thing.'

'What mind thing?'

'He's a telepath. You know, can speak to people in his head.'

'And I'm a great tracker.'

The Ape is on a mission. He is thunderously angry and his rage is emanating from him like a hot shimmer on a road.

'We need you,' I tell the Ape.

But he keeps on walking.

'*I* need you,' I add, hoping to reach him on another level.

He ploughs on.

Johnson leaps through the air and lands in front of the Ape.

'We'll come back as soon as Other-Johnson has located where the Moth is. I swear to you,' I tell the Ape.

We have to keep backing up because the Ape won't stop.

Johnson tries again. 'Daz, you've got to think straight.'

Which is the Ape's big problem. He only thinks one thought at a time and goes straight for it.

'They took the Moth for a reason, and that makes me think they need him alive. So we'll find him. All of us. But for now, I promise you, he's safe,' I explain to the Ape.

I'm backing up so fast now that I trip on the edge of a

sleeper and crash onto my backside. But the Ape barely glances at me as he walks straight past. At any other time he would have stopped to help me.

Johnson helps me to my feet and then speeds up to the Ape and grabs his shoulder. 'Don't make me do this.'

The Ape turns with indecent speed and punches Johnson straight in the gut. Even in his new body Johnson doubles over as the breath escapes from him.

The Ape turns and heads down the track again. I scramble towards Johnson as he straightens and rubs his belly. 'Think I got through to him,' he jokes.

I have no option but to sprint after the Ape. My body is cut and bruised and my muscles would prefer that I didn't use them for the next month but I pound after the Ape and leap onto his great back. 'For chrissakes!'

The Ape staggers forward under my momentum but then rights himself. And keeps on walking.

'You can't bring him back,' I wail and realise I'm crying again. 'Even if you find GG he will not – he just won't be . . . He won't. He's not coming back.'

The Ape begins to slow.

'I want him to be stuck in a tree or a hedge, just like you do. I want that so much but what are the chances?'

The Ape finally stops.

I'm clinging on to him, just like I clung on to Johnson and I'm sniffling and snuffling and shuddering from the horrible bleakness.

'He's gone,' I croak. 'He's gone.'

The Ape stands stock-still.

'I was hoping. I was. I was praying and praying. But his shoe . . . His outrageous shoe that no one else would ever wear . . .' My words are escaping between great sobs. 'I would give anything not to have seen that shoe.'

I slide from the Ape's back but keep my arms wrapped round him as best I can.

Johnson walks quietly up to us, wary of breaking the moment.

The Ape's breathing starts to calm but he won't turn and look at me.

'The Moth?' he asks quietly.

'We'll think of something.'

The Ape lets out a long slow breath and scans the world around us, hoping for a sign of GG.

'So where's G-Man? If he's dead where is he?'

The Ape's alarmingly straightforward logic cuts to the heart of everything.

And he's right. Apart from the shoe there's no sign of GG.

'Dead don't walk,' the Ape says simply.

Johnson scans the area. It is totally silent and nothing moves apart from the breeze whispering through the leaves.

This world is very good at giving you a sliver of hope and then snatching it all away again. It loves to tease. And torment.

'If he's OK he would have headed down the track, wouldn't he? We'd have met him,' I say quietly, wishing I was wrong.

Johnson stares at the trees, hoping to find a sign that GG was swept up onto a branch.

But there's nothing.

The Ape slips his hand into his coat pocket and squeezes GG's shoe.

Could the Moth Twos could have found GG and taken him away?

Would they do that?

Or has GG been thrown somewhere we'll never find him? Neither option is a good one.

The Ape unzips his jeans and lets a torrent of urine hit the track. He has his back to us but we can clearly see the spray as he directs it in an arc across the track.

After he finishes and zips up he turns to us. 'I was here,' he announces, but I have no idea what he's doing. Maybe even he's been tipped over the edge.

Johnson whispers in my ear. 'I think he's marking his territory.'

The Ape roars suddenly. 'I! WAS! HERE!!'

His bellow echoes across the emptiness. A defiant war cry, a call to arms and battle.

It sends a quiet chill down my spine as he glares at whatever he thinks is out there. Challenging them to come for him. Daring them.

And I know they will come. I know it just like Johnson and the Ape know it.

I don't know why they took the Moth or why they tried to bring Non-Ape down but they've played their hand and revealed something I'm only just starting to grasp.

The two people who can help us go home are Non-Ape and the Moth.

Non-Ape can unearth the papers.

The Moth can read them.

Someone really doesn't want us to go home. Someone with incredible powers but who still fears us finding what we need.

Well, whoever they are, you're going to have to try a lot harder.

GG, probably lying broken and battered somewhere in the

miles between here and King's Cross, gave his life to give us a chance.

But he has also given us something more than that.

He has given us anger. And if this person – thing, world, whatever! – wants a fight then they've got one. GG would be spinning in his leopard-print coffin if he thought he'd floated away for no reason.

CROSS OF KINGS

Non-Ape has eaten everything.

There is literally nothing left in any of the kiosks or delis or fast-food outlets. He is back on his feet and all of his wounds are already beginning to self-repair. Seeing him looking better is the only positive thing in the past few hours.

With him there's still a chance to find the papers.

The cuts that penetrated his hide – I can't think of it as skin – are starting to disappear, or rather new hide, I suppose, is forming over them. He looks bigger now and like any teenage boy all he really needs to do to be happy is eat and eat and eat.

And then fart.

We reach the concourse in time for the noxious gas to hit. I've got my mouth open because I'm panting from the long walk back and I accidentally suck it down into my lungs.

And immediately retch. 'Good God.'

Non-Ape farts again and it's a borderline sonic boom.

'Ape!?' Other-Johnson waves the stench away as Non-Ape laughs.

'Breathe that!'

The Ape lurches from his silent mourning and leans his head forward, breathing in as much of the disgusting smell as his lungs can hold.

He exhales. 'Channel number five!'

Non-Ape laughs in return. 'Number five from a number two!'

They seem to have an instinctive repartee that only they understand.

Non-Ape farts again. 'Bombing the coast!'

The Ape responds. 'Coast is toast.'

I briefly wonder if they have the same gassy scent. Would that happen? If you're a complete double, then I think it's got to be more than likely.

The farts at least seem to have roused the Ape a little and pulled him out of the painful reality he has been enduring.

On the way back we have made a pact, a solemn promise, to find both GG and the Moth. We are going home with them, make no mistake.

Other-Johnson is pleased to see us. Or me at least. 'Any luck?' Then: 'Sorry. Stupid question.'

'We couldn't find either of them.'

'So what now?'

'We carry on,' Johnson says.

'Any idea where that hotel is? Was.'

GG had texted me the name a few days ago but my phone is still not working. I rescued it after hurling it into the snow, but it's still useless. If it was working I'd be able to read the text and this would run as smooth as smooth. But nothing seems to happen like that in this world.

'London,' I reply.

'That narrows it down.'

The black cab the Ape drove all the way to the ticket barriers when we were last here has been tipped on its side and flattened by the crashed train.

'We'll need a car,' he says.

'Bigger than a car. Non-Ape has eaten so much he won't fit in one.'

There is no one to make any outrageous or inappropriate GG-style jokes when Johnson returns from one of the clothes shops that make up part of the small shopping area set off from the main concourse.

'We should get changed.'

We are still covered in the splatter of drying black blood and he has found an American-style outlet. His taste isn't as exquisite as GG's but there are showers in the toilets on the mezzanine and after using one and then drying myself I pull on jeans and a white T-shirt. I emerge from the toilets to find that everyone is wearing jeans and white T-shirts apart from Non-Ape who will have to find an extra-large-man shop somewhere. His clothes are cut to ribbons and hang off him. The rest of us look like we've walked out of a fifties rock 'n' roll musical.

I can't fault Johnson for grabbing whatever he could find but it makes me think of GG even more acutely and again I have to suck it up and keep it together.

When I emerge there is no sign of Billie.

'Anyone see where she went?'

The Apes and the Johnsons look at one another but have no answers.

'Can you scan the airwaves?' I ask Other-Johnson.

He does so and looks momentarily confused.

'What?'

'I can't scan anyone.'

After pouring every ounce into harnessing Non-Ape, Other-Johnson's mental powers have faded alarmingly, which could mean he won't be able to switch back, even if he wants to. Johnson will hate this but if Other-Johnson has a plan then it's all working out beautifully. He's going to make it impossible for Johnson to belong in my world.

'Give me a moment.' He takes a few silent breaths and tries to focus.

I wait. But I also wonder, *Is he faking this?*

'Anything?' Johnson asks.

'Sorry.' Other-Johnson's sigh seems forced. Or maybe he's just exhausted like the rest of us.

'Doesn't matter.' I suddenly know where she'll be. 'Dazza?'

'Yeah?' They both answer but it's my Ape I want. 'Fancy a walk?'

'Just been on one.'

'It's not far. Just across to St Pancras.'

Non-Ape straightens. 'I'll come.'

'If he's going, I'm going,' the Ape responds.

'If you're going, I'm going,' Non-Ape responds.

'You already were going,' I tell him.

'So I'm going too,' Non-Ape replies.

'I'm not getting left out,' the Ape says.

'You never were,' I tell him.

'How come I was getting dumped?' Non-Ape asks.

God, please help me. I have no idea how to hold a conversation when they get like this.

'No one's dumping anyone.'

Non-Ape pouts. 'No?'

'Did I say that?' My voice turns into a taut frustrated whine

251

and I catch Johnson grinning to himself. It's the tiniest light amid the grief and tragedy.

'Did you?' Non-Ape asks.

'Listen! All I want to do is go to the Eurostar terminal. It's not a trip to Disneyland.'

'So who's going on that?' the Ape asks.

Johnson slips a hand over his mouth to stop himself from laughing.

I'm standing there between the human equivalent of a hill and a mountain, dwarfed by them.

'I want to go on that trip,' Non-Ape declares.

'If he's going, I'm going,' the Ape declares.

I try and spell it out as simply as I can to them. 'We're just walking across the street to another train station. I didn't want to go alone.'

'Never been to Disneyland,' Non-Ape says. 'So going to punch that big mouse.'

'Forget it, I'll go on my own,' I mutter, hiding my face in my hands.

'So you don't want me?' the Ape says.

'Yes! Yes I do!'

'What about me?' Non-Ape looks hurt.

Johnson has to turn away he is laughing so hard now. Other-Johnson has wandered away as he tries to come to terms with the loss of his telepathic powers. He looks bereft, or at least pretends to, but that's the price you pay for wanting to be a measly human.

'Let's just go.'

'Where?' Non-Ape asks.

I wave my hand in a big open gesture. It encapsulates half the entire world as far as I'm concerned. 'Anywhere!' I snap.

'Just had to say,' Non-Ape says.

'Moo-dy,' the Ape adds.

'Why would Billie be at St Pancras?' Johnson asks.

'Because she wants to escape. While we're getting her, can you find us a street map, or something that lists all the hotels in London. We might recognise the name.'

Johnson gives his lazy salute, but this time he uses a talon to do it, and it doesn't quite work or look as cool as it did before. He did it almost too naturally. I'm scared he's changing from the boy he used to be.

The Apes and I emerge into an empty street that is usually heaving with traffic and people. Commuters and holidaymakers are either jumping in and out of black cabs or dragging tons of luggage while they try to shepherd their families.

I've never been to this station because I've never been to Europe; in fact, I've never been out of England. Mum isn't much of a traveller and gets nervous at the thought of aeroplanes. I used to beg her to at least get on a ferry to France or let me go on a school trip but the reality was she couldn't afford it. Besides, she'd worry horribly if I were in a place she couldn't come and rescue me from. She is a professional worrier and I can only imagine the state she would be in if she could see what I'm going through right now.

I remember my non-mum finding the power to bring a town to a stop. It's the same strength my real mum possesses when she thinks she has to fight for me. They are both lost in their worlds, almost invisible as they crouch and cower from their lot in life, but put their daughter in danger and they'll bring hell with them if they have to. They have passed that on to me and Rev Two, and I will bring more than hell if it means getting what I want.

The Apes flank me as we climb the steps to the entrance to St Pancras. The shopping area is completely deserted but I check the signs and the Eurostar platforms are only a few metres to our right.

There is no sign of Billie but I quicken my pace and reach the sleek automatic barriers that prevent access to the platforms.

I jump up and climb in the least ungainly way possible over the nearest ticket barrier. The pathway to the trains looms ahead of us as I hear Non-Ape wrench the barrier out of his way. 'Tickets please!' he yells, laughing.

The Ape copies him. 'Tickets!'

'TIIICCKKKKKEEEETS!!' Non-Ape bellows even louder.

His voice echoes around the station as a lone Eurostar train waits patiently on platform one. It's a long bullet of a train composed of carriages that all but disappear into the distance.

I still can't see Billie but I'm sure she's around somewhere.

'TIIICCKKKKKKETTTTTS!' Non-Ape bellows again and my ears ring.

'All right, I get the joke. I got it the first time.'

'Double moo-dy,' Non-Ape mumbles.

'Such a girl,' the Ape whispers to him.

'Yeah, a real girl,' Non-Ape whispers back. Only their idea of whispering is not whispering at all because I can hear everything they say.

I raise a hand and press the ENTRY button on the first carriage. The door hisses with a sigh and then unfolds and opens wide, revealing a carriage that is much bigger than I was expecting. It's first class and there are plush seats and tables with crockery and cutlery set out on them.

I can feel my shoulders tingle.

The world is playing with me again.

The obvious thing would be for me to climb aboard the train and for it to miraculously start up and kidnap me all the way to another country, where I'd be stuck for good. Only I wouldn't be stuck because I'd load up with supplies and follow the track all the way home, on foot no less. But that's what I'd do. No matter how many weeks it took I would trek all the way back here. So take that and eat it, world.

The Ape steps forward and peers into the carriage. His great head moves slowly one way, and then the other.

He does it twice for good measure then steps back. 'Empty.'

There must be at least eight long carriages coupled to each other and all of them stand silent and still. I'm convinced Billie is aboard one of them. 'Let's try the next one.'

We move to the next carriage and a squabble breaks out because the Apes want to press the OPEN button.

'My turn,' the Ape says.

'No, mine.'

'You can do the next one.'

'I want this one.'

I jab the button to bring the foolishness to a halt. Both Apes look miserable.

'Wasn't your turn,' Non-Ape says to me.

I lean into the open carriage but I'm not tall like the Ape and can't see half as much as he could.

I dare to edge in closer. Billie could be seated in the carriage but I can't see past the interior door. I put a put a foot into the carriage and lean further in.

'I'm pressing the next button,' Non-Ape declares.

The carriage seems empty.

'No you ain't,' the Ape warns.

But I should make sure. Billie is struggling badly and is not herself. I climb into the carriage but I'm careful to keep very close to the open door. It couldn't possibly have time to shut before I could leap out.

'Am,' Non-Ape says.

'Billie?' I call out.

'Ain't.'

'Am.'

'Ain't.'

'Am.'

At the far end of the carriage the adjoining door between the carriages opens with a very gentle hiss of air. It catches me by surprise.

But the invitation is obvious.

Come this way, Rev.

Behind me the Apes set off along the platform, charging to be the first to reach the OPEN button on the third carriage door.

The next carriage awaits me but at least the Apes will be there.

I venture forth.

The door to the platform closes behind me.

But I was expecting that.

I gather myself and head down the carriage, reaching the open adjoining door. I step through and more silence and stillness awaits me.

I hear the Ape wins the race to the next button and jabs it hard. 'Yowza!'

But the door doesn't open. The Ape tries it again. It doesn't work.

Non-Ape joins him. 'Ha!'

I can see them outside and know that Non-Ape could tear

this carriage apart if he wanted. So I'm all right. I'm not in any danger.

Except the idiots decide to charge for the next carriage, which takes them further down the platform – and further away from me.

What the hell?

I go to the window and start banging hard on it. 'Hey! What are you doing? Come back!' But the window is triple-glazed or reinforced in some way because my banging fists make a dull thud and little more. I sprint for the nearest carriage doors and start jabbing at the EXIT button.

Nothing.

They refuse to open.

The Apes are already finding that the next carriage down is similarly locked and are charging further down the platform again, racing to try and beat each other in their stupid button-pushing duel.

I step back from the doors and kick them hard. I don't even make a dent. I remember the emergency hammer that Carrie found on GG's train, which we used to hack open the driver's door. I look all around but can't see one.

'*Johnson!*' I try to send a message to Other-Johnson, but then remember that his brainpower isn't functioning.

OK, I think. *Stay calm. It's coming and you know it's coming so be ready. Clear your mind. Clear it of everything but the need to find Billie and get her away. I promised her that nothing would happen to anyone else, and I'm not going to let her down.*

I head for the next adjoining door between compartments but it won't open either. It's thin and mainly made of glass or Perspex so I start kicking hard at it.

A gentle hand alights on my shoulder and I half scream and spin.

Billie stands before me.

I have no idea how I missed her. Was she hiding under another table? She looks like she's got a fever. Her skin is clammy and her eyes are bloodshot. And black.

I throw my arms round her. 'Billie!'

Billie wriggles away and takes a couple of steps back. 'Don't, Rev.'

'Billie. C'mon, we've got to go. I was so worried for a second.'

She looks like she's been crying again and what little mascara she had left is running down her cheeks, some of it trickling into the gouges in her cheek. 'How pathetic was I on the train?' she asks.

'Doesn't matter.'

'I wanted to fight, I did.'

'It wouldn't have changed what happened. They came for the Moth. We were overrun and . . .' I trail off. I can't get GG out of my head and try hard to stay focused. 'We've got a hotel to find.'

'What?' She looks shocked. 'You're really still thinking about finding the papers? What's the point now without the Moth?'

'And what's the point in giving up?'

'I found this train.'

'No one knows how to drive one of these things.'

'It can't be that difficult. Press a few buttons and *bonjour*, Paris.'

'Billie, forget it. We are not running.'

'You don't even know where the hotel is.'

'We'll find it.'

Billie slowly shakes her head. 'We're beat.'

'No.'

'There's only three of us left. Me, you and Johnson.'

'Don't forget the Apes.'

'They don't count. They belong with their own subspecies. I'm scared, all right. Petrified,' she says

Billie takes a seat on one of the tables, leaning back, arms crossed as if the debate is over. Even through the reinforced glass in the windows I can hear the Apes thundering down the platform, getting further and further away.

Billie's skin has developed a sheen of perspiration that glistens under the carriage lights.

'My head hurts,' she says.

'I'll get Johnson. He's great. He knows medical things.'

'It's spinning. Can't focus.'

'Wait there.'

I make to move away but she grabs my wrist. Her movement is staggeringly quick.

'Did you know we were together?' she eventually asks.

'You and Johnson?'

She smiles the smile of someone in love. 'He's amazing, Rev.'

'Yeah – uh – about that.' I can tell Billie is halfway delirious. 'Tell you what, why don't we go see him?'

Billie is lost to her imaginings. 'We got trapped in a rainstorm.'

This is getting awkward now. 'We've talked about this, Billie. We dealt with it, remember?'

'I kept getting a drip down the back of my neck.'

'That wasn't real.'

Billie's eyes flick to blue then black again. 'Of course it's real.'

'Listen to me.'

She stops.

And smiles.

Not a proper smile of happiness, more one that would accompany scorn. It's a jeering smile.

'I get it. You think he should be with you.'

My shoulders tingle.

'Enjoy your little piggyback, did you?'

Billie climbs to her feet, steps closer. She looks weak and is unsteady on her feet. 'Johnson and I . . .' She sways and has to sit back down on the table. 'That was amazing. What we had, what we *still* have. It's perfect, Rev. I can see why you like him so much.'

She smiles again.

And something glints in her mouth.

'I totally get it.' She is panting, and her breathing is laboured and she has to steady herself in case she slides off the table. 'It's just a shame I got him first.'

The overhead lights in the carriage bounce off something metal in her mouth.

'We shouldn't be here, Billie. You should be rehearsing *Hamlet* and I should be dyeing my hair a normal colour and thinking about Kyle and what my mum's going to say when she eventually sees me and asks me where I've been. And I've seen my dad! I need to tell her that.'

Billie stiffens. It's tiny and almost unnoticeable.

'When?'

'What?'

'When did you see your dad?'

260

I hesitate.

Her black eyes give little away. But I'm tingling all over now.

'In the supermarket,' I tell her, backtracking as fast as I can. 'Where he got burned. You were there.' Instinct is screaming at me not to tell her about the hospital.

'No. You didn't mean then.' Her clammy skin ripples. It's like a small wave as it runs the entire length of one arm and then back down the other. Non-Lucas's skin did the same once.

'Yeah . . . I did. When . . . when else would I have meant?' I stammer. Though to be fair I wouldn't believe me either. I'm a rotten liar.

'Where did you see him, Rev?' Her eyes flick from black to blue and back again. 'Where?' She says it quietly, intimately, almost a whisper.

I think quickly. 'In my dream.'

Billie is surprised.

'I dreamed I saw him,' I tell her and because it's the truth I can talk more convincingly. 'He was back at the train station and I climbed across the track to see him. But it felt realer than a dream, you know? So I guess it feels bigger than that.'

In the dream my dad was standing at the train station in our home town. He was wearing a suit and shiny shoes and the dream was so real I truly thought that he'd somehow reached out to me.

He'd told me to run for my life.

Billie's skin ripples again.

'A dream,' she says, almost to herself. But the way she pounced so quickly onto any thought of my dad is worrying. Something about her attitude makes me think that the last thing she wants is for my dad to help us.

Where the hell are the Apes?

'But it was just a dream,' I add. 'And anyway, maybe it was the other Rev's dad. Maybe they helped him get better and took him home.'

'They went home? How would you know that?'

'I-I don't,' I stammer.

Billie presses her face closer to mine. She scans every aspect of my face, as if sniffing out my awkward lies.

'It's just we never saw them, so I presumed,' I offer.

'They left their Ape though,' Billie says quietly.

'Who wouldn't, right?' I add a smile to this, as if we're in on a little joke together. 'Who wouldn't leave an Ape if you got the chance.'

'You wouldn't,' she says simply. 'And that other Rev is also you.' Billie is processing me, evaluating me in ways I really don't like. 'You'd make sure we all went back together.'

'Yeah but—'

'And you wouldn't leave Johnson behind.' Which is her coup de grâce, her thick iron nail driving deep into the tissue of half-truths I've been selling her. 'Would you?'

Her eyes switch to the deepest black yet and stay that way. I don't know if she's even aware of it happening but she looks like a lion who has cornered a lamb.

'So Rev Two and the others must be still here ... which means your dad hasn't gone anywhere.'

'Of course he has.'

A talon slides from Billie's index finger. It takes her completely by surprise.

'Billie!?'

Her mouth drops open. 'Rev!?'

'It's all right, Billie. It's all right.'

'Oh my God, oh my God!' Billie staggers back, as if she can

262

get away from the talon, but it's attached to her and she can't escape it.

'What the hell?' The shock has sent Billie tumbling back into her human state. She's now a panicked sixteen-year-old with a talon sticking out of her finger.

I try to stay calm for her. 'Billie, take some breaths. Breathe. OK? Breathe . . .'

Another talon slides out of the tip of her middle finger.

'Rev.' Her voice is faint now, barely a whisper as her brain fails to make sense of what she is seeing. She backs down the carriage, bumping into a seat and almost falling before steadying herself.

'Breathe, Billie . . .' I have no idea why I'm saying that. It's not as if she's about to give birth. 'Just keep calm.'

Billie stops backing away and takes some deep lungfuls of air.

Where the hell are those stupid button-obsessed Apes?

Billie raises her hand. She looks at the talons in quiet wonder, as much baffled as bewitched by them.

Her teeth glint and I can see that they have turned to metal. The thing I feared the most – in fact, the one thing I tried my best to ignore, as if that would make it go away – has happened. When Non-Lucas cut her with his talons his DNA somehow bonded with Billie's.

There's no two ways about this.

She's one of them now.

Billie runs the tip of her other index finger along a talon until it reaches the hideously sharp point.

'Rev?' she says, her brain still unable to accept what her eyes are telling her. 'Say something.' Billie's internal war between shock and grim fascination has been won by shock.

'It'll be OK—'

'OK!? You call this okay!?' Her eyes are as black as coal now, but the panic is still evident. 'What's happening to me?'

'You must've noticed.' Which sounds so, so lame.

'Noticed what?'

'The way you-you've changed ... You've been sort of behaving like one of them – on and off – for a while now.'

Being hit by a nuclear explosion would have less impact on Billie than my words have just had. She opens and closes her mouth and tries to speak but her eyes are filling with tears.

'Billie, you must have felt something inside ... The anger, the way you've been with the Ape, with me ...'

Billie starts crying and she is about to clasp her hands over her face when I leap forward and grab her wrists.

'Don't, you'll stab yourself!'

Billie comes eye to eye with the talons in front of her face. She can barely see them through the blur of her tears but it's enough.

'Rev, kill me.'

'What? No! Don't say that!'

'Look at me! I'm a monster!'

'Billie, please, you've got to take control, all right. You've got to try and-and ...' *What?* I think. *What, what, what?* 'Billie, try and put those-those things away.'

Billie stares at the talons and while she does another slides out slowly and sleekly.

She screams.

Another talon follows it.

'I can't stop them!' She starts to back away again, as if she can outrun them or something. Her brain has overloaded and can't process anything.

Billie turns and as she does the tips of one talon rake a plushly upholstered seat. They slice through the material and the stuffing with obscene ease.

She stumbles and this time the talons slice the head off one of the table lamps.

I go to her but she can't connect her brain to the talons and she comes for me, needing me to hug her or hold her, but the talons drive straight towards me as she flings her arms out and I have to duck fast, shielding my face and head with my forearm. I feel the swish of air as the talons miss my skin by millimetres.

'Oh God ...' Billie turns away, lurching back down the carriage.

I go after her. 'Billie!'

Billie stops so suddenly I almost crash into the back of her. She doesn't turn but her chest is heaving as she takes a long moment to try and find a shred of sanity.

'OK ... OK ...' she says over and over.

I give her all the time in the world.

'OK ...'

Seconds become minutes.

The Apes must be at the far end of the train by now. Why haven't they come to find me?

'I can't go home, can I?' Billie says eventually.

'We're all going back. I won't leave you.'

'Not like this.'

'Billie, we'll deal with it.'

'How?'

I don't have an answer, which is an answer in itself.

'You did this to me.' I'm not sure but I think she is crying again. 'You and your stupid dad.'

I stay silent because anything I say will probably only inflame her.

'I *hate* you right now.'

Billie finally turns and faces me. Her look cuts right through me. 'We are not friends.'

'Billie—'

'We are nothing.'

Billie raises one of her hands and the talons look sharper and deadlier on her than even Evil-GG's did.

'Billie—'

'You should've had a proper dad.'

'That's not fair,' I cry.

'A proper normal dad wouldn't have caused any of this. And what do you do when you realise what a mess we're in? You treat it like it's one big wild adventure.'

'No . . .'

'And at the centre of that adventure, there's you, being the hero. The big brave girl, leading everyone on. But what really matters, what's more important than anything, is that you get to moon over two boys. Because you've never had that have you? Never really been noticed that much, or wanted, apart from that leprechaun Kyle. So it goes straight to your head and you start dangling the Johnsons on strings, turning them into lovesick puppets waiting for you to make up your mind. And it goes straight to your head and you think you can somehow have both of them.'

'That's-that's not true.'

'And when it looks like I'm with Johnson, you can't wait to destroy that.'

'Billie, that was someone else doing that. They were playing with you, with all of us.'

266

'You're the one playing with us, Rev.'

I try my best to stay calm and hold it together. I have to reach Billie. 'This isn't you talking.'

'Ask Lucas, Carrie, GG – the Moth. They'll tell you the same thing. That this is all on you. But wait, they can't talk any more, can they?'

'You can fight this,' I tell her. 'You can be Billie again. Take control of it.'

'You want to know who the monster really is, Rev? It's you.'

Her words cut deeper than any talon as Billie fixes me with the deadest eyes I've ever seen. *Do not come near me again.*

It's a warning.

A threat.

Speak to me again and you're dead.

Billie sucks in one last breath, then turns, heads for the doors that refuse to open and slices the EXIT button, before driving a talon deep it into its electronics. The doors give a dead man's sigh and shudder open with an aching whine.

'Don't get burned out there.' She mockingly echoes Johnson, her voice dripping with bile and venom.

She drops from the train and glides away. She moves with a new grace and power and her transformation is complete.

She is definitely one of them now.

NO ONE KNOWS

Johnson still hasn't returned and Other-Johnson intercepts me as I return shaken and pale from St Pancras with the Apes.

'Stupid trip,' Non-Ape grumbles.

'No big mice anywhere.'

Other-Johnson takes my arm and leads me away. He is anxious, which is not the natural state for a Johnson. 'Well?'

'I, uh . . . I didn't find her.'

Other-Johnson doesn't need to be a mind reader to know that's a lie.

'Try again,' he tells me.

'She's . . .' I start again. 'She's not what she was.'

'Explain.'

'She's like one of you now. Talons, metal teeth, black eyes.'

Other-Johnson sucks breath in through his teeth. 'That's different.'

Which as understatements go is up there with the biggest of them. Having your best friend turn into a murderous alien that hates you is not how most friendships pan out.

'She didn't come back this way?'

'Didn't see her. But I've been thinking, Rev—'

'Read her mind. Find out where she's gone,' I snap.

'All I'm getting is static,' he says.

'You're hopeless. We have to find her!'

'Give me time, OK? I'm not what I was either.' He almost looks wounded.

'I want my dad's papers,' I tell him. 'While I'm doing that, start getting your head fixed. Then when you've done that, you can find Billie and the Moth. OK? We don't have time for you to fail now.'

'Yes, ma'am.'

But I'm not inclined towards humour right now. I know I'm being bitchy, but I can't help it. In just a few short hours I've managed to make everything a thousand times worse. 'Just get it done.'

I call to the Ape. 'Dazza. We need transport.'

Both Apes look at me, but the Ape knows I'm talking to him because he grins.

'Something big enough for all of us,' I add.

The Ape scans the street that runs in front of King's Cross and then marches towards it, eyes keenly peeled for the perfect vehicle. 'Easy,' he purrs.

'What about me?' Non-Ape asks, already looking lost and exposed without his new best friend by his side.

'Do what you do best. Stay strong, stay tough,' I tell him. Which he grins at, pleased.

I feel like I've turned into a sergeant major from the army but I am sick of this world.

I scan the huge station. Johnson should be back by now. There are newsagents everywhere and it shouldn't have taken him long to find one, grab a map and get back here.

I check the time on the arrivals and departures board: he's been gone over half an hour.

Non-Ape pulls off the remains of his slashed clothing and is practically naked. He doesn't seem to care and from what I can tell of most Ape-types they love stripping off and bearing their vast bodies.

'Can't you find a blanket or something?' I ask him.

He proudly slaps his big hairy belly. 'I don't do cold.'

The slap echoes through the ridiculously quiet station.

I check the time on the giant board again. As if that's going to get Johnson back sooner.

Other-Johnson senses my concern. 'Maybe Billie found him,' he says.

'Don't say that.'

'She didn't come this way so maybe she went looking for him.'

'It wasn't real – what they had. So why would she?' My temper is fraying by the second.

'I'm just saying, Rev. Chill.'

But I can't 'chill'. I just can't do it. With every hour that passes I seem to lose someone else.

I keep watching the seconds tick by on the giant display. Each silent movement means we have increasingly less time to find the papers and then track the Moth down.

Where the hell is Johnson?

Is Other-Johnson right? Has Billie found him and convinced him to run away with her? What if they've both changed and right now they're skipping away, talons entwined.

'I'm thinking it came with us on the train,' Other-Johnson says quietly. 'The person from my world. I think they're here, Rev.'

'Can't be, we'd have seen it whoever it was.'

'You didn't see it arrive in the classroom so why would you see it now?'

It makes sense but it also doesn't make sense. 'So where was it on the train? Riding on the roof?'

Other-Johnson looks reluctant to say. 'What if it's invisible?'

My stomach switches places with my heart, or at least that's what it feels like.

'I'm not saying it is but . . .'

'Can your kind do that?'

'It'd be a first. But then so would making it snow in summer . . .'

Strangely enough I don't feel like celebrating the fact that we're witnessing some kind of new phenomenon. I've seen enough to last a lifetime as it is.

'That is some serious mental power,' he adds, beguiled by the wonder of it. Which is so not any Johnson's way. 'When you think about it, they could make anything happen.'

My eyes find Other-Johnson's as we both hit the same hideous thought together. 'If it's been with us this whole time, then it created all those Moth Twos.'

We both take a long moment to let the thoughts settle. I am trying my best to sense another presence and I know Other-Johnson is too.

'It's got to be close, Rev.'

OK, so it's able to alter reality, reanimate the dead, cause static for telepaths and now it's invisible. That's just too much. It's not a fair fight. It's really not.

'Why did you have to go and say that?' I tell Other-Johnson.

'Someone had to.'

I lean closer to Other-Johnson and whisper in his ear. 'You have to get your head fixed.'

'I'm trying,' he whispers back.

The giant digital clock stops.

It takes me a moment to realise it but the read-out has stopped turning over. Lights flicker all around the station. Non-Ape stands stock-still, alert and listening.

A ripple of alarm runs from one of my shoulders to the other. Then it comes back again, a slow shiver. A very gentle alarm.

Non-Ape starts to look around, turning three hundred and sixty degrees.

We're not alone.

Other-Johnson's eyes flick left then right.

'Rev?'

'I know.' I try to stay calm as I can.

Other-Johnson calls to Non-Ape. 'Ape. Be ready.'

Non-Ape might be slow of mind in almost every aspect, but the merest whiff of danger turns him into Einstein.

'Already there,' is all he needs to offer as his eyes skim our surroundings.

We are completely vulnerable, standing on the open concourse and with no chance of hiding from whatever is out there. And where's Johnson – and the Ape for that matter? Why did I send them away?

I look to Other-Johnson and I know he's trying his level best to mind read whatever is out there.

'I'm not getting anything,' he tells me, sounding frustrated. 'Still just static.'

Non-Ape stands taller, listening hard. He's definitely got enhanced hearing considering he seemed to be able to find me in the pitch-black of the alley outside the private hospital.

'Anything?'

He holds up a massive finger, as in be quiet.

But it's coming.

I know it is. This world gifted me with a spider sense, and at first I thought it was a blessing. But the way this world has been coming after me I think it's more of a taunt. As if it's saying, *Trouble is coming your way, little Reva, and guess what, I'm going to make sure you're scared first. I want to savour every last drop of your fear.*

The footsteps are fast. Leather on cold tile.

We turn as one.

It's Johnson. He's moving quickly, inhuman legs pumping. 'Let's go!'

'What? What is it?' Other-Johnson is looking all around. 'I don't see anything!'

'Johnson?' I can't see what he's running from.

Johnson lets himself skid the last few metres across the polished concourse, as if he's on ice, before he stops right in front of me. Gliding as if he's in slow-mo.

He waves something in the air and it takes me a while to work out that it's a map.

A London street map to be precise. An A to Z.

'One map, madam.'

He presents it to me with a flourish, like a knight from the realm.

My shoulders are still buzzing with danger. Non-Ape and Other-Johnson are on high alert too.

We stay silent for a long moment and Johnson frowns. 'What?'

'We thought . . .'

'Something was coming,' Other-Johnson tells him.

273

'It was. Me.'

'No . . .'

'Something bad.'

'You were running like crazy,' I say to Johnson.

'Who wouldn't with legs like these?'

'There's nothing chasing you?'

'No.'

'Did you see Billie?' I ask him.

'Didn't you find her?' He looks concerned.

I want to explain but I keep thinking something is going to arrive any second to try and kill us. Someone stopped that clock. Someone made the lights flicker. And that someone has to be right here amongst us. Or even worse. Inside one of us. Is that where they're hiding?

Non-Ape looks around the empty station. Eating everything in sight has somehow made him grow huge. He must be ten feet tall. Everything about him, from his eyebrows to his toes, must be about fifty per cent bigger. There are no clothes that will fit but GG would have tutted mightily and fashioned a toga from a bedsheet. If he was still here of course . . .

I can't think of him without wanting to double over in agony.

Non-Ape hears something and leans forward a few inches before angling his head towards the station entrance.

Non-Ape straightens. He's definitely heard something. He bunches his fists. 'Worm. Get ready.' His voice has dropped about two octaves because his voice box must be half as large again as it was before.

Other-Johnson tenses. 'What is it?'

Non-Ape doesn't answer but he is facing the huge

274

entrance/exit of the station, eyeing the empty streets and shops outside.

Johnson slips the map into his back pocket and then watches as the talons in his fingers appear. He still isn't comfortable with them.

'Careful with those,' Other-Johnson tells him. 'They could come in handy, especially where you might end up.'

'And where would that be?' Johnson replies.

They square up to each other and I have to get between them, being mighty careful not to get a talon in the eye.

'Johnson!' I warn them.

Non-Ape cracks his knuckles. 'It's here.'

The roar of an engine fills my ears and I turn to see a bus heading straight for us. A gleaming red London bus. The shadows from the huge roof of the station blot out the windscreen and the driver but whoever is behind the wheel seems intent on driving straight for us.

Non-Ape drags me behind him. 'I got this.'

Even their catchphrases are the same. The Non-Ape has grown so tall, my head is barely above his fleshy buttocks and if he were to fart again he'd probably blow me back onto the tracks.

Johnson turns to me. 'It's OK, Rev, nothing's going to—'

With a colossal mind wrench Other-Johnson swaps bodies with Johnson. And finishes Johnson's sentence for him.

'—get you, Worm. Not while I'm around.'

Johnson staggers as he finds himself back in his old body. 'What the hell?'

Johnson can't find his feet. He looks like people do when they step off boats. He's also directly in the path of the oncoming bus. Placed there on purpose by Other-Johnson?

I rush out from behind Non-Ape and grab him and pull him out of the way, glaring at Other-Johnson. 'Not funny!'

The bus horn sounds loudly. Once. Twice. It's a challenge. A call to arms.

Whatever its intention, the sound is all Non-Ape needs because he sets off and charges straight for the bus.

The horn sounds again. Non-Ape is twenty metres from it when the bus starts to brake.

Hard.

But impact is imminent and it is only now that I can see who's behind the wheel. It's the Ape! He's driving a bus!?

Non-Ape draws his mighty arm back, fist bunched. He flattened a hotel so this bus is going to disintegrate in seconds.

'No, don't!'

The Ape is practically standing on the brakes as Non-Ape's fist looms up in front of him.

'Stop!' I scream.

Fist is about to meet bus when Non-Ape is wrenched out of its path. Other-Johnson mentally drags the behemoth to one side but the bus still clips his mountainous body and bounces off him. The Ape loses control of the steering wheel and the bus crashes straight into the huge wall that obscures the intercity train lines behind it.

An airbag blows up in the Ape's face, the windscreen shatters and the station wall crumbles around the bus, bricks and mortar crashing down. I'm already running for the bus when the doors hiss open and the Ape, stunned and dizzy, steps from it and falls to his knees. I catch him as he tries to stay upright but he's too heavy for me and he pitches forward and I end up pinned under him.

His massive weight crushes me and we're in a highly

276

indelicate and unfortunate position as he slumps on top of me.

'Ape?' I exhale.

The Ape looks down at me and I know his head is ringing from the impact. His eyes won't focus.

'Ape, say something! Ape.'

The Ape looks down at me, his big head inches from my face. I can smell beer and cigarettes on his breath.

'Dazza? Darren,' I say.

'Huh?' His tongue flops from his mouth.

'It's me, Rev. You know me, right?'

His eyes open and shut and when they open again he's turned cross-eyed.

'Dazza!'

But then he grins. 'Gotcha!' He uncrosses his eyes and sucks his tongue back into his mouth.

'You big idiot!'

The Johnsons have joined us and they start pulling the Ape away. 'You're crushing her.'

'She's loving it.' He grins again and then climbs to his feet. He turns and checks the crashed bus. 'Skills.'

'What? What skills?' I say.

'I'm a great parker.'

'If you hadn't already been braking ...' My eyes are scrunched up and I can feel tears behind them. 'I am not losing you. You listening? I am not going to lose you.' I can't believe he doesn't get how close he came to dying. I know we've been there before. I know I've almost lost him time and time again but this – this would have been the most stupid death imaginable. I beat at his great chest. 'You're an idiot! An absolute idiot!'

He winces and I realise I'm beating at his bruised or broken ribs.

'Easy now, easy,' Other-Johnson says.

The Ape looks down at me and I wipe my eyes and nose with the back of my hand. 'I'm just saying, OK – go careful. For me. I need you.'

'Got it the first time.'

The Ape climbs stiffly back into the bus. He crunches the automatic gears into reverse and a shrill ear-splitting reversing beep echoes over and over as the bus pulls away from the wall.

The Ape opens the bus doors with that customary hiss.

'Tickets!' Non-Ape pushes past us so that he can be first onto the bus. 'I'm sitting at the back.'

His huge weight makes the floor of the bus bow and dip.

Johnson stops me as I head towards the bus. He leans in close to me and whispers in my ear. 'I don't trust him.' He means Other-Johnson. 'These things that are happening. He could be doing them.'

'You think he's capable of that?'

'All I'm saying is we don't know anything about him. He can put thoughts in our heads. He can jump around inside of us. But what if he can do a whole lot more?'

My mouth dries a little. Is Other-Johnson creating all of this just to be with me? Removing anything that gets in the way? I've seen him lie so easily to get round people. He is dark and dangerous and yet so hard to resist.

'He couldn't possibly be able to,' I whisper.

'But he wants to be with you, Rev.' Johnson meets my eyes. 'And I know what that feels like.'

I wait for him to follow up on that but he looks like he

already thinks he's said too much. He breaks eye contact and climbs on board the bus.

He had the perfect opening but he didn't go for it. I am still wondering if he ever will.

I watch Other-Johnson stretching and getting accustomed to his old body. He clicks his neck and slips into the body like it's a new suit.

He spots me watching him.

'My power suddenly came back. How about that?'

'Yeah,' I practically whisper. 'Amazing.'

'I missed this. Being stronger. And better.' He grins.

But I don't return his grin.

If he's back in his proper body then maybe he wants to go home to his world after all.

And maybe . . . just maybe, he's planning to take me with him.

PUKUS ERUPTUS

It has taken ages to not find the rubble that was once a hotel.

Two horribly gnarly hours of the Ape's singular inability to listen to anything anyone tells him.

We have driven past every possible London landmark in a fast-moving, non-stop sightseeing tour that no one wants to be on.

We have passed Marble Arch, Buckingham Palace, the Tower of London, St Paul's Cathedral, that battleship in the Thames, famous London theatres, the statue of Eros and Buckingham Palace again.

Non-Ape lies along the rear seats, holding his hairy stomach. He has remained very quiet and when I catch sight of his pale face I think he must have been really hurt by the Moth Twos. I have no idea how many stabs or swipes it took to eventually penetrate his skin but he suffered countless cuts as he ploughed through their ranked masses.

The wounds have healed, but I'm worried that he looks feverish and maybe there's some internal damage that we don't know about.

He doesn't seem to be aware that Billie is no longer with us. The old Non-Ape would have been all over that. He's her shining knight.

The Ape is driving too fast, swinging the bus round corners as if he was in a dodgem car. The continual swaying is playing havoc with the Non-Ape. 'Slow down!' I shout for the millionth time.

'You said we were in a hurry,' the Ape responds.

'We need to stop and try and establish our bearings. We can't just drive down every street in London.'

The Ape dings the bell to drown me out. His thick hairy arms pull the power-assisted steering wheel one way and then the other.

Other-Johnson joins Johnson and I can't get over how if I was blindfolded I wouldn't be able to tell which was which. Their voices are the same, their inflections are identical, even the words they choose are exactly alike. 'Can you remember the name of the street?'

'It was posh,' Johnson says. 'The hotel.'

'So it's in a posh area.'

'You hear that?' I rap on the thin plastic divider that keeps the bus driver from his public. 'We need to go posh.'

The Ape spins us round a tight corner and it's too much for Non-Ape who retches violently.

He's at the back of the bus and projectile vomits all of the sandwiches, cakes, cookies and coffees he gorged himself on.

I try to get out of the way as the torrent of vomit rushes down the aisle. 'Open the door!'

The acrid reek of Non-Ape's stomach contents burns our nostrils and sting our eyes.

The Ape, for once, does as he is told but the putrid torrent reaches my shoes just as the Ape yanks the bus round another sharp corner and I slip and slide and roll straight out of the open door.

I thrust out a hand but can't find anything to stop me crashing into the street. We are on a bridge. I'm not sure which one and I don't really care as I land in a pitiful bone-jarring heap. I hear the bus braking hard and skidding to a halt. I gingerly feel for any breaks before I'm ready to sit up. My left shoulder is numb, both knees are grazed and I can feel a swelling at the back of my head, but as I stagger to my feet and lean against the stone wall of the bridge my eyes find the River Thames flowing below me.

But it's not the Thames that grabs my attention.

It's the pile of rubble on the other side of the bank. The rubble that used to be a hotel before Non-Ape punched it senseless.

We've found it, I think, then realise I really am the most stupid person ever to draw breath.

Now that I can see the hotel in all its demolished glory I can safely say that this was actually the ultimate in idiotically desperate ideas. Cement and great chunks of wall, metal and plaster lie broken and doomed in a crushed mass. The rubble is piled higher than a small block of flats and the thought of finding a sheaf of scientific papers lost amongst it is ridiculous. Hopeless. We're never going to escape. We don't even have the Moth to read the papers that we'll never ever find.

The Ape sounds the bus horn from the bridge. 'Found it!' he yells.

He sounds the bus's horn over and over. 'Found it! Rev! I'm a great tracker!'

By the time I catch up with them he is outside the bus, leaning on it as he surveys the destroyed hotel.

'Yowza,' he purrs at his handiwork.

Johnson lights a cigarette and probably feels the same way I do about the impossible task ahead. He blows a smoke ring and watches it float away. 'Jeez, Rev.'

Billie was right all along. I'm a useless fool, charging from one disaster to another while being torn between two boys and I don't deserve to be with either of them.

'*Have you heard from Billie?*' I ask Other-Johnson telepathically.

He doesn't reply.

'Hey!' I say out loud.

Other-Johnson turns to me and frowns. 'What?'

'Billie?' But if he didn't hear me in his head then he certainly won't be able to find her.

'*Give me a minute.*' His voice sounds faint and distant in my head.

'I thought you were back to your best.'

'It comes and goes. It's not like before.'

'*When you can, you need to find out about my dad. Has he woken yet?*' I literally force the thoughts into Other-Johnson's head. '*He might be our only chance now.*'

'*I'll do my best,*' Other-Johnson replies.

But I don't know if he's lying or not.

I really have no idea. Johnson's doubts have started to make me question how much I can trust Other-Johnson. Maybe *he* locked the classroom door. Or maybe it was always open and he just made it look like he couldn't open it.

And is my dad in danger now? Perhaps he always was. What is the Other-Johnson planning? He's smart and deadly and I'm starting to fear him more than I've feared anyone or anything.

'Can you move all that rubble?' Johnson asks Non-Ape.

'Need to eat.'

'But you can move it?'

'Course. I got skills.'

The Apes knock knuckles. 'Skiiiiillllllllssssssss.'

As they do I think of Billie.

I can't bear the thought of her roaming the city alone. She'll be scared and panicked and, despite what she said to me, people need their best friends when they sprout talons and metal teeth.

You have to hand it to GG; he had a taste for the finer things in life. The hotel he picked for us the last time we were here was pure five-star luxury. It's rubble now of course, but in the good old days of yesteryear he found us the most amazing place I have ever stepped foot in. GG knew class when he saw it.

Unfortunately Other-Johnson has less of an eye for luxury. I'm not complaining – the hotel he's found is still huge and has hundreds of rooms, but it's not quite what GG would have chosen.

This hotel is older and not as exuberant, and sits two streets away from the river. It looks onto the world-famous Strand, though the usually busy street remains eerily empty.

Night has closed in and forced us to find sheleter and wait for morning. Time is of the essence but Non-Ape needs to gorge himself and build his strength up again and we can't see well enough to find the papers in a rubble-haystack anyway. No one has the energy to go shopping for torches.

I went into a bedroom and yanked a bedsheet from one of

the beds. I then managed to knot it round Non-Ape's huge body, so that he now looks like he's on his way to a toga party. The Apes marched straight into the kitchen and have been in there for well over two hours. I meant to tell them to ration whatever they do find because there could be long hard days of rubble-clearing ahead of us but my tired brain has all but closed down for the evening.

The shower in my room is compact but modern compared to the rest of the musty hotel. I step into it, fully clothed, and turn on the hot tap. Water cascades onto me and I stand under it, rubbing soap and shampoo into my clothes and hair and skin. I am so tired I don't even have the energy to get undressed. In the morning I will go 'shopping' while the boys – I never thought I'd be the type to say 'the boys' – start moving the rubble.

The hot steamy water soothes and lulls me, and barely being able to stand I slip down so that I am sitting under the shower, arms propping me up, legs stretched in front of me. My plan is to strip off after the shower and hang my rock 'n' roll clothes up to dry while I sleep the sleep of the dead.

My eyelids are heavy and I don't think I can keep my eyes open any longer. Maybe if I stretch out a bit more and lean my head back against the shower wall I could sleep here, while the soothing warmth of the water gently pummels my aches and scratches and cuts and bruises and burns.

Yeah.

Aches and scratches.

And bruises and burns oh my.

Lions and tigers.

And bears oh my.

Bruises and burns.

And cuts oh my.

286

Lions and bruises.

Tigers.

Cuts.

Oh.

My . . .

There's a hard rap on my hotel door.

I jolt awake.

'Rev.'

It's Johnson/Other-Johnson. I have no idea which one. I'm having trouble remembering if they've swapped back or not. I think they did.

'Knock, knock.'

I turn off the taps and wrap the Union Jack towel round my soaking-wet clothes. My eye finds the spyhole and Johnson/Other-Johnson is standing there.

He must sense me. 'Room service.' He smiles.

It's Johnson. My Johnson. He's back in his human body and a bright blue eye appears at the spyhole. We are the thickness of a door apart.

My eye, his eye.

'How you doing?' he asks through the door.

'Living a nightmare. How about you?'

'Same.'

'Listen,' he says, then hesitates. 'I'm staying with you tonight.'

He takes me by surprise. 'Oh . . . Really?'

'On the floor,' he adds.

My eye studies his eye. 'The floor.'

'Yeah – the floor.'

I remove the chain and turn the double lock. 'I'm soaking wet,' I warn him as I open the door.

287

He stands there, all dark curls and skinny-legged jeans. He has a tray of food and drink at his feet, which he bends to collect. I hold the door open for him and let him pass. It's a tight squeeze and only the tray prevents us from brushing against each other.

'Grabbed what I could before the Apes ate everything.'

I let the door close and follow him into the room as he slides the tray onto the large double bed.

'Hungry?' he asks as he opens a bottle of beer for me. There are crisps and sandwiches and even fruit, which looks like it's turned a little too ripe now.

'Starving.'

I bite into the sandwich and it's the best thing I've ever tasted. I have ignored my hunger all day but this thick doorstep-sized cheese and pickle sandwich is the greatest meal of all time. Washed down with cold beer the meal becomes a ravenous feast as I eat and eat and then eat some more.

'God this is good.'

'Michelin star.'

Johnson sits with his back against the headboard, legs stretched out, just watching me eat and drink.

'I'm sorry I went away,' he says.

'Wasn't your fault.' I'm speaking with my mouth full. Which isn't polite or sexy. But I don't care right now. I didn't realise just how hungry I was.

I feel a burp rising in my chest, which is so unladylike. I grab the cotton napkin he brought for me and pretend to wipe my mouth while letting a low soundless belch escape into it. Boy, I'm a real catch.

Johnson watches me for a few more silent minutes.

'Not eating?' I ask.

He smiles. 'There's not a lot left.'

I finish a second beer and look down at an empty plate. I've even eaten the slushy fruit and barely realised it. Some of the juice dribbles down my chin and I sit there, drenched, wrapped in a Union Jack and fighting a wave of belches. Johnson might think better of staying to watch over me.

But he doesn't move apart from raising his arms and linking his fingers behind his head.

'You know, I meant what I said earlier. There's only one person who can manipulate our minds.'

He means Other-Johnson.

'He can't make it snow.'

'You don't know *what* he can do.'

'He was as shocked as us at the sight of the Moth Twos.'

Johnson falls silent for moment. 'Maybe. Maybe not.'

Is he right? Is Other-Johnson playing games with us? Why? Because he's worried that I'll go away and never return? So he's finding ways of keeping me here? Keeping me in peril. Needing help.

Needing a hero.

Needing him.

It makes a terrible sense but I can't accept it. 'There's something else here,' I tell Johnson. 'I'm sure of it.'

He probably thinks I'm being ultra defensive of Other-Johnson but he doesn't push it.

'I was going to get out of these wet clothes,' I venture.

He raises an eyebrow.

'So, if you're going to sleep on the floor—'

'Which I am.'

'Well, I'll need to, uh, get in bed.'

Johnson doesn't move for a moment. His eyes find mine.

I clear my throat, and fight another belch that is brewing.

How to ruin a moment by Reva Marsalis.

Johnson unlinks his fingers and swings his legs off the bed. He looks down at the floor. 'Looks comfortable.'

I move the empty tray to the bedside table. The double bed now looks too big for one person. 'Then again ...' I start.

He waits.

'The bed is pretty big. We could, uh ... We could, you know ...' My heart has started beating a little faster.

Still he waits for me to finish.

I gather my thoughts. 'I'll go get undressed and ...'

'Yeah?'

'We can re-discuss the sleeping arrangements. If you want to that is.'

He smiles gently. 'I'm just trying to be here for you, Rev. I miss the others. I want GG here telling me jokes. I didn't get to know Carrie that well but I would've done. And the Moth and Lucas. We'd have partied on down after this.'

'We so would've done.'

'I haven't been any good, and I want to be, Rev.'

'You've been amazing,' I assure him.

'Going to keep you safe though. Swear on that. Nothing's going to happen to you.'

'I'll ... I'll take that.' *More gratefully then you'll ever know*, I think.

He is about to respond when the phone in the room starts ringing. It surprises us both and I gingerly reach for it.

'Hello?'

'Hey.' It's Other-Johnson. 'I'm still not operating like I used to. Haven't used a phone in years.'

I clear my throat. 'Must've saved on bills.'

'Want me to come round?'

'Uh . . .'

'Keep you company, protect you, be your guard dog.'

My eyes find Johnson's. He looks away. He knows who I'm talking to.

'I'm OK,' I say into the phone.

'I can be there in seconds to kiss you goodnight.'

I can feel my face burning. I turn away in case Johnson sees. 'Have you been drinking?' I ask Other-Johnson.

'A little.'

'Well, you just, you know, stay put. We've got a big day ahead of us. Lot of digging to do.'

'I'm lonely. I'm lying in this massive bed and it feels like I'm on a desert island.' His easy tones and confidence have been boosted by the alcohol. 'Come rescue me, Rev.'

'No. Sorry.'

'C'mon.'

'Sleep tight,' I whisper and hang up the phone.

I turn round to Johnson, only he isn't there. I crawl over the bed and find him on the floor with a pillow and a quilted throw from the bed.

'Oh,' I say.

He nods to me. 'You said it yourself, big day tomorrow.'

He settles down and I think back to when I first met Other-Johnson and he told me that my Johnson would never push hard enough, that he'd need to step up if he really wanted to win my heart.

I don't know what is holding Johnson back but we seem to get close but never close enough.

UNBIDDEN

Johnson was up early and filled every pan in the kitchen with water. He used every hob to start boiling all the dry pasta he could find. He had left me to sleep and slipped out of my room. We never did get to share a bed.

When I finally woke up it was to the sound of a ringing phone, and Other-Johnson was calling me again.

'You dead or asleep?' he asked.

'Both,' I said fuzzily.

By the time I reached the kitchen, what was left of the pasta had boiled dry and stuck to the pan, but Non-Ape was still scooping it out with a huge ladle and letting it slither down his throat. He looks stronger than ever.

He belches and the Ape belches in return and they are sniggering like naughty schoolkids, and I suppose that's what they are really. We all are.

The Johnsons are out assessing the rubble. Both are eager to come home with me and even though I think I know that it has to be Johnson, I have to be on high alert, because after sleeping on it, I'm pretty sure that Other-Johnson can't be trusted to let that happen.

The Ape sits down opposite me in the empty dining room and stares at me.

'What?' I ask him.

'We going home?'

'Eventually. If we beat odds of a billion to one, then yes.'

'We're staying.'

'We?'

'Me and Big Me.'

We've been through this before and there is no way I am leaving the Ape here. He wanted to stay in the empty world all on his own, but now it seems he has a buddy who shares the same thought.

'The plan is he goes back to his world, then we go back to ours. And we have to make sure that we never, not ever, meet again,' I tell him.

'We're best mates.'

'So are me and you.' That comes out so naturally and truthfully it takes me by surprise.

'You're a girl.'

'So?'

'So you're a girl.'

I want to reach over and take the Ape's hand and squeeze it. To not let go until we are back home.

'This world isn't safe,' I tell him.

'You think? We've been naming our ten best things about this place.'

'There's ten good things?'

'Well. Six.'

'Six good things?'

'Maybe four.' The Ape rubs his chest. Which has now taken the brunt of two vehicle crashes in this world alone.

'What are the four good things?' I ask.

'It's more like one good thing.'

'So there's no list,' I tell him.

'There is a list. A list of one. But it's written ten times because it's so good.'

'It's really, really dangerous here,' I tell him. 'I thought it was a nice world but it's not. It's evil. It does things to try and kill us. It started off great and full of all the things we need, but that was a trap. I think that's what it does – it leads you in, it lulls you. It wants you to love it because then it can come and get you when you're off guard. My dad didn't come here to find me – he came here to warn me.' The more I talk, the more I can see the bigger picture. 'My dad somehow knew that I'd be taken here, or was about to be, and he tried to warn me. This world kills, Dazza. It killed Lucas, it killed Carrie . . . and now, well . . .' I have to check myself. I start again. 'It killed . . .' I can't say it. I can't bring myself to say his name.

The Ape knows I'm talking about GG. At least I think he does.

'That'd be on another list,' he says quietly. 'All that would be on a Not Good list.

'It's not just us it's killing. It's *them* as well. Our copies, doppels, other versions. You have to think of this world like the Colosseum.'

'The what?'

'You've seen *Gladiator*?'

'That's on another list. Top films I never saw.'

'Well, this world is a big fighting arena and it sends lions and tigers and slaves to fight in it.'

'Tigers. Cool.'

'No. No, it's not cool. People don't get out alive.'

Until I voiced this I never even knew I was thinking it, but it's so obvious. The world is empty because like any other arena it would be. It bends the rules and puts in trapdoors and surprises, but all we've done so far is fight. And die.

'We're never coming back here.' I say this with absolute conviction.

'But we made a list.'

'Forget the list – please.'

'It's like we're in a video game. We love it.'

Only two Apes could get together and come up with a positive for a world that wants so badly to kill you.

'But this is real,' I counter. 'You don't get killed and then just get up again and start all over. No extra lives.'

'Yeah there are.'

'What?'

'Black Moth came back.' He means Moth Two but Black Moth seems to fit better. Black for their eyes and black for their evil hearts. So Black Moth it is. 'Then there's the Other-Lucas. Johnson's twin.' The Ape continues counting his fingers. 'They were dead, now they're not. See? It's a game. We've been talking.' The Ape eases back in his chair and the excitement behind his eyes is as bright as the sun. 'It's a game we're good at.'

I want to argue. I want to grab the Ape and shake him, yell at him. But his logic is so simple and so pure that you can't bend it or break it or prove how stupid it is because to him it's perfect.

'We've got skills,' he adds, eyes bright with all kinds of excitement.

'Skilllllllls.' Non-Ape joins us, his huge form blocking out half the view of the Strand.

'We love it here,' the Ape repeats.

'Love it,' Non-Ape echoes.

'I don't want you to not come home though.' A lump comes from nowhere and settles in my throat. 'Who would look after me?'

The Apes look at one another as if one of them is going to answer.

'I'll Snapchat you,' the Ape tells me.

'I dunno if that would work,' I say. 'We'd need to ask the Moth that if he wasn't gone too. But it doesn't matter because you're not staying here.'

'You going to stop us?' Non-Ape asks. Not threateningly for once. More like a child asking his mum if he's done something wrong.

'If I have to.' I offer a not very convincing smile.

'Then he comes back with us,' the Ape tells me. 'Those are the rules.'

'And we get to come back here,' Non-Ape adds.

'Whenever we want.'

'That should be on our list,' Non-Ape emphasises for good measure.

I can't make that promise to them so I nod. It's a pretty weak nod and doesn't mean anything or have any real guarantee behind it but they seem to think it's enough. 'Let's talk more later.'

'Best game ever,' Non-Ape says.

'Skilllllllls.'

'Skilllllllls.'

Non-Ape belches loudly again and the Ape immediately belches a response. It's true love.

I lower my voice, leaning closer to them while trying to

ignore the lingering belch breath. 'Let's make sure we find the Moth and the papers. Then we can work on the other stuff.'

I don't like lying to them and I feel terrible that sooner or later I will have to bring their blossoming friendship to an end.

'Listen.' Non-Ape's gargantuan head looms towards me; he has more face than anyone I have ever met. 'You two need to be on constant alert.'

They both nod but don't think to ask why.

'I don't trust this world or anyone else here,' I add. 'But that's between me and you two. OK?'

The Ape leans forward, copying me, until our noses almost touch. His huge brown eyes have a depth I hadn't noticed before.

Non-Ape copies the Ape and looms even closer to me so that it feels like I am surrounded by great Ape heads and there is something almost comforting in this.

'OK?' I ask again.

They both nod.

'It's us three against the world,' I whisper, which they seem to like because they both let the exact same beefy grins run along their mouths.

'Three's enough,' Non-Ape declares confidently.

There's going to be one hell of a problem if and when we get the chance to go home because it'll mean splitting them up, but I'll keep working on a plan. I'll get Johnson to work on it as well. We gelled before and we can gel again.

'We've got to find G-Man,' the Ape announces. 'Been thinking about that a lot.'

I nod. 'OK. Once we've searched the rubble, found the papers, then we'll find GG.'

'Big Me can push a train.'

'Skills,' Non-Ape adds again.

'Skilllllllls,' the Ape responds.

They want to go back along the track again and find GG. The Ape is clearly not going to rest until he has done so. I'm amazed they've even had this deep a discussion.

'Then we'll do that,' I say, nodding again.

'Yeah, he's . . .' The Ape leans back and stares at the empty street outside. 'GG's OK,' he adds, which for him is a huge statement of affection.

'Billie can touch him,' Non-Ape suggests.

I'm stunned. Why hadn't I thought of that? Of course we need to find GG and take him to Another-Billie. It's so simple and so obvious. I could hug Non-Ape, but I doubt my arms are long enough to slip even halfway round him.

This is the first sign of hope I have experienced since GG sacrificed himself.

I need to make my own list now:

Get the papers.

Save the Moth.

Get GG.

Heal GG.

Grab my dad.

Go home.

Six steps. Easy.

I get to my feet. 'I'm going to go find myself some fresh clothes so if you're feeling strong enough why not start moving that rubble?'

The Apes rise with me and hold out their massive fists. I knock my fists against them and it's like we're bonded in some Ape/Rev/Ape fisty triangle now.

The best thing about any Ape is once they've decided that you're their friend then you're friends for life. They see no need to be otherwise and I totally trust them with my life. They don't want anything but a bit of friendship and kindness. To be included, a part of the gang, to be useful and helpful. It's so simple it's beautiful.

DARK TIMES

The Thames is filling with rubble. Non-Ape is lifting and hurling great chunks of hotel masonry into the majestic river. The Ape is helping by picking up smaller chunks of concrete and cement and heaving them as far as he can. Other-Johnson joins the Apes and back in his old body and with his increased strength he is a big asset. I try not to look too closely after he removes his T-shirt and reveals his tight sinewy body as he heaves a chunk of plaster into the Thames. He soon builds up a sheen of sweat and it's only then that I realise that I'm still watching him.

I turn and head for the nearest clothes shops, which I think must be near Covent Garden. I'm not sure of the general direction and I really shouldn't be wandering around on my own but I aim to be as quick as I can.

The boutique I find is in a row of shops that ring part of the square in Covent Garden. It is high-class fashion but there are jeans and a cool jacket on one of the mannequins and so I go in and grab them. My stabbed thigh and blistered hands need fresh bandages and as soon as I find a chemist I will ask Johnson to work his magic again.

I get changed in the changing room and when I look in the full-length mirror I see a body I barely recognise. I am bruised and cut all over. I think my arms have developed muscles and I have definitely lost a few pounds. It's not a diet I would recommend, but running for your life really does burn the calories.

Billie would love this shop. She's got the sort of elegance the more expensive clothes cry out for. I hope she is close by, and hasn't tried to find a way out of London. No matter what she thinks, she can't deal with what's happened to her on her own.

I grab a pair of high-fashion trainers and wear them in by walking all the way around the cobbled square. I love the emptiness and will probably never be able to do anything like this when I get home. For a few seconds at least I am totally free.

I know it's a lethal world but there's something spectacularly beautiful about it as well. The Apes think it's a violent video game, but for me it's a big secret garden, a fabulous fantasy world that I just wish had been kinder towards us.

On the way back to the river I find a chemist and ransack it for all manner of ointments and bandages. My thigh feels like it creaks every time I take a step and I am concerned it's become infected. I am hobbling now and the tear in my leg is howling in protest. I pass an underground ladies' toilet and nip down the steps so that I can wash and treat the wound.

The toilets are a little on the dank and mildewy side, and date back to Victorian times with their tiled walls and uneven flooring. A sign proclaims that they are cleaned every hour and I have to marvel at how this empty world operates. It has got everything right, down to the finest of details.

I peel off the old putrid bandage and have to turn away when I see how infected and pus-filled the slice in my thigh has become. I grab some paper towels and fill the sink with warm water, being careful to dab around the wound until it's clean enough to apply whatever super-creams I have found.

I do what I can and wrap a clean bandage round the wound. I check my burns and other cuts in the mirror and decide that if I carried on bandaging them I'd end up looking like a mummy. It's only when I am washing my hands that I sense I'm not alone.

I straighten up and press the hand blower fixed to the wall. There are two of them and I press both, one for each hand, and they blast hot air over my sensitive palms.

While I do this I try to get a glimpse in the rust-speckled mirror fixed to the wall above the sinks. I can't see anyone, not even a shadow. But there's definitely someone there; my tingling shoulders are never wrong.

The blowers are loud and I keep drying my hands as I try to locate something, anything, that I can use to defend myself with.

All I can see is a row of cubicles and a tiled wall. Whoever is waiting for me expects me to get dried and dressed and then come happily whistling up those stairs, like one of the seven dwarfs after a good day's diamond mining. That's when they'll strike – when I'm least expecting it.

Overhead are opaque glass bricks that let in some daylight but they're as thick as normal bricks and I can't see myself busting through them.

What would the Ape do?

What would that King of the Ring do?

The blowers stop.

302

I want to press them again and keep on pressing them in the vain hope that whoever – whatever – is lying in wait for me will eventually grow totally bored of waiting for me.

'*Johnson,*' I whisper in my head. '*Johnson.*' I don't care that my voice is panicked. As soon as he hears it he'll do everything in his power to save me. '*Pick up!*'

I'm not sure if I said that last bit in my head or out loud. I often find myself mouthing the words I'm speaking telepathically, which makes me a pretty rubbish psychic type.

Catching sight of myself in the mirror again I can see I'm screwing my face up, trying my hardest to send my SOS. '*Mayday! Mayday! Come in, over!*'

A shadow moves.

It's the tiniest movement but the light streaming down the steps has thrown a shadow across the floor. It's lean and thin and elongated.

I'm thinking it has to be Evil-GG. The worst of the worst. He's back and he's probably got Non-Lucas with him.

It makes sense. Moth Two came back from the dead so what's to stop anyone else doing the same? Has Other-Johnson resurrected them? If it is him doing this . . .

The shadow moves again. Whoever it is, is coming silently and slowly down the steps. But at least it's only one person. That's a positive, right?

The shadow creeps along the floor and starts to rise up the wall.

'*Mayday! Mayday! HEY! FOR GOD'S SAKES!!*'

Why isn't Other-Johnson answering? He said he needed time to recover his powers, but this is worse than being on the crappy Internet back in my flat.

'*Come on, answer me!*'

The shadow stretches its thin shape all the way to the ceiling.

I think back to what Johnson said. What do we really know about Other-Johnson?

But then, what if it's Evil-GG? This world is so perfect it brings people back to life. Well, nasty vicious people anyway. So maybe not so perfect.

The shadow is turning back on itself as it runs along the ceiling.

What would the Ape do?

He'd find a weapon. Or he'd charge at them. Yes. He'd charge at them before they were even ready.

Evil-GG is fast though. If it is him, he'd cut me down in the blink of an eye.

I need a weapon.

Or I could just scream.

It's a silent world and sound carries. But I'm underground and that would muffle my scream to a squawk.

The shadow stops.

There's got to be a weapon in here. I could wrench the hand heater from the wall and expose enough wiring like I did with the lamp in the private hospital. I could have ten thousand volts in each hand.

I feel movement behind me. There's something in the mirror.

A reflected face.

But not Evil-GG's.

It's my dad's.

'Reva,' he says. 'I'm awake.'

OMG

I have met my dad in a dream that was or wasn't a dream before. He told me to run.

This time it's different.

'Come back.'

His voice is rich and gentle and he is healthy and his eyes are alive with promise and honesty.

'How are you doing this?' I ask him, but my voice is a croaky whisper.

'It's time, Reva. It's time we fixed all of this.'

He smiles and his handsome face beams back at me from the mirror.

'You can't be here and also there,' I tell him. 'You can't be.'

My dad is calm and confident. 'It's that sort of a world,' he says and then disappears from view. I swivel but he is no longer behind me. Assuming he ever was.

I have to take stock, to get control. I have no idea what is real and what isn't any more. But I do know one thing. I know that I believe him.

I grab my bag of bandages and creams and am about to charge up the steps that lead to the street when a thought grabs me and drags me to a halt.

Does a dream cast shadows over the walls and ceiling? Does it creep up on you and wait in silence?

That wasn't my dad's shadow. Someone is still outside.

Waiting for me.

I can't hide down here for ever and I've got the added motivation from my dad now so I creep up the steps, taking them slowly and quietly. Daylight spears into the cold brick stairwell and then a shadow blots it out.

Here we go again.

Who's it going to be this time?

'God, you took for ever down there!'

'Billie.' I edge up the steps. 'You, uh, you came back.'

I should be glad to see her but her eyes are coal black and she is grinning way too much to be friendly.

'I just needed some time.'

'Did it help any?' I try to look calm and casual, easy-going, friendly.

'I'm here, aren't I?' She keeps smiling and her metal teeth glint.

'That's ... That's great. Can't believe it's you.'

'I think it's me.' She laughs and it shouldn't do this but it unsettles me. 'Who knows who I am any more?' She hesitates. 'Or what I am.'

The laughter dies away.

I'm not sure what to say next.

'Anyway. You found me,' I say.

'I remembered the hotel.'

'Always were smart. Took us hours.'

306

Billie looks at her hands and she seems to have managed to get her talons under control.

'You OK?' I ask tentatively.

'Getting there.' She smiles again.

'I was trying to make Other-Johnson scan for you—'

'—Nice jeans.' she cuts me short. 'Been shopping?'

'Uh yeah. Yes.'

'Rev, don't look at me like that.'

I didn't realise I was looking at her in any particular way.

'I'm going to be OK.' She adds, 'I was in shock. Who wouldn't be?'

I nod. 'True. We still friends then?' I venture.

Billie smiles again and I have no idea how we're going to explain her metal teeth when we get home.

But that will be a problem for later.

'Listen, I think we can go home,' I say.

'You're always saying that.' Her black eyes are unreadable.

'But my dad . . .' I take a moment, because this is going to sound crazy but then again it's pretty much on par with everything else. 'He spoke to me. In a vision, a dream. But it was him, Billie, and he's awake and he wants me to—'

'What d'you mean "awake"?'

'I'll explain on the way, but we've got a better way out of here.'

I want to hurry back to the Johnsons and Apes, but Billie's hand snakes out and catches my wrist. 'Explain now.'

'Later. C'mon, we've got to get the others and go.'

'You're going to leave the Moth?'

'No. We're going to find him – somehow. Other-Johnson can do that, once he's back to full power.'

I want to see excitement in Billie, but instead she takes a step forward and draws close enough for me to feel her quiet breath on my skin. 'Who do you want?' she asks. 'I need to know, Rev. Who do you really want? Which Johnson?'

'What? Didn't you hear me? My dad can probably get us home.'

She lays a hand on my bicep and gently squeezes my arm. 'It's like you've got two hearts. One for Johnson, one for Other-Johnson. But in truth people only have one heart.' Billie's words sound exactly like some of the mushy melodramatic poetry that Carrie used to write. She entered it for competitions but, surprise, surprise, never won a thing.

I twist out of her grip. 'My dad's healed. I didn't tell anyone because I didn't know if it would work or not. But it did, he's better.'

'You need to make up your mind,' she tells me, unable to think about anything but Johnson. 'You can't have them both.'

'There's more at stake than that.'

I head away but within a heartbeat I feel a swoosh above my head and before I know it Billie has leaped over me and landed in front of me. 'Which one, Rev?'

I have pined and mooned for the Johnsons and dithered and been torn one way and then the other. I have been as honest as I could be in such a mind-bending, heart-jangling situation. It's not my fault that I keep fluctuating, who wouldn't? But I certainly don't need Billie making my mind up for me.

Her fingers snap round my wrist again and she tugs on my arm, wanting me to come closer. I resist, digging my new trainers into the tarmac road.

'Tell me,' she says gently, but tugs a little harder.

I'm completely at her mercy and I think she likes seeing the fear in my eyes. *Well, you can*, I think, *you can look into my petrified eyes and you can see what you've become reflected straight back at you.*

'Billie, my dad's alive and he can help fix everything. He's in a private hospital,' I say. Not knowing how else to make her let me go.

'He's what?'

'They didn't go home. The other me and you are still around. My dad's been healed.'

I know it's a risk, but she has to snap out of this somehow.

Billie takes a moment.

I've played the only card I have left.

She lets my wrists go. Then she nods. 'Well, that's . . . That's amazing. Why didn't you tell me before?'

'I never . . . Never really got the chance,' which is sort of true.

Billie dredges up a smile. 'You should tell the others. Before one of them gets brained by a piece of hotel.'

'It's going to be good, Billie. All of it. You can meet your doppel and she can probably – help – you.'

Billie nods, warming to the idea.

'This isn't about boys,' I tell her. 'It's never been about that.' Even though it sort of has. 'We'll do what we've got to do. You and me. BFFs.'

Billie nods again, keenly lapping up my words. 'I'm right there, Rev. I'm right there.'

I go for an awkward hug but Billie keeps me at arm's length. 'Enough with that . . .' she jokes.

I grin at her. 'Everything's going to work out,' I promise her and realise that I'm starting to believe it. 'C'mon, let's tell the others.'

'I'm right behind you.'

I'm out of breath by the time I reach Johnson who is also now helping to move the rubble.

They have been going since early dawn and the mountain of dead hotel has shrunk a little. Masonry and plaster splash into the Thames.

'Boys!' I yell breathlessly.

Non-Ape has cleared tons of rubble and the Thames now has the beginnings of a concrete island sticking out of it.

'Stop!'

Everyone stops bar Non-Ape who keeps hurling concrete.

Johnson is also topless now and, be still, my beating heart, I've got two lithe torsos to gawp at.

'We need to go back.'

Other-Johnson stops. 'How come?'

'My dad's awake.'

'Whoa!' Johnson suddenly calls out.

I turn and see a lifeless body hurled into the Thames.

'What?' Non-Ape asks.

'You just threw a girl in the river!' Johnson tells him, semi-stunned.

'A girl?'

'Didn't you notice?'

Johnson and I run up to the bridge and peer down at the fast-flowing river in time to see Carrie's lifeless body being swept towards us.

'It's Carrie,' Johnson says.

'You mean Evil-GG,' I say. 'He's inside her. But we can get her fixed I think . . .'

My mind is alive with possibilities. With Another-Billie we can bring everyone back to life . . . Everyone we can find, that is.

Johnson is wary. 'Fixed?'

'Long story, but it could be possible.' I'm thinking Another-Billie is going to have her work cut out when we return. We could even get Lucas from his house.

'You just said it's not Carrie,' Johnson says. 'She's in Evil-GG's body. And who knows where that is.'

Carrie is swept under the bridge and Johnson and I run to the other side to watch.

'We can't just let her be ... carried ... away,' I murmur to Johnson. 'We could get her back, get her swapped, get her healed and get her home.'

'Love your optimism.'

I climb onto the wall of the bridge.

'What are you doing?' Johnson asks.

'If it was you in that river, would you want me to leave you?'

Carrie crashes hard into a moored river dredger, crunching her bones and gashing her brittle body. I always end up watching Carrie get hurt in some way. Even when she's categorically dead I still have to bear witness to even more pain.

Johnson hesitates. He knows he should do the heroic thing and try and reach her somehow. But in the split second that he wavers there's a splash behind us.

Other-Johnson dives into the Thames.

He's beaten Johnson to the punch.

He surfaces after a few seconds and looks around for Carrie's body. It has almost completely submerged so I shout to him, pointing and gesturing. 'There, up ahead!'

Other-Johnson swivels and sees Carrie slipping under.

He is about to swim after her when a chunk of masonry splashes down a metre away from his head.

'What the hell?' I yell. Non-Ape is still intent on throwing lumps of concrete into the river. 'Stop! Hey – stop!!'

Non-Ape hasn't heard me and more pieces of hotel rain down around Other-Johnson.

There is stupidity and then there is Non-Ape.

Johnson watches for a moment and I wonder if he'd be quite happy for Other-Johnson to be crushed by an internal wall from the hotel.

But then he gathers himself and starts waving and shouting at Non-Ape. 'Quit throwing stuff! Hey!'

Johnson's voice is louder and carries further than mine and Non-Ape stops, a huge piece of floor raised over his head ready to hurl into the Thames.

My voice joins Johnson's. 'Find GG's body – only wait a bit, OK? Just wait a second!'

Non-Ape considers it for a very long moment until he drops the piece of floor at his feet.

The sun has almost reached its highest point and we're baking underneath it. The river looks inviting as Other-Johnson treads water, desperately hoping he won't be crushed to death.

'*He's dangerous even when he's doing good,*' Other-Johnson whispers in my head, his relief evident.

'*You're back!*' I tell him.

'*What? Oh. Yeah, yeah I am. I'm switched on again.*'

A huge lump of concrete lands near Other-Johnson.

'For God's sakes!' I scream at Non-Ape.

He raises a meaty paw by way of an apology. 'Forgot.'

The Ape joins us on the bridge. He is on high alert. 'I think I heard something.'

'Like what?'

312

'I don't know.' The Ape takes a moment to look around the street.

Carrie is still caught up against the river dredger but the current is starting to tug her free. Other-Johnson needs to reach her before she is dragged away again.

'*I'm on it, Rev.*'

He dives under the surface.

He is gone for ten seconds.

Twenty.

Thirty.

He breaks the surface at forty seconds and is much closer to Carrie now.

But her body is pulled free of the river dredger and gets carried along by a new stronger current.

'Hurry!' I yell.

Other-Johnson plunges back under the water and moves at amazing speed, swimming more like a seal than a person. He is under the bridge one second then resurfacing fifteen metres past it in the next moment.

'Glad all that metal in his body isn't dragging him down,' Johnson remarks. But I hear a faint wistfulness in his voice.

But when Other-Johnson surfaces he can't see Carrie's body and I yell to him, 'She's being dragged away!'

As Other-Johnson twists and turns, fighting the current, he looks agitated.

'Johnson!' I yell.

Carrie has travelled at least another fifty metres away. But Other-Johnson is treading water again. Then he goes under again. But this time it's like something has got hold of him and yanked him out of sight.

Johnson, the Ape and I clamber from the bridge down a stone stairway and run as hard as we can along the riverside.

'Johnson!' I cry again, more in panic this time.

I don't know how we're going to get down to the actual water's edge but there's got to be a way of reaching him.

'Boat,' Johnson declares, as if reading my mind.

There is a row of pleasure and sightseeing cruisers moored by the river and all of them have a gangplank leading to them. That's the easy part.

The hard part is knowing how to drive a boat.

Other-Johnson resurfaces and starts swimming for the bank. He has given up on rescuing Carrie/Evil-GG because there is something in the river with him. And that something grabs him and drags him under again.

'Can you drive one of those boats?' I ask the Ape.

'Easy.'

'You can? Wow.' Even Johnson is impressed.

'They're just buses that drive on water.'

Other-Johnson breaks the surface and yells at us, not bothering with telepathy. 'There's something in the water!'

He gets tugged back under and we charge onto the gangplank of a sightseeing boat.

Johnson, thinking much more clearly than me, remembers to uncoil the ropes tethering the boat to the bank.

I run to the cabin and find myself face to face with a bank of controls and read-outs that mean nothing to me. There's a key in what I pray is an ignition but other than that I am lost.

Something hard hits the side of the boat and rocks it. It must be a wave but I have no idea what caused it. The river had been pretty still moments ago.

'How do we start this thing?' I yell.

'I'm a great sailor.' The Ape stomps towards me but when the boat rocks again he lurches forward and flattens me against the control panel.

'Ape!'

The Ape pushes himself from the console but the boat rocks again and again he falls into me.

'For God's sakes!'

'Ain't me,' he says and pushes himself back from me.

Only for another wave to smash him back into me. It's like some misguided mating ritual as another lurch pins him even tighter to me.

'What on earth is doing that?' I shove at his shoulders, pushing him away.

'Chemistry.' He grins. And flies forward once more, only this time I spin and clamber away.

The boat rocks again as I race out of the cabin. 'Just get it started!' I yell back at the Ape.

I head for the side and look over the edge. The boat rocks again but I can't see anything.

Johnson has finished untethering the boat and joins me to look over the side for Other-Johnson.

The Ape must have twisted the key in the ignition because I can hear the engine whine and then die. It sounds dry and lifeless.

I can't see Other-Johnson.

He hasn't resurfaced yet.

The boat rocks again but the Ape, pressing buttons, twisting the key over and over, swearing and hammering the console with his fist, finally gets the engine to fire. I have no idea how he manages it but the large boat thrums into life.

Other-Johnson breaks the surface and is panting hard.

I wave frantically. 'We're coming!'

He sees me and his eyes widen. 'No! Rev! Get off the boat!'

He starts swimming towards me as I run to the nearest lifebuoy and get ready to hurl it into the river for him when another shunt sends me staggering backwards.

The Ape is still pressing all manner of buttons and twisting the boat's wheel one way and then the other, but finally we are moving away from the bank.

'Rev!' Other-Johnson calls again. 'Get off the boat!' He is treading water again, looking all around for whatever is in the river with him.

Johnson staggers towards me as the boat is battered again. 'What is down there?'

The Ape is putting the engine through some major distress as he does his best to sail the boat. In reality we are just floating – going with the current now that the boat is free of its mooring.

I find one of the ropes that was used for the mooring and quickly tie it to the lifebuoy. I head back to the side and get ready to throw it to Other-Johnson but he has disappeared again. I can't see him anywhere.

The boat rocks violently and is shoved further into the middle of the river.

It feels like it's been hit by a whale.

The Ape joins me and Johnson.

Johnson is surprised to see him. 'You're meant to be driving this thing.'

'Boats aren't that much like buses,' he says.

Other-Johnson's voice crashes into my head. '*I know who's doing this, Rev. I know who—*'

Other-Johnson's voice snaps out of my head.

I run up and down the side of the boat trying to find him but he's been dragged under again.

Johnson is looking at the increasingly turbulent waters. The sun has disappeared behind a dark cloud and turns the day into momentary dusk. 'I can't see him,' he tells me.

The Ape heads back for the cabin and after a few moments the boat lights up, as lines of multi-coloured bulbs snap on at once, more for decoration than anything else but at least they shed red, white and blue light across the Thames.

'*Johnson?*' I keep trying our mental phone line but I can't pick him up. '*Johnson!?*' I yell inside my head.

The pleasure cruiser is moving fast now, as the huge shunts have forced us out into one of the river's major currents. Up ahead is what might be Westminster Bridge and it is odds on that we'll crash into one of the stone arches that have propped the bridge up for centuries.

We have come so close to a chance of going home but with every second we head further east, where if we don't figure out how to steer and stop this thing we'll eventually end up being washed out to sea.

We'll probably see France after all. If Billie was here, she'd be happy.

Billie, I think. She was right behind me a few minutes ago, but she never made it back to the hotel. I thought she was right behind me. Did something or someone get her?

Did they know she was powerful enough to pose a threat?

'*Johnson, are you there?*' I whisper but there's no answer. '*Johnson!*'

An empty silence descends.

We're not going home anytime soon.

In truth we never were.

THREE FOOLS IN A BOAT

We are heading for one of the magnificent arches of the ancient bridge, when there's a mighty shunt from underneath and it alters our course so that we squeeze under the arch, one side of the boat scraping and scratching loudly on the stonework.

Johnson is at the rear of the boat looking back to see if there's any sign of Other-Johnson. I wonder if any part of him feels guilty for wanting to change back into his old body. If he hadn't, it could have been him jumping into the Thames to try and rescue Carrie's corpse.

'Anything?' I ask.

He shakes his head in silence.

The Ape has given up trying to steer the boat. Every time he does the boat gets hit by whatever is in the water and shoved onto a different path.

A chill is creeping through the air. The sun remains trapped behind gathering grey clouds.

'We could jump,' I tell Johnson.

'And be dragged under by whatever's down there?'

The smashed hotel is probably over half a mile away now, maybe more. London looms on either side of us as we are propelled to who knows where.

With Other-Johnson drowned . . . I have to catch myself and take a moment to stay calm. He can't be drowned. That can't have happened. But a small shiver runs through me and Johnson slips an arm round my shoulders. I let myself lean into him and wonder who or what is doing this when a Moth Two appears on the next bridge up ahead.

Oh.

My.

God.

A Black Moth as the Ape calls them.

Then another.

'Johnson?'

'I see them.'

The Ape has also seen them and readies himself. 'Get behind me.'

Another of his tried and trusted war cries.

He scans the boat for a weapon and his eyes light up at the sight of a long wooden pole with a brass hook on the end of it. It must be used for hooking fallen guests out of the river or maybe helping to push the boat away from the quayside but he picks it up, inspects the tip and seems satisfied.

More Black Moths line up on the bridge. It's probably four hundred metres away and we're drawing ever nearer.

Johnson stands alongside me. 'We beat them before.'

'They ran away,' I remind him.

'Still felt like a win.' He's staying brave and keeping calm for me.

The bridge is fast becoming littered with Black Moths as

they leap onto the bridge wall, squatting and crouching, getting ready to greet us.

As soon as the boat reaches the next bridge they are going to rain down on us.

The Ape weighs up the possibility of more violence with relish. 'They ain't so tough.'

Johnson scans the boat. 'Boats have anchors.' He looks up and down and from right to left. 'They have to park them, don't they?'

Johnson and I head for the rear of the boat and as the metres are eaten up by our inexorable drift towards the gathering Black Moths we find an anchor. It looks like it weighs a ton and Johnson searches for the mechanism that will send it to the bottom of the Thames, mooring us.

Can Black Moths swim?

I have no idea, but as long as we can buy ourselves some time we still have an ace up our sleeve.

That ace is Non-Ape and he is thundering along the riverbank, trying to catch up with the boat. His mighty footsteps rock the foundations of the closest buildings. Non-Ape is on his way.

Boom.

Boom.

Boom.

Thank God for the Apes. Thank you God for creating them and bringing them into existence. The world cannot spin without an Ape to turn it.

Non-Ape is closing on the boat but we are getting uncomfortably near the bridge that is now teeming with Black Moths. They can barely wait. Even from here I can see row upon row of smiling metal teeth and sharp talons.

God alone knows how they knew where to find us, why they've come back, or what they want. Do they still have our Moth?

Johnson presses a button that may or may not be connected to the anchor. Nothing happens. He jabs at another one. Still nothing.

Boom.

Boom.

Boom.

Non-Ape is closing on us.

But the Moth-laden bridge is closer.

They'll be on us before Non-Ape can reach us.

Johnson jabs another button and the anchor moves. It starts sliding into the Thames.

The boat is rocked again and sends us off our feet.

'What the hell is doing that!?' I cry.

'It's going to smash a hole in the boat,' Johnson says, climbing back to his feet. 'So, either the Moths get us or whatever's down there sinks us and ... Shall I go on?'

The anchor keeps falling.

Johnson grabs my wrists and drags me to my feet. The boat is starting to slow.

We're barely twenty metres from the bridge.

Non-Ape isn't fast but he eats up the ground as best he can. He has to – his best friend is on the boat.

The Ape braces himself, pole at the ready, eyes scanning the dark hateful Black Moths. 'I'm going to take them all.'

A soaking hand grabs the side of the boat and another follows it.

Something is coming aboard.

THIS REALLY IS END OF THE ROAD

'Ape!'

Ape swivels, sees the hands gripping the side of the boat and charges.

Other-Johnson pulls himself into view and gets the fright of his life as the Ape aims the pole straight for his throat. He ducks as fast as he can and the Ape almost topples over the side, his momentum pitching him forward.

He throws out a slab of hand and only just stops himself.

Other-Johnson, breathing hard, dares to pull himself up again. 'Jesus.'

I go to him as the boat lurches to an anchored a stop barely thirty feet from the bridge. Johnson joins me and together we drag Other-Johnson aboard.

'I thought you were . . .'

'Me too.' Other-Johnson retches and coughs up a lungful of Thames.

'What is down there?'

'I don't know. It's too dark. But that's not your biggest problem.'

I point to the rows of Black Moths, a hundred large and evil crows perched and ready to swoop down. 'I figured that.'

Other-Johnson scans the bridge but then shakes his head. 'They're not your biggest problem either.'

Before he can say more he bends and coughs up more of the Thames.

The Ape is on high alert as he turns back to await the Black Moths.

Non-Ape has drawn level with us but we're too far out for him to jump aboard. Not that that was ever his plan because he thunders straight past us.

Boom.

Boom.

Boom.

He's going for the Black Moths.

Other-Johnson pulls himself straight again, wiping his mouth with the back of his hand. 'Rev . . .'

I know from the look on his face that it's bad news.

But I also know he doesn't have to tell me. It's been staring at me the whole time.

I turn to Johnson. I can't believe what I'm about to say.

Up ahead Non-Ape punches the bridge with all his might.

'Johnson.' My voice is caught way back in my throat.

A crack runs all the way along the bridge.

Black Moths are shaken from their perch and some pitch headlong into the Thames. Others swarm towards Non-Ape.

But he punches the bridge again and it buckles and groans and the Black Moths are thrown this way and that.

Johnson can see tears in my eyes. 'What is it?'

Another punch lands.

Then another.

But there are too many Black Moths and despite how many plunge into the Thames enough still manage to reach Non-Ape, leaping on him and attacking with a savagery that far outdoes their earlier attack.

The Ape looks on, for once unable to do anything.

I don't know how much strength Non-Ape used up throwing half a hotel into the Thames but there is no way he can be on full power. The Black Moths intensify their attack.

Other-Johnson plunges into my mind and starts yanking images and memories from me. He does it so hard I cry out in pain. But he doesn't apologise as he rifles through me, searching and scanning and searching some more.

The first of the fallen Black Moths climbs from the Thames and onto the boat. They can swim then. The Ape is on him in an instant, driving the pole straight into his throat before heaving him into the air and flicking him back into the Thames.

The Ape is watchful as he grips and re-grips his weapon. I look at him and realise that he wants this. The video game to end all video games.

Another Black Moth leaps onto the boat and the Ape charges for him.

Other-Johnson is wrenching more images from my head. They are speeding by at a hundred miles an hour.

There's a flash of white light and we arrive back in the school. The Ape can hear footsteps. I am listening with him now, and then I'm following the footsteps as they hurry out of the school and leave footprints in the snow.

The Ape was right.

There was someone in the school with us.

Then I'm in a deep river that shouldn't have been so deep. Not enough to drown me anyway.

There's the winter that was never winter. The snowman. The bleak freezing cold.

I see Johnson and Billie entwined.

Behind me the Ape kills another Black Moth as it leaps onto the boat. The Ape marches forth, smashing and slashing as more of them swim for the boat and climb up its sides.

Black Moths are being torn apart by Non-Ape on the riverside, and their limbs and heads and bodies land beside us after he hurls them away. But they keep coming for him, talons slashing and teeth biting. There are too many for him this time, I am sure of it.

More images come.

Billie crushing me a little too tightly in the church, nearly squeezing the life from me. She'd already started to change and didn't know how powerful she was becoming. I didn't think of it before but how did she know I was there?

Then the Ape miraculously finds Johnson in the blizzard. In ten minutes exactly. A miracle.

Or a manipulation.

Billie raining kisses on Johnson as he comes in from the cold.

Non-Ape roars and shakes free of the Black Moths. He digs his fingers into the base of the bridge and tears it from its mooring. Black oil drips from a hundred cuts in his skin as he summons all the God-like power he can and heaves one end of the bridge into the air, snapping it in half. Black Moths are suddenly plunging into the river, but this time half a bridge is coming down after them. God knows how many he kills but what's left of the bridge sags and bows and then collapses into the Thames, taking the rest of the Black Moths with it.

More images are plucked from my head.

Non-Ape attacked on the train. The attack that seemed only focused on him.

Johnson completely unscathed on the train. Not one curl on his gorgeous head was touched.

The Moth kidnapped.

Images keep gathering as Other-Johnson ransacks my brain.

The winter that never was.

Escape.

Europe.

Black Moths are still climbing on board, coming from all directions. Their talons and sleek bodies dripping water.

The Ape's pole is covered in black oil but even he can't take all of them down.

Non-Ape bellows as he wades into the river, trying to reach us, crushing anything that gets in his way.

Not the river, I think. *Don't go in the water.* 'Don't!' I yell. 'There's something down there!'

But on he ploughs.

'Get back!' Johnson yells at him.

'What?'

'There's something—'

That something drags him under.

One second the river is up to his chest and the next Non-Ape is gone. He doesn't even get the chance to bellow.

So this is it.

This is our last stand.

The day has turned even darker as the Ape backs up in front of us, eyes trained on the advancing Black Moths.

All along someone has been making it impossible for us to leave. They took our brain and they tried to take our muscle. Both vital to my grand quest.

326

But how could they possibly know that was my plan?

The Black Moths keep climbing aboard. Even though their numbers have been decimated by Non-Ape there are already too many of them to fight. Without Non-Ape we're dead.

'*Rev.*' Other-Johnson is in my mind again. His voice is barely a whisper.

'*Yeah?*'

'*I'm sorry. Really thought we had a chance.*'

He doesn't think this is going to end well and who can blame him?

Johnson stands side by side with the Ape who breaks his pole in half over his knee and hands one half to Johnson.

'You're some man,' Johnson tells the Ape, his eyes never leaving the Black Moths. They've got us surrounded and they have all the time in the world.

The Ape stays tall. '*We've* got this.' He has no give up in him but the odds are impossible now. There must be over twenty Black Moths on the boat with more still climbing up the sides.

I think of the Moth, trapped somewhere, alone and unable to do anything more than crawl. With us dead no one will come for him now.

I have made an unholy and tragic mess of this.

Other-Johnson mentally arrows in on the footsteps in the snow again. He takes me all the way with him as together we track the footsteps.

We glide down the steep hill that leads into town and the footprints lead all the way to the town square. The snow appears from nowhere and thickens with each step.

And standing there, as snow appears all around her, is Billie. I watch as the snow spreads throughout the centre of town.

An entire winter springs up around her in seconds.

It's only now that I realise he is dragging these images from her head and putting them in mine. Which means she must be close by.

I almost choke. 'Billie . . .'

Other-Johnson is running short home movies of Billie through my mind.

Billie on the train thinking that she needs to stop us getting to London, that Johnson will never be hers if she doesn't. The train rattles a speck of the dead Moth Two's oily blood into the air. Her eyes settle on it through the train window and she wills reality to change.

Moth Twos spring up all around the fast-moving train.

She has so much power.

Being cut by Non-Lucas and having her DNA spliced with his has given birth to something incredible.

Another image.

Other-Johnson kicking a classroom door that just won't open.

There is no Invisible Entity. Nothing came back with us.

The enemy has been amongst us all along.

There was no way Billie was going to let us leave. No matter what the cost . . .

Other-Johnson leaves my head and I realise I have nothing left now. My best friend has taken the last of me and snuffed it out.

'For what it's worth she's not one of you or one of us any more.' Other-Johnson is genuinely heartfelt.

But there is one last battle to be fought and I drag myself upright and join the Ape and the Johnsons. The Black Moths stop, waiting for the signal to lunge. I don't even have a weapon.

My shoulders are on fire. My spider sense is burning me from the inside and the slowly sinking boat rocks as another big wave hits it. Is Non-Ape underwater fighting whatever it is that dragged him under?

Something leaps through the air – just like Non-Lucas could leap – and makes it from the bank of the river all the way to the boat in one silky graceful bound.

Billie lands on the deck. Behind the Black Moths.

They hunker down low, on all fours, and with her supermodel height she towers spectacularly above them.

'We were going to be so happy,' she tells me. 'It was a gift. A world all of our own. Me and Johnson.'

Clearly the Moth didn't figure in her romantic plans.

Johnson tightens beside me. 'It wouldn't have lasted,' he whispers drily.

'I went to the school as soon as we got back in town,' Billie tells us, but looks directly at me the whole time. 'I ran up that hill and when you weren't there I realised what was meant to be. It was written in the stars, Rev. It always has been. I'm meant to be with Johnson. Not you and him. It was never going to be you and Johnson.'

'Billie, there's no need for this,' I tell her but I know it's not Billie any more. I don't what she is now but maybe it's better that way. I need to keep this impersonal, because if she gives me an opening then I'm taking it. 'All this over a boy?' I try and smile.

'But then I saw the white light and suddenly you were back,' Billie says, ignoring me.

'Told you I heard footsteps. I've got great ears,' the Ape tells anyone who cares to listen.

Johnson stands taller, and fixes Billie with an honest and

329

defiant look. 'You might as well stop there because I'm not going to love you. Look what you're doing! What you've done! How could I love someone like you?'

Which isn't what any girl wants to hear, let alone a super-powered, reality-manipulating she-devil.

'Great line, Johnson,' I whisper heatedly. It's right up there with Non-Ape for stupidity. What is it with boys?

Billie's eyes blaze and she lets out a snarl.

Other-Johnson flashes a glare at Johnson. 'Yeah, that went down well.'

Johnson shrugs. 'Just saying it like it is.'

The Ape takes a step forward. He can't help himself; he doesn't do hanging back.

'I'm going to kill them all,' he says. 'Anything that gets in my way is dead.' He's never been so focused. Or determined. 'Rev – I'm killing every single one of them.'

'Wrong,' Billie replies. 'And so, so stupid.'

The Ape moves first, charging forward, his bulk gaining momentum and giving him power as he ploughs into the Black Moths. He thunders through them and I already know what he is doing – he's going for Billie. Of course he is. He knows how to win.

Goosebumps break out all over my skin as he takes the fight to Billie. I know what he's thinking. If he can take her down then all of this will disappear. His gut instinct is telling him to get to her, whatever, however. And he cuts and slashes his way, a boy against a tide of unbeatable odds, but still he keeps going – one step at a time, one centimetre, one millimetre, always going forward, always moving towards and not away, never being beaten back, never giving ground. Black Moths leap upon him and he lashes out as Johnson joins the fight.

Other-Johnson grabs me round the waist and leaps me through the air, trying to find safety. But three Black Moths rise with us and bring us down with a bone-crunching thud. They set about Other-Johnson as I roll to my feet and come up in time to see the Ape crunch through the swathe of Black Moths and take aim at Billie with what's left of his pole. He's about to hurl it like a javelin when a Black Moth cuts him across the stomach with a bright and shining talon. The pole spears through the air even as the Ape falls to his knees, blood pouring from his wound.

Billie takes great delight in flicking the pole away, making sure the Ape knows how futile his attack was. He kneels before her, holding his stomach with one hand while trying to push himself to his feet with the other.

Billic looms over him with all the hatred she can muster.

Oh God no.

I am already running for the fallen pole as she brings the Ape's face up to meet hers. 'You animal.'

A talon slips from her fingertip and with one hand snapping the Ape's head back she exposes his neck. 'You vile, vile animal,' she says calmly, and swings her talon towards his throat.

But no one beats the Ape. No one. And he lurches forward, driving hard with his mighty legs, shoving Billie backwards, carrying her, half in a fireman's lift, back towards the edge of the boat. She is taken by surprise and can't quite fathom that while she is an arrogant hateful teenager he is a warrior. And like any warrior he was born to fight.

'Come on then!' he bellows and Billie is so shocked by the attack that she is barrelled over the edge of the boat. The Ape roars like an animal as Billie splashes down into the river. He

331

turns and tries to find me through the blur of Black Moths who have pinned the Johnsons to the deck. More of them surround me and the Ape launches towards me, weaponless, bleeding profusely, but still coming. Coming to save me.

The first Black Moth leaps for me and I jam the end of the pole straight into its throat. But they're clever and smart and the Black Moth hurls himself over the edge of the boat, whipping and twisting the pole from my hands even as he dies. A selfless kamikaze attack that leaves me utterly defenceless.

His sacrifice paves the way for Black Moths to converge around me.

The Ape barrels towards me, trailing blood. 'Rev!'

He has almost made it when he is caught and cut down before my eyes. Black Moths leap on top of him and even the Ape, the mighty Ape, can't wrestle free of them.

I don't even know I'm crying as Billie climbs back on board, soaked and angrier than ever. All of us are trapped, pinned and with no hope of escape as Billie walks straight up to me, shoving Black Moths out of her way. She spits river water out of her mouth and snarls again. Billie's blazing darkness envelops her and she is lost to it. My best friend is no more.

All of her talons slide into view. 'Want to hear something funny?' Billie lets out a slow sad sigh. 'I didn't even know I was doing it, not at first. I honestly had no idea.'

Billie shows her taloned hand to me. 'Which hand would you like? The left or the right?'

'How about neither,' I reply.

She manages a smile at that. 'How about both?'

She is about to plunge her talons into me.

'I told you to choose your Johnson. I gave you a chance.'

This is it, Rev. Your race has run. And I apologise to Lucas, and to Carrie and GG and the Moth. I am so sorry that this happened.

And to you, Johnson. I so wish it had been different.

And you, Ape. I love that you were there for me, and I'm sorry that it's over now.

Billie's hand arcs towards me.

THE END OF THE END

'Billie, wait!'

It's Johnson. He is being held down on the deck but he can still see that Billie is about to slice me in half.

'I'll go with you,' he shouts. 'I'll go away with you.'

Billie stops. Her talons are within millimetres of striking me.

'Wherever you want. I don't care as long as we're together,' he tells her

No, I think. *You can't do that.*

Billie gestures to the Black Moths and Johnson is allowed to climb to his feet. The Ape is still alive but he seriously needs medical attention. Other-Johnson, even with his extra strength, can't break through.

Johnson doesn't look at me. I know he can't because he has to focus everything he's got on Billie. 'Billie, we'll go away, and we'll make it work. Me and you. That was your dream, right?'

Billie's eye flicker to blue for a moment. 'You're just saying that.' But in her voice is a desperate desire to believe what Johnson is telling her.

'Let them go home and I'll stay. It'll just be us in a world of our own.'

'Johnson, don't,' I whisper.

But he continues to act as if I'm not even there. His eyes meet Billie's. 'You and me and a Harley-Davidson. That's all we need.'

Tears are rolling down my cheeks because finally I know which Johnson I want. Maybe I always knew and maybe Other-Johnson did as well, considering how hard he tried to win my heart. He's been inside my head and probably my heart, so he saw it there and he tried to act as if it wasn't. But the boy I love is standing right before me. Long dark curls frame his perfect face, his taut bare torso and his long thin legs ready to take him away with Billie.

I didn't even get to kiss him, I think. *Or tell him how I felt.*

'How about it?' he asks Billie. 'I'm ready to go now.'

Billie can't help herself. She finally has her heart's desire. 'Promise?'

'Hope to die.'

Billie is in heaven.

'I'm all yours, B. All yours,' Johnson tells her.

My heart snaps.

I'm surprised no one hears it because it definitely snaps in two.

Billie glances around the boat and I can imagine the fantasy that is overpowering her. They could sail away together. They could be lovers in an empty paradise.

Johnson senses the same. 'We've got the Garden of Eden all to ourselves,' he tells her. I don't know how he's keeping so calm and measured.

Billie smiles and one by one the Black Moths pop out of

existence, leaving drops of black blood to run between the cracks in the decking.

The black oil mingles with the Ape's rich red blood as he manfully tries to get himself into a sitting position. 'Told you, told you I'd get them all.' But his breathing is laboured and he has turned very pale, and perspiration is running into his eyes.

The boat is still taking on river water and it won't be long before it's dragged down into the murky depths.

Free of the Black Moths, Other-Johnson springs to his feet and is already moving fast for Billie.

But Johnson jumps in his way. 'Don't touch her!'

Other-Johnson, talons fully extended, skids to a stop.

'That's my girl.' Johnson gestures to Billie. Protective. Heartfelt. Loving. 'That – is my girl,' he repeats.

I know it's an act because Johnsons aren't great liars. In fact, the term 'great liar' is all wrong anyway. If people know you're great at lying, then by definition you're not great at all. But Billie hears what she so desperately wants to hear and slips into a deep swoon. She has found her heart's desire.

Johnson knows that to attack her now would mean the end of everything. He takes a quiet breath and finally looks my way.

Our eyes meet.

The boat sinks further.

Please let Non-Ape kill whatever is in the water and charge to our rescue. He's been underwater for minutes now but surely his massive lungs can hold gallons of air.

I'm desperate to tell Johnson all the things I should have told him from the very beginning. But I can't, not in front of Billie.

The thump of his heart tells me he wants to hear it but his eyes say no.

'See you in another life, Rev.' Johnson touches his finger to his temple and then cocks it my way.

And with that Johnson turns to Billie. 'We've got a road to hit.' He takes her in his arms and kisses her full on the lips.

The boat receives a giant shunt. A wave hits it and turns it towards the riverside. But the anchor holds the pleasure cruiser in place so all the wave really does is push the front of the boat until it's facing the riverbank.

The kiss ends and Billie looks breathless. 'This is where we get off, Johnson,' she tells him.

'I've got this . . .' The Ape's voice is barely a whisper now as he sinks onto his back, hands cupping his slashed stomach. His breathing is shallow, barely audible.

Billie takes a cruel delight in this. 'You've got nothing.' She laughs and takes Johnson's hand in hers. 'I'm the one with everything.'

I look back to Johnson. And probably for the first time in his life he has true fear in his eyes.

I can't let him do this. We have to keep fighting. We have to. He sees it in my eyes, the raging, desperate desire to have one last attempt at bringing Billie down. But he slowly, silently, shakes his head.

'Goodbye,' Johnson mouths to me.

The boat rocks again. *Come on, Non-Ape, c'mon!* The wave rises and settles as the hull fills with water. '*Where is he?*' I transmit to Other-Johnson.

'*I can't reach him.*' His telepathic voice is panicked, fearful.

'I'm not letting you do this, Billie.' I can't help myself. The one thing I've learned is to never give up.

Billie knows this and fixes me with the deadliest look of all.

'Spend time fighting and your precious gorilla'll die. He'll fall into a coma and never wake up.'

'This is nothing,' the Ape pants as he tries once more to get to his feet. But he can't do it. He hasn't got the strength. His hand slips in his own blood and he crashes back down to the deck.

Billie looks to Johnson, revelling in the sweetest of moments.

'Let's go. We can walk in the fields again.'

Other-Johnson transmits a thought to me. A simple courageous thought. *'Your call, Rev. I'm with you whichever way you want to take this. Make your move and I'll move with you.'*

The Ape's breathing shallows and I know for certain he will die if I don't help him.

'Billie, please!' I beg.

Her metal teeth light up her mean smile. 'It's your choice, Rev. You can try and save Johnson or the Ape. But you can't save both.'

To Be Continued . . .

The apocalyptic detention continues in . . .

ESCAPE

The Ape is dying, Johnson is with
Billie and Rev is about to be
rocked to her core. Nothing can
prepare her for the astonishing
truth of what is really happening.
A realisation that will change her
life forever and leave her alone
and with nowhere to run.

But Rev is Rev, and if there is one
thing she's learned, it's that you
must never, not ever, give up . . .

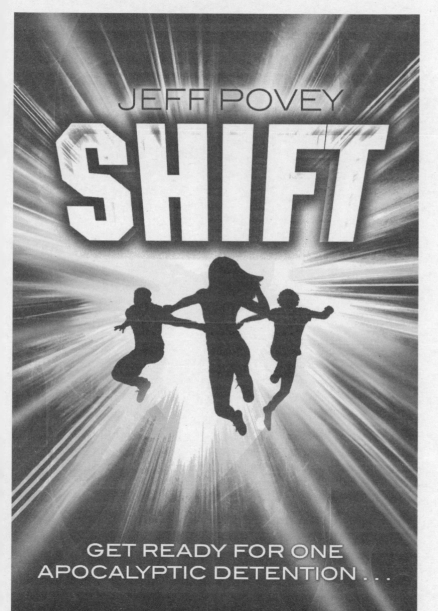

Acknowledgements

It's lovely to think that an author is the only person that matters when writing a novel, but I can assure that's far from the truth.

So first and foremost, huge thanks to my editor Jane Griffiths whose good taste and wisdom remain matchless. My agent Valerie Hoskins played her part as always, but special mention must go to Sara Moore and Rebecca Watson for their invaluable input. And obviously to my wife Jules who all but shredded the first chapter and told me to start again.

Thank you also to all at Simon & Schuster. But most of all thanks to all of the children and teachers etc. that I spoke to last year. Too numerous to mention by name, but you know who you are and I hope this book meets with your approval.

As ever, if you happen to love either Johnson, Tom Wiggins remains the real deal.